DAUGHTER OF SWAN & SWORDS

I would like to acknowledge the following for photography or artwork used on the cover: Sascha Bosshard, Ricardo Cruz, Caspar Rae, Lazarescu Alexandra on Unsplash

ISBN: 979-8-9873348-6-7
E-ISBN: 979-8-987-3348-7-4

DAUGHTER OF SWAN & SWORDS

FAY SMITH

Contents

Terminology   1

1   2

2   17

3   33

4   50

5   62

6   75

7   91

8   106

9   119

10   134

11   146

12   158

13   171

14   190

15   203

16   216

17   About the Author   231

18 Also by this Author   232

Terminology

Hrafn (h-RAH-fn)- our hero, it means raven
Jeger (YAY-ger)- Hrafn's consort, it means hunter
Faen (faan)- fuck
Faen ta deg (faan ta day) - fuck you
hva faen (hva faan) or
faen i helvete (faan HEL-VET-eh) - fucking hell
Fitte - bitch or cunt
Dritt - shit
Mikill Sumar (Mik-il Soo-mar) - "Great Summer" Hrafn's country
Fimbulvetr (Fim-byl-VETr) - "Mighty Winter" country to the NE
Konungr (Ko-noon-gr)- King
Kriger (Kree-GHER)- Name of the enemy prince, means warrior
Jævlig (YA-vlig)- fucking or devilish
Banamaðr (Bana-mathr)- Olwen's sword, it means slayer, killer
Jeg gir faen i det (Yay jeer faan det)- I don't give a fuck
Dúfa (Doo-fa)- Jeger's cousin in Fimbulvetr, means dove

Olwen

The raven's screech was punctuated by the pounding coming from her front door and through the house. Olwen grabbed the fabric tightly in her pruney fingers and dragged it over the scrubbing board before the banging disturbed her washing again. The large raven in the nearby tree cocked its head at her thoughtfully, drawing her attention; the incessant noise at her door continued, and her head fell in frustration. There would be no avoiding this confrontation. She let the sopping wet fabric of the dress slide back into the soapy water as she pulled herself up to her feet and headed to the front door.

"Henrick, you can't hide yourself away forever," A loud voice boomed through the door. "You'd best come out and deal with me now."

Olwen pulled the door open just as a large fist was descending to pound once more, and she stepped to the side quickly to avoid being hit. The large man on her doorstep pulled his arm back with a surprised jerk. He scowled as he realized that it was not Henrick standing before him.

"My apologies, good lady; I am here to see Henrick about a debt."

The man stood tall and proud, and his clothes were of fine quality.

Olwen had no doubt he would use his fists to get what he wanted, but he certainly looked to be merchant class and not her own labor class. He was a man of means, whereas her husband was not. Still, the narrowing of his eyes told her he suffered no fools.

"I am sorry, good Sir, but my husband has not returned just yet. He left for the forge early this morning, and I've not seen him since."

The man watched her with distrustful eyes, taking in her modest dress and disheveled appearance.

"He has not returned for his evening meal?" the man asked curiously.

"No, Sir, I've not seen him since he left me, before the sun was risen."

Olwen shuffled her feet nervously, trying to look every bit the shy and naive bride. She was neither cowed nor shy, but he didn't need to know that. The man looked her over one last time, seeming to evaluate her, before shaking his head with whatever decision he had come to.

"You will give him a message. You will tell him Dirst is growing impatient, and if he cannot pay the coin he owes, then he shall have to make arrangements for some... other form... of payment."

Olwen didn't like the way his eyes lingered on her body, and she nodded quickly and closed the door on his lewd glare.

This was the third visit she had received this week from the people who had loaned her husband funds. She was well aware that her husband gambled more money than he earned, and that he owed debts all over their small town, but it did her no good to speak on his behalf. He wouldn't appreciate it, regardless. It was better to appear a foolish woman, good for nothing but warming her husband's bed, birthing his babies, and tending his household. They didn't need to know she could better manage their money than her spendthrift husband; there was only room for one leader in their marriage, and her husband had already claimed it. Regardless, it was unheard of for a woman to have any sort of control over her life or homestead, even if she was better suited.

This last visitor, Dirst, had left her feeling uneasy. She had seen many money-lenders come and go over the years, but she had never had so many in one week, and they had never left a veiled threat with her before. She was a simple housewife; most gentlemen accepted that women were beneath such matters and left her alone. He had been nicely dressed, but it was clear from the scars on his knuckles he would use force or violence if crossed, potentially on innocent wives.

And where was her husband? He was the town blacksmith and had left for his forge early that morning. He often came home for his evening meal before going out again. While he would never deign to explain himself, or his absence, to his wife the ale on his breath told her where he spent most of his free time. But tonight, he had not returned for his meal. Had he gone directly to the Ale House for his supper, spending more of their money on himself while Olwen fended off his debtors? She blew out a frustrated breath, which chased a few stray golden locks of hair from her sweaty forehead.

She looked around their small home unsure of what she should do. The laundry was still sitting in the back but her anxiety kept her where she was, making her want to take action of some sort. Unfortunately, there was nothing she could do at the moment. Anxiety crept into her limbs like insects under her clothing, making her itch to move.

The fire had burned down dangerously low, and she wasn't allowed to feed it more wood. Her husband had said they couldn't afford it; in truth, he didn't want the wood 'wasted' if he wasn't home to enjoy the heat himself. He would call her wasteful, even though he spent every evening enjoying the warmth of the fires of the Ale House, spending money they couldn't afford on drink and games. She would spend her evenings chilled and alone, waiting for her drunken husband to stumble home in the dark of the night.

She slumped into a chair, staring at the dying flames in the hearth. Her hands fell uselessly in her lap. This was not the life she had anticipated or wanted, and she fought back tears of frustration that threatened to burst from her eyes. She could do so much more if she wasn't held back by a husband. She was a good woman, a strong woman; there was no reason at all that she shouldn't be allowed to live on her own and support herself without a husband to control and diminish her. But that was not the way of things in this small town of Espar, or the surrounding country.

Her father had been a swordsmith, one of the most sought-after in the realm. He had married a foreign beauty, the daughter of a famous foreign smith, with the promise that she held the secrets to smithing the metals in new and miraculous ways. Her mother had filled her childhood with fairy tales of how she had been raised with the magic of metal, a gift bestowed on her family by the Fae. In her youth, Olwen had been blessed with a life of freedom and privilege. But the magic of those fairy tales died with her mother when she was still very young, leaving her with a broken-hearted father and the weight of reality crashing onto her shoulders.

As the only daughter of the widower swordsmith, she had lived a very unconventional life by local standards. They traveled often, moving every so many years to a new location and setting up a forge again. But her father's work was legendary, and no matter where they went, people sought them out for his fine swords. They lived well; there was always food and heat, and she was gifted many fine dresses, although she hardly cared to wear them. She was happy in trousers, running through the woods and climbing trees. She was a wild thing and a child of nature, taking after her mother. They were rare golden-haired angels in a sea of brunettes.

Another point that set Olwen apart was that she was educated and could read and write, something many of the common folk in Espar could not do. She had kept this information to herself, as the people in her town did not appreciate women having, or using, a brain. Likewise, she hid the fact that she was, herself, an expert swordsmith. Her work rivaled even her father's. If her reputation was known, she would never have to worry about money again. Unfortunately, it would never be known. Her skill was kept from public knowledge as well, owing to the insecure and controlling nature of her jealous and mediocre husband. Where she could have provided them enough coin to live very comfortably, he saw only that his wife outshined him.

Her blond hair further set her apart. She had not seen another blond since she was a child, other than her own mother. When she stood in the sun it sparkled like gold, whereas the local women all had some variation of auburn or brown hair. This earned her a lot of unwanted attention, and a jealous rage from her husband, who accused her of flirting anytime she left their home.

When Henrick was still her father's apprentice, he had asked for her hand in marriage and Olwen was sure her father would refuse. Henrick was an untalented smith, and there was always something about him that Olwen just didn't trust. She had never had to live under the yolk of ownership or suppression in her life, as her father encouraged her to learn and explore. When her father agreed she would marry Henrick her shock turned to grief, and then to rage, when it became clear Henrick would inherit the forge.

Now her father was dead, and she sat in their small cold house, waiting for her useless husband to come home so she could warm herself. How had it come to this? Was this really what her father had wanted for her? How could it be, after he had spent most of her life encouraging her to learn, do, and be more? Tears surged to her lashes.

Another resounding round of 'THUMPS' echoed from the door, announcing yet another visitor, regardless of the early evening hour. Olwen jumped to her feet, startled by the noise. Dirst wouldn't be back so soon, would he? Would he insist on searching the house for her husband? And when he didn't find her husband, what would he do?

The pounding echoed again in the emptiness of the room.

For a moment, Olwen considered simply not answering the door and instead hiding. But where was there to hide in a house as small as hers? Their door wouldn't keep anyone out who was determined to get inside, and when they did find her... would her fate be worse? Where was HENRICK?!

Steeling her shoulders, she moved to the door, unbarred it, and threw it open to receive her next visitor. The figure on her doorstep was cast in the dark shadows of the early evening with his cloak pulled low, his face hidden in its depths. What dim lighting did escape the door illuminated the fact that he was foreign; his cloak and cuffs were of a fine fabric not available nearby. His boots were highly polished, in a foreign style, not the rough thick leather the locals preferred. His voice was a deep smooth bass.

"Are you Olwen, wife of the swordsmith?"

Olwen watched as the visitor pulled off his fine kid gloves and moved them into his pocket as he shifted his weight onto his other foot. A feeling of dread moved like icy fingertips up her spine, making her shiver. She opened her mouth to answer, but nothing came out. She had no reason to fear this stranger but fear him she did.

The stranger made a small noise of irritation and stepped forward into the light, pulling his hood back.

"I am not in the habit of repeating myself. Are you, or are you not, Olwen, wife of the smith?"

The stranger was the most beautiful man Olwen had ever seen. He was very tall, with broad shoulders, an imposing wall of masculinity looming over her dainty frame. His hair was blue-black like a raven's plumage and pulled back in a tail behind him. His cheekbones were high and sharp; his jaw was squared and equally sharp. His eyes of deep sky-blue seemed to pierce her soul with his stare. His features made him appear both otherworldly and like a predator; she could appreciate him in the same way she would a lion or a tiger. Both were breathtaking, and both were lethal.

His eyes narrowed, staring intently, and he slowly brought himself to hover over her; she realized he was waiting for her to answer, and she swallowed loudly.

"I... I am Olwen. But my husband isn't home! He's due back any minute–"

The words spilled from her mouth as if she could shield herself with them. Whatever deal her husband had breached had found its way to their home and to her, and it looked like she was finally going to pay the price for his sins. She silently cursed him and simultaneously prayed that he would return home to deal with whatever was about to happen. She realized she didn't even have a sword in the room that she could grab to defend herself.

The man didn't wait for her to continue but instead rudely pushed past her into her small home and made himself comfortable on a chair. He spoke to her as he took in her meager home with disinterest.

"Well, I am glad we cleared that up. I am in the right place, although this hardly seems like the quaint homestead Henrick described."

Olwen clenched her hands at her side. "You've talked with my husband? Where is he? You should not be here without him present; it is inappropriate." She hoped she glared at him in a way that said she was strong and capable because inside her chest, her heart was pounding, and she was finding it hard to breathe through her rising panic.

"Oh, yes," the stranger said as he rested his feet on the chair in front of him, "I spoke with him alright. He won't be coming home tonight, I'm afraid. You see, he and I have entered into a bargain and, well... let me cut to the chase. Your marriage to him is now nullified, and you are to be my wife instead. Gather up whatever necessities you may have; we are leaving." He pulled himself back up off of the chair and stood expectantly, gloves in hand.

Olwen stood completely still, allowing the words to register in her mind. She didn't know who this idiot was, but there was no way she was foolish enough to believe a stranger peddling tales. Henrick would set him straight.

When she didn't move to comply, the stranger rolled his eyes with impatience and breathed out a huff of a breath.

"I don't have all night. This is no way to begin our marriage, *Wife*." He hissed the last word.

That spurred Olwen into motion. "I am NOT your wife. You'll forgive me, *My Lord*, if I do not take a stranger's word that my husband has simply bargained me away. I am not going anywhere with anyone until my husband comes home."

"I AM your husband now, and I AM here, Olwen. You will gather your things, or– never mind. There cannot be anything here of value to you. Don't say I didn't give you the opportunity."

The man shot his hand out as if he was going to grab Olwen's face, but he stopped with his palm bared, fingers splayed in front of her.

"I will not argue. A deal is a deal. I don't care if you come willingly, or if I have to drag your unconscious body with me; either way, you are coming. We cannot remain here any longer."

Olwen opened her mouth to argue, but darkness filled her vision and then took her completely.

Olwen groaned. She slowly became aware that she was laying face down on her stomach, and her body was draped and swaying with movement. The soft 'clopping' of hooves on packed dirt met her ears, and she smelled the horse before she could even open her eyes to see it. Based on her level of discomfort, she must have been sprawled over its back for quite some time... enough time to be far from Elspar.

"Ah, good. You're awake."

The deep voice reverberated through her sore body, and her memory flooded back into place. Slowly her situation clicked together in her mind: she had been taken by the raven-haired stranger, she was on a horse with him, and she didn't know where he was taking her.

"I want to speak to my husband." She tried to demand it, but her unused voice came out sounding like a pathetic croak.

"I am your husband," the deep voice reminded her flatly.

"No. My REAL husband: I want to speak to Henrick."

"I think I liked it better when you were asleep," he growled.

"You have abducted me against my will! I will report you. Henrick will see you jailed if you lay a hand on me!"

Olwen began to struggle, but she wasn't in a position to be able to do much. She tried to push off with her arms so that she could slide off the horse, but the rider's arms clamped tightly around her sides, and his voice had an edge of anger.

"You are becoming more trouble than you are worth, *Wife*. Henrick assured me that you were compliant and agreeable. Do not flatter yourself thinking that I have stolen you away like some prize, little mouse. I have the agreement Henrick signed if you should like to inspect it, not that I imagine you can read. I did not seek a bride from this agreement, so do not make me choose to become a widower so soon after I have been married; my patience wears thin."

His hands squeezed her ribs tightly once more before he pushed her back down onto her stomach on the saddle in front of him. He kept his hands on her back, but there was no way she could force her way up even without him wieghing her down. To her horror, she realized that she was laid out over his lap as he sat in the saddle.

She allowed herself to lay limply, conserving her energy as she considered her situation. She was a practical woman, and if time was all she had, then she would use it to best find a solution to her dilemma. She didn't want to take the word of a stranger; however, it would not surprise her at all if her dolt husband had gotten himself so deeply in debt that he would use anything, including her, to free himself. She would look at the agreement the stranger said he had. She would read the truth for herself. Regardless, she was now far from her home and her... and Henrick.

Perhaps this was a blessing in disguise. Hadn't she just bemoaned the turn her life had taken with Henrick? This stranger didn't seem to want a wife, so maybe he would be willing to abandon her. Perhaps she could now have a life of her own making. If he wouldn't abandon her, well, at least he wasn't a drunk laborer who blamed his miserable life on her. Maybe he would take her somewhere far away and she could escape.

They rode on in silence as the shadows grew deeper. Other than the rare birdsong, the only noise to interrupt their thoughts was the rhythmic plodding of the horse's hooves over the earthen pathway. When the sun was fully set, and they were immersed in the darkness of the night and the trees around them, the stranger brought the horse into a clearing in the forest and pulled him to a stop. He climbed down off the horse and then pulled Olwen by the hips so that she slid down her belly over the horse's back until her feet touched the ground.

Olwen tensed as she stood pressed into the horse with the stranger behind her, his hands on her hips intimately. Understanding her reaction, he pulled away from her as if she had burned him, stopping only to snag one of her elbows in his hand.

"I cannot trust you not to run yet, and I have a bargain I must fulfill," he said by way of explanation.

Pulling something out of one of his bags, the stranger clamped a set of manacles around her wrists and locked them with a key which he then pocketed. Olwen stared at her wrists in horror. She had always felt like Henrick owned her life, but never had she felt so much like a slave. The man clearly knew how to use restraints, because there was no way she would be able to manipulate or maneuver her hands to shuck them off.

"Is this how you treat your wife?" she asked sarcastically with a growl, her fear mixing with her indignation.

"I wouldn't know," the stranger replied in a bored tone, pulling her along. "I've never been married before today. But seeing as my wife is you, and you've already made an attempt to escape atop a moving horse, then yes. This is how I treat my wife so that I know that she remains safe and *with me*."

As much as she wanted to, Olwen couldn't argue with his logic. That didn't mean she liked being tied like an animal. She was going to have to get him to trust her if she wanted the shackles removed. Then she could see if he was open to renegotiating their 'marriage' if she didn't simply escape before that.

"What is your name?" she asked as he secured a length of chain through the manacles and around a sturdy tree.

"You may call me Hrafn," he answered, not looking up.

"Raven? Very fitting," she replied.

His movements stopped, and his deep blue eyes met hers. "You speak my language?"

"No, but I know a great many things. I should like to look at that contract you drew up with my... with Henrick. I should like to know what my value as a wife was worth to him."

Olwen held her head high when she asked, but she didn't miss the unmistakable flicker of emotion that flitted through his look before he resumed his mask of indifference. She had seen pity there. The thought only made her anger burn hotter at her former husband.

"I will set up camp here and prepare some food; then I will show you everything."

Hrafn turned and moved away leaving Olwen chained to the tree near the horse as if she was just another beast of burden. He unrolled a tent and set it up efficiently, then he started a fire and set food to cooking. Olwen couldn't help but watch him move. She had been married to Henrick for six years, and never in that time had she ever seen him lift a finger to make a meal for himself. Other than his work in the forge, he had done no work to maintain the household. None.

The smell of fat sizzling got Olwen's attention, and her stomach growled loudly with approval. When was the last time she had meat on her table? She hoped her new 'husband' was at least willing to share his food with her; it had been a few days since she had a proper meal. She ate ground oats but reserved most of the vegetables and bread for Henrick. And if there was meat, it all went to him as, "He needed his strength in the forge." He didn't know she did more work than he did in that forge, even while he starved her. Her stomach growled loudly again, getting Hrafn's attention.

"Are you hungry, Wife?" His tone was playful and his words softer, but he still kept his distance and his eyes were still cold.

"There is no shame in saying that I am. I am a hard worker." She shrugged her shoulders. There was no point in lying.

Hrafn made his way over to her and unchained her from the tree, leaving her wrists bound together in front of her. He walked her to a place by the fire and bade her to sit while he dished out some food into two bowls. After he handed a bowl to Olwen he sat down and took up his own.

Olwen groaned with delight despite herself.

"You like it?" Hrafn asked before taking another spoonful of the stew into his mouth.

Olwen moaned happily again, and replied, "You make this just like my mother did. No one else uses frav berries in their stews around here. I have not had this flavor in a long time; it brings me back to my childhood time."

"If your mother used frav berries then she was not born here. Your mother was foreign?"

"She was. She was born in the heart of the Black Mountains to the East. My father met her on his travels there."

"Did you travel much?"

"Yes. My family moved often. My father was Ignar Cygnus the Swordsmith, and he was needed all over the continent for his work."

Olwen finished her bowl of stew and looked longingly at the cauldron by the fire. Hrafn motioned for her bowl, and he refilled it with more stew for her silently. Olwen sent a silent prayer of gratitude to the Old Gods; no matter what else would happen, she would not go to bed hungry this night.

"It was your father I came here to meet," he confessed. "I was told by the merchants that he had surrendered his mortal body a few years ago."

Olwen stopped chewing. The ache in her heart still burned at the mention of her father's death.

"Yes. My father arranged for me to marry his apprentice, Henrick, and he died soon after we were wed. The forge went to Henrick when it should have been my birthright." She couldn't keep the bitterness out of her voice. The only joy she had after her father's death was to continue his work, and Henrick had forbidden it. He didn't want a woman in the forge when her place was in the kitchen, especially when her metalwork was far superior to his own.

Hrafn watched her closely. "So Henrick became the swordsmith because he married you and inherited your father's work?"

Olwen huffed and shook her head. "Henrick is a general smith and a mediocre one at that. He never had the talent for swords that my father had, and very few people came to him for that work. He worked more in tools and horseshoes, and the occasional plow blade."

Hrafn leaned over his forgotten bowl as if to push the issue physically. "There have been stories that 'Ignar the Swan' Swordsmith still works from beyond the veil. There are men who swear that they have gone to his old forge, and found swords waiting for them, stamped with Ignar's own seal. How would you explain this, if Henrick is so subpar?"

"I would not explain it," she answered simply. "But I will guarantee that no sword of any quality was ever smithed by Henrick, and he does not have my father's seal to use."

Hrafn scowled. He sat quietly as Olwen finished her second bowl of stew. She collected the bowls and motioned to him that she was going to clean them in a basin of water he had collected earlier. Prisoner or not, she would earn her keep, and she was thankful that he had fed her as an equal. He waved her off and sat with his chin in his hand, lost in concentration. After their dinner was cleaned, Olwen approached Hrafn by the fire.

"May I see the contract?"

Hrafn looked up in surprise; he had been lost in thought and seemed startled that she had remembered. He got to his feet and went to his bag, returning to her with a rolled piece of parchment which he handed to her with a flourish.

Olwen unrolled the paper with uneasy hands and scanned down the fancy script until she came to the terms of their agreement. Hrafn would receive free use of Henrick's likeness in appearance and name, so long as he was not in the same place as Henrick, for as many years as he should desire. For his part, Henrick would receive a large sum of coin, and be free of his marriage to Olwen to pursue a life of his choosing, the one stipulation being that Hrafn would agree to take Olwen on as his own bride and ensure that she was not neglected. Both men had signed their names at the bottom.

Olwen's stomach dropped like a ball of lead. Henrick had bartered her away.

He had effectively sold and married her off to some stranger. Why? What had she ever done to deserve this treatment from him? Was it because she had never borne him children? He had barely shared a marital bed with her, so she never really had a chance to try to fulfill that demand for him. If anything, he had failed to give her anything to work with in the bedroom, and she knew nothing but frustration from him.

She had learned to keep her mouth shut and censor her opinion in favor of his, even though her experience and education far outweighed his. She sat by silently while he spent his time and money drinking and gaming in the Ale House while she toiled to keep their house clean and waited dutifully for his return. She had done everything, everything she could think of to be a good wife.

So why, then, did he give her away? She re-read the page twice, but it made no more sense the second or third time.

"You said you were not in the market for a wife, so why agree to marry me?" she asked as tears of anger and embarrassment gathered on her lashes.

Hrafn looked up at her. "I was not. It was never my intention to be married, ever, if I could manage it." He sighed deeply. "I told you I came looking for your father; I have need of a swordsmith of his legendary skill. What I got was Henrick, who clearly doesn't know the combat end of a blade. I had been assured I would find what I needed with him, but that was not the case. I found I would have to search elsewhere, but I have a great many enemies and spies circulating at all times; once my presence here was discovered, I needed a way to hide so I could try to find another swordsmith of Ignar's caliber, if one even exists.

"I knew of Henrick's debt and offered to resolve it in exchange for his face and identity; with it, I can work with other swordsmiths without alerting my enemies to my actions, and if smiths will think I am the heir to Ignar, they will be more likely to help me. It was Henrick who insisted I take you on as a part of his price; that was not my doing. If I did not need this swordsmith so desperately, I would have refused. No offense, Olwen, but I do not want or need a wife."

"And why do you need a swordsmith like my father?"

"That... I cannot tell you. Only that it is urgent that I find one and convince him to help me."

Hrafn rolled himself up slowly until he was standing. The hour was late, and the air had a chill in it as the sun had long since sunk, its warmth long gone.

"It is late. Get some rest in the tent. I will stay by the fire and keep guard."

"You can't stay awake all night, Hrafn. You need sleep too."

"Worried about me already, *Wife*? And here I thought you hated me for stealing you away." Hrafn smirked.

"Well, now that I know what a disloyal beast Henrick was, perhaps I have a new appreciation for you, *Husband*. After all, you have rescued me from living a life with *him*."

"How do you know that I am any better?"

She turned to him. "Hrafn, I have known you less than a day, and I can assure you that you are a much better man than Henrick will ever be. But don't let that go to your head; I am still angry with you both at having been bartered like goods in a marketplace. Goodnight."

Olwen climbed into the tiny tent and was surprised to find a small sleeping roll with thick blankets waiting for her. She wanted to take her dress off but couldn't with the shackles still attached to her wrists. In the end, she chose to simply sleep with it on. Perhaps she would find an opportunity to escape once Hrafn fell asleep, anyway.

He couldn't stay awake all night, after all.

2

Hrafn

Hrafn watched his new mortal bride enter the tent and shut the flap behind her. He was glad to have her out from being underfoot at last. He resolved to himself that if he ever met Henrick again, he would kill him for the sheer nuisance the man had caused him. Fortunately, Olwen was human, so she wouldn't live long enough to truly be a burden beyond temporarily. And if she was unmanageable, he could simply drop her off in his homeland and wait out her lifespan.

But as much as she was a distraction, she was also fascinating to him. She had recognized the foreign nature of his name and had clearly traveled. That was unusual for a female. She could also read, quite the novelty. She also spoke her mind clearly, and argued well; she was not a dramatic emotional well of tears that most women were. While he had expected a screaming tantrum, she had instead reasoned her situation out. She seemed to have accepted it, albeit unwillingly. And she was right about one thing, Henrick didn't deserve her.

To further complicate the situation, she also had an amazing body. Even though she was half starved the thin peasant dress she wore did nothing to hide her lithe figure and womanly curves. If he was not bound to her, he would have loved to ride that body until he ran dry. Unfortunately, he was obligated to her. He could not have an anonymous passionate night with her while he was responsible for her: if she was even interested in that with him. He was saddled with her.

Suddenly finding himself married was an inconvenience he had not counted on. It simply made his quest more difficult and more dangerous now that he had to worry about her safety as well as his own. He was sure Henrick was not smart enough to have realized that he had accommodated her safety with his wording in their bargain. Otherwise, Hrafn could have simply killed her from the start. Even now, he could not just allow an enemy to kill or take her, as he had promised to ensure she was "not neglected." Given more time, he would find a loophole.

In the end, it would probably mean establishing her in his household with a few servants until she passed from the mortal world. He didn't have time to worry about her, with his current situation becoming more dire by the day. Having set the wards around the outskirts of their camp, Hrafn closed his eyes for a few hours of sleep before they had to move on with the rising sun. He would deal with his problem of marriage later.

A violent shock wave tore at his midsection, pulling him from a sound sleep by the dying fire. He leaped to his feet, reaching for his sword belt and finding it missing. Luckily, he still had his shortsword strapped to his thigh. He rushed to the tent to find it empty, as he assumed it would be. The ripple of magic from the wards made him aware that someone was either trying to sneak into his proximity or that someone was sneaking out. The empty tent told the tale.

Growling under his breath, he listened for her movement. She was human and clumsy and made enough noise to broadcast her location to anyone with superior hearing. Had he not been sound asleep when she left, he would have easily heard her movements. He stilled and listened for the telltale rattle of branches and thumping of feet as she ran. He rushed into the bush, following her sounds and her faint scent. She wasn't far.

"*Wife*, I am in no mood for games. Return now, and I shall spare you punishment beyond a lecture."

His long legs carried him quickly, and she turned with terrified eyes as he closed in on her small running form.

"Why do you run, *Wife*? You are only going to anger me further," he barked at her retreating form.

Her breathing was ragged; she was clearly terrified as she ran. He caught up with her easily. She screamed as she turned forward and pulled out all of her energy for one last push for freedom. Just as he reached out to grab her shoulder, the earth shook beneath their feet, throwing him backward a few steps and knocking her to the ground with another scream. He jumped to his feet with caution, moving to recover her when the earth, again, shook violently. This time a gash was torn in the ground beneath them, opening into a deep and wide cavern cutting into the earth. As the ground split open, the soil and roots broke and rolled down the steep embankment and into the depths of the crevasse.

He and Olwen were both swallowed into the earth before they could reach for something to anchor them on the surface. Their bodies tumbled and rolled, crashing through tree roots and bouncing off bedrock jutting from the earthen walls before they both rolled to a stop at the bottom. Clumps of earth and debris rained down onto them, partially burying them in the dark soil.

Hrafn was furious and turned to reach for Olwen but noticed that she hadn't moved from where she landed. He froze in terror, but she groaned loudly. He noticed there was no shackle on the wrist he could see; her other one was hidden beneath her body. Finally, she stirred. Still groaning, she slowly pushed her upper body off of the ground, and with effort, she managed to bring herself into a sitting position against the wall of earth. She was heaving in breaths, and her face remained downcast.

A slow realization worked itself through Hrafn's mind, and his stomach sank.

"Why didn't you tell me you were Fae?!" he demanded heatedly.

Her head slowly rose to meet and match his glare.

"How DARE you?" she hissed. "I am no Fae. I will not have you sully my character, so."

Hrafn's face hardened as he knelt in front of her sitting body. His brows were drawn in anger, and his lip curled with distaste.

"I will tell you how I *dare*, Wife. I know of no mortal woman who can remove shackles without fae magic or a key, and yet I see you wear none. Do you care to explain to me how you, a normal human mortal woman, could achieve such a feat while I hold the only key on my person?"

Olwen never dropped his eye contact, although there was a moment of fear in hers as she realized she would have to divulge her secret to her captor. She took a deep calming breath before delivering her answer.

"That is easily explained, *Husband,*" she sneered as she spoke his supposed title, "I removed the shackles with Fae magic, a gift to my mother and her family. It does not make me a Fae."

"A fae gift, you say?" he retorted with a mocking chuckle. "And tell me, dear *Wife,* how does this gift work? Did you simply make the shackles disappear?"

"Not that it is your business, *Husband,* but no. I did not make them simply disappear. I ... I sang to them." She held her head high, but her cheeks flushed, and Hrafn could feel discomfort rolling off of her in waves.

Again he laughed a mocking laugh. "You SANG to them? Oh, *Wife,* THIS I must see!"

"I have nothing metal to demonstrate with. I am sorry to have to disappoint you. We should find a way out of this trench." She tried to pull herself up to standing, but the earth around her simply caved further, carrying her back to the ground as she struggled to move up and away from him.

"Fear not, *Wife;* I have metal." Hrafn pulled the shortsword from his scabbard and drew the point to the center of her chest, his voice heavy with sarcasm. "Show me, *Wife*. Show me how you sing to the metal."

Olwen eyed the blade and then looked up at him with large eyes. She seemed to be considering her options, but finally, she closed her eyes and took a deep breath.

"It will ruin your blade, *Husband*," she said without anger. He simply nodded and waited for her to demonstrate.

Placing one hand on either side of the flat of the blade gently, she hummed a small tune. Hrafn watched as the energy emerged like a gentle plume of smoke from her throat. It glowed a beautiful brilliant blue and slowly made its way to her hands. The energy then entwined itself between her hands and around the blade. He nearly dropped the sword in shock as he watched the metal begin to swirl and melt like liquid around her fingers. He watched as she moved her hands expertly, pulling at the liquid metal and urging it. She weaved her fingers and the metal followed as she guided. When she was finished she pulled her hands away and the music stopped. The energy dissipated into the air like steam evaporating. His sword blade was tied in a perfect knot.

"There, now you see, *Husband*; I am no Fae, only a girl gifted by a family of swordsmiths." She spoke calmly and rationally, but he saw the fear in her eyes.

"Yes," he answered slowly, inspecting his ruined shortsword, "it would seem so. You have explained the absence of the shackles. So tell me now how the earth was rent asunder as I moved to retrieve you."

She looked up at him suddenly. "I have no idea what caused the earth to tear. You cannot think I had anything to do with that." Her words were less heated than they had been before.

"Oh, but I can," he answered. "Tell me, *Wife*, can you lie?"

She looked at him with wide eyes, incredulous. "What kind of question is that? Of course I can–"

She stopped suddenly, seeming to swallow her next word before she slowly thought it through and tried again. "I'm sure I can tell a lie; however, I usually choose the truth. Why, *Husband*, would you have me be dishonest with you?"

Hrafn smirked. "Of course not, *Wife*." He rubbed his thumb and forefinger over his chin as he contemplated before he turned to her again with a mocking smirk. He was going to exploit his newfound weakness.

"So let me ask you this; were you a good wife to Henrick?" He crossed his arms over his chest and gave her a pointed look with an eyebrow raised. He knew it was unfair to take advantage of the situation, but her attitude vexed him. He wanted to see her squirm just a little.

"I fail to see how that is relevant, *Husband*," she answered quickly, looking away.

"Indulge me, *Wife*," he answered, eyebrow still cocked, knowing he was poking at her.

"Well, I... that is to say... I did everything he asked of me. I performed every duty. How would you define 'a good wife?'"

"Alright, let me be clearer; by YOUR definition of 'a good wife,' were you a good wife to Henrick?"

"I was loyal. I was dutiful. I did what I was expected to do. Is that what you want to know?"

"But were you a GOOD wife?" He leaned in closer, pressing his advantage at her discomfort.

"I do not wish to discuss my relationship with my former husband any longer," she barked. Her face was slowly turning red, and she couldn't look Hrafn in the eye.

"All I wanted to know, *Wife*, was whether you were a good wife. Why can you not simply tell me–"

"I did everything that man asked of me!" she shouted suddenly, enraged, staring Hrafn in the eyes. "I allowed myself to be made small and quiet. I made myself meek so that he could feel stronger. I bit back every word I would have said if it would contradict him, no matter how foolish he was being. That bloated waste of a man used my body for his own satisfaction, completely diminished my validity as a thinking being, and made me a slave in my own home! I despised him, and I would have been far better off without him. Even still, I did everything that was required of me! So you tell me, *Husband*, was I '*a good wife?*'"

Tears streamed from the corners of her eyes, but they were not tears of sadness. Her body vibrated with rage. Hrafn slowly pulled himself to standing and extended a hand down to Olwen, who slapped it away as she tried to stand by herself. He recognized that she had spoken her truth. If he had a conscience, he would have felt guilty in the face of her tears and rage. He changed his tone and the topic.

"Olwen, I need to tell you a few things, and I need you to consider them. You are a smart woman, so I know you will at least give them the fairness of weighing their truth. Olwen, the Fae cannot 'gift' magic to humans. It is not possible. Humans do not have the inherent magic within their bodies to make it work.

"When you 'sing' to the metal, you are using magic, and only Fae can use magic. I'm willing to bet that the same magic which speaks to the metal also speaks to the earth and that your fear created an escape route for you when you felt endangered. There is no other explanation for the earth pulling itself apart beneath our feet.

"Also, Fae cannot lie. They can tell an untruth if they believe it to be true, but they simply cannot let the words of dishonesty leave their tongues. It cannot happen. Can you think of a time that you have purposefully told an untruth successfully?"

"This is ridiculous!" she exclaimed, throwing her hands up. "I am human. I have always been human. My parents were both human."

"Did your father 'sing' to the metal? Is that how he crafted his swords?"

"No, he smithed like every other smith over a fire and anvil. My mother..." Olwen stopped in her tracks. Hrafn could see her eyes tracking whatever thoughts were running through her mind.

"Your mother taught you to sing to the metal," he volunteered.

"Yes... but she was human. She died. Fae are immortal; she would not have died if she was a Fae." Olwen turned to him. She looked like she was pleading for it to be true, her denial evident in her posture.

"Fae are not immortal, Olwen. Yes, they are very long-lived; however, they can be killed, and they can die. If they live too long in the mortal realm, many of them become very ill and succumb to death."

Olwen shook her head emphatically from side to side, closing her eyes against the possibility that it was true.

"Humor me, Wife. Close your eyes and imagine that there is a staircase beside us, climbing out of this trench. Please. Close your eyes, and imagine a staircase, right beside you there. See a staircase made of earth that would free us from this pit."

"This is absurd," Olwen huffed, but closed her eyes and did as she was asked. She envisioned it, and then again, before finally sighing loudly. "Can I open my eyes now, *Husband*? I fail to see what this–"

Without waiting, she opened her eyes and then she screamed, falling into Hrafn as she jumped. There, beside her, was a perfectly cut staircase in the earth, packed firm so that they could easily climb out.

"HOW?" she stammered, but Hrafn only groaned.

"Come, it looks like there will be no sleep tonight." Hrafn relieved her of his sword and belt and took Olwen by the wrist to pull her up the stairs and out of the dirty cleft in the earth. In her shocked stupor, she allowed him.

Olwen

Hrafn pulled Olwen back to the center of their camp, where the fire had all but burnt out. Only a few warm coals remained against the chill of the night. Olwen was still in her light dress, and shivers wracked her body as the wind licked at her skin.

Hrafn pulled off his expensive cloak and put it around her shoulders when he noticed her shaking with cold. She wanted to tell him to keep it. She wanted to hate him and anything to do with him. He had said those hateful things and accused her of being Fae. But she was a practical woman with no desire to freeze to death. She also had to believe what she saw with her own eyes.

Unless it was a trick! What if HE was the Fae? What if he made the ground tremble and part so that he could catch her? What if he had created the staircase? What if he had fed her lies to make her doubt herself? Yes, that was something a Fae would do! She desperately wanted to believe that. She needed to believe that.

Her whole life, she had been told stories of the wicked Fae. They were tricksters, bending the truth to rob people through unfair bargains. Some said they were nothing more than pranksters, while other stories said they would lure ladies into their faerie circles and make them dance until they died of exhaustion. They were reported to have stolen children and left changelings in their place. What they did with those stolen babies was never explained. They were dangerous and not to be trusted. Olwen knew she could not be a Fae. She could not.

And why had Hrafn questioned her about her previous marriage? While she had not loved nor appreciated Henrick, that did not make her evil or a Fae. Just because she had not borne him children did not make her a bad wife. She was simply a barren human woman: nothing more. She *was* human.

"Promise me you will not run again tonight, *Wife*. I am tired, and we have very little time before we must be off again," Hrafn said, his voice low with warning, as he threw himself onto the ground next to the cooling fire and began to feed it wood. He didn't spare her a glance.

"I promise you, *Husband*," she said, staring into the darkness of the woods around her and snuggling deep into his warm cloak.

"Wake up, Wife. We must leave soon."

Olwen jumped as she realized a hand was shaking her shoulder. She looked up to see Hrafn standing over her in only his britches. His chest was on full display, and it was magnificent. His sculpted muscles were a work of art as they flexed and rippled with his movement.

He smirked at her when her eyes finally looked up to see his locked on her. He had seen how she had ogled him. She averted her gaze immediately as her cheeks flushed red, and she climbed to standing. It was then she realized she still had his cloak wrapped around her, warmer than any blanket or quilt she had ever had. It was far too long and dragged the ground if she tried to move. She gently unclasped the neck and pulled it away, allowing the cool crisp air of the early morning to kiss her skin, bringing gooseflesh.

"Thank you," she stated as she held it out to him, still looking away. She couldn't look in his direction, not while he had no shirt on.

"Never thank me, *Wife*," he said flatly, taking the cloak from her hand and dropping it on his bag.

"But why?"

He stopped what he was doing, and she purposefully brought her eyes to meet his, using all of her willpower not to let her vision drop to his sculpted chest.

"I am your husband, and I am asking you not to thank me ever again. You claim that you took direction from Henrick, and he was ... what did you call him... "a waste of a man." I would think it would be a lot easier for you to accept my requests than his, considering I treat you better." He spoke with a neutral face and no emotion as if it was a logical argument that he made and not something so painful to her own heart.

"Fine," she answered flatly, matching his tone, "If that is how you wish it to be, I shall comply with this wish." She turned and moved to start packing up whatever she could.

The two of them moved around each other easily and silently until there was nothing more Olwen could do to help. Hrafn knew how everything packed down and where it went, so she simply sat and waited for him to finish. When most of his belongings were loaded into the packs on the back of the horse, he sat next to her and handed her some bread and some dried meat. The two of them ate in silence.

"I am a man of my word, *Wife*. My bargain with that useless husband of yours stipulated that I must not neglect you. To do that, I must keep you with me. This presents a problem, as I often find myself in danger-ous situations." He paused and took another bite of his bread, chewing briefly before continuing. "I can forcibly restrain you from running, but

I would rather not. I also do not want to have to beat you to make you fear running from me."

He turned his head until she was looking into his eyes as he spoke.

"I want your word that you will not run from me." His gaze pierced through her like it had when she first met him.

"How can I give you my word when in truth, I want only to escape you?" she asked calmly.

"Am I so vile then? You would stay with Henrick, but you feel you must run from me?" he asked. There was a slight heat of anger in his words and he scowled down at her.

She chewed her food and considered her answer before speaking. "No, I would not say you are vile. I would have left Henrick if I thought I could have gotten free and stayed free. But the entire village and region believe that women are owned by their husbands. Even if I could get away, if I was caught I would be beaten or killed for being a faithless wife.

"Several years ago, a girl named Marjorie ran from her abusive husband. She was a simple girl, and he would rape her and beat her almost daily. Everyone knew he did; he didn't try to hide it. She walked with a limp due to a broken leg he had given her and then refused her medical treatment. She met some traveler, a foolish idealistic boy, who talked her into leaving with him. I think he thought he was saving her. It was only a few moons later that they were both found. The boy received public lashings, but Marjorie was hung in the town square as a lesson to all other would-be faithless wives.

"So this is the first time I have been away from the village and without a father to protect me. There is still the very real danger that I would be caught and punished for being faithless, but I would be *your* faithless wife, and you do not want a wife. Perhaps you would even abandon me? There must be some agreement that we can come to where we both get our lives back. You don't want a wife, and I don't want a husband." She eyed him steadily as she chewed.

He considered her words in silence as they both finished their meager breakfast. As they got up and got ready to leave their camp, he stopped her.

"I agree that neither of us wants this marriage, Wife, however, I am bound by it... for now. Let me make a bargain with you: if you will promise not to try to escape me until such time as I have returned safely to my homeland with my quest successful, I promise that I will grant you your freedom of our marriage and arrange for you to live your life as you wish."

"I need more information," she interjected, "What is your quest? If it is a fool's errand, then I cannot agree to those terms."

"I would hardly call it a fool's errand..., but it is going to be difficult, yes. I must find someone who can make enchanted swords like your father's. I must have enough for my armies in my homeland."

"Why do you–"

"I cannot tell you more than that. Only that I need them, and I must find them. Failure is not an option."

Olwen fought to keep the smile from spreading across her face. She knew where he could find a swordsmith like her father. In fact, she knew where there was a large stash of enchanted swords waiting for her return. This would be too easy.

"I accept your bargain." She held her hand out as she had seen merchants do in their negotiations.

Hrafn's head whipped up in surprise. He must have been sure she would say no. He took her hand eagerly and shook it. Olwen felt a pressure tighten on her skin and a sharp snap, like the flick of a belt, on her entire body. She winced, and then it was gone as if it had never happened.

"The bargain is made; let us be off." Hrafn held his hand out to her to help her up onto the horse, and then he climbed up behind her.

Olwen had told Hrafn to bring her back to her forge but he had silenced her saying he had plans. He would not discuss it further. And so they rode.

They had ridden for many hours, the road taking them in and out of forested areas, through long meadows, and over rivers. The hot sun beating down on them, in concert with the soft plodding of the horse's hooves, made the ride exceptionally tiring. Olwen's ass ached from sitting in the saddle for so long. She shifted her hips, trying to relieve the throbbing against her thighs and cheeks. Hrafn's hands grabbed her hips roughly and held her in place.

"I would suggest that you stop fidgeting with that ass unless you wish to consummate our marriage, in which case, I would happily oblige you," he gritted through clenched teeth.

Olwen was suddenly aware of the large protrusion within his pants jutting into the crevice between her cheeks. She squealed and tried to pull her hips forward, only to slide back on the saddle, impaling herself on his hard ridge again.

"Is that a yes?" he asked with a smirk.

"That is a NO," she growled. "I need to get off of this horse for a little while. I am sore in places I should never be sore."

"If you build up stamina, it won't hurt as much. I can help you with that," he said with a cruel chuckle.

She turned to glare at him.

"What? If you ride more, you get used to it," he explained innocently.

Begrudgingly he pulled the horse into a small copse of trees and stopped. He climbed down himself before lifting Olwen off of the saddle as if she were weightless and depositing her on the ground. She noticed he didn't remove his hands from her waist.

"Than– ... er. I'm all set now." She pulled out of his grasp and gingerly waddled away with as much dignity as she could. Behind her, she could hear Hrafn still chuckling.

"It's not polite to laugh at other people's suffering," she growled over her shoulder.

"I offered a solution, *Wife*. You didn't seem interested." He laughed harder.

"Is that how you lure all of your women? Offering to help them with their sore asses and thighs after trapping them on a horse for hours?"

All laughter stopped.

"I can guarantee you, *Wife*, that I have never had to lure a woman to me. They come to me willingly. As for you, maybe if you had someone tend to your ass and thighs, you wouldn't be such a prudish shrew. Now, if you'll excuse me, there is a river nearby, and I intend to bathe. I suggest you do the same. Don't let me catch you trying to sneak a look at my naked body, either." There was a hint of anger in his words as he taunted her.

Olwen's jaw dropped with indignation at his words, but she was too stunned to even retort. Hrafn grabbed a cloth from his saddle bag and made his way down the hill and away from her swiftly. She closed her mouth and ground her jaw unconsciously as the anger seethed through her. Seeing that there would be no one to defend her honor, she chose to take advantage of the river he mentioned. She found another cloth in his pack and headed down the hill in another direction, away from the direction he had gone.

Within a few minutes, she could hear the rushing water, and she pushed through the trees to get to the river. A huge smile lit across her face as she took in the beautiful scene before her. There were mountains in the background, and the river was wide but appeared to only be deep in the middle. There were small pools of clear water surrounded by large stones where she could rest and bathe.

Stripping her clothes off quickly, she left them on the shore and walked into the cool water. Instantly her nipples pebbled, and gooseflesh rose on her arms and legs. The cool water felt refreshing as she stood in the heat of the midday sun. She made her way to a small pool surrounded by rocks where the water was deep enough for her to wet most of her body but also where the current was not so fast that it would tear her downstream.

She dunked herself beneath the surface of the water, pushing back up while blowing the water off of her face. She felt rejuvenated. The cool water worked miracles on her sore muscles. After a good scrubbing, she climbed out onto one of the large flat rocks to lay herself out and dry. The sun was warm, and there was a gentle breeze tickling her skin and keeping her from overheating. She sighed contentedly. It was the first moment of peace she had felt since before she had left her home.

A noise at the treeline caught her attention, and she cracked her eyes open to see movement in the trees. Hrafn! Had he been spying on her? She was furious at the thought. His innuendos were bad enough, but to violate her privacy like that was unforgivable. She slipped off of the rock and gathered her clothing; throwing only her dress over her head, she charged into the woods.

After a few minutes of climbing the hill, she slowed; nothing looked familiar. She was certain she must be heading back to where they had left the horse, but no matter how far she climbed, she never saw or heard the horse or Hrafn. She didn't remember the river being that far away. She slowed her climb to one footfall at a time, scanning the trees, trying to find something that would tell her she was going the right way.

A strangled groan broke through the trees. Olwen clutched her clothing to her heart, looking for the source of the noise. It had never occurred to her that there might be others on the hill; she suddenly didn't feel safe calling out for Hrafn. She could see movement ahead of her, so she crouched low and slowly approached some bushes to use them as cover. Once she was in the thicket of bushes, she gently pushed a small branch aside to create a small hole in the foliage to look through.

When she saw it was only Hrafn, she breathed a sigh of relief and then prepared to let him know how angry she was with him. She stopped when she noticed he was acting strangely. She could see Hrafn leaning on a tree with one arm; he was groaning like he was in pain. With his other arm, he was–

Olwen clamped a hand down over her mouth.

Hrafn was pleasuring himself with his hand, pulling on his length, grasping it from root to tip, quickly shuttling his hand back and forth over it while he groaned quietly. She could see he was well endowed, not that she had seen a lot of men's appendages in her life, but she had seen enough.

She knew she should back away quietly and leave him in privacy, but she couldn't. There was the practical issue of the noise she would make pulling herself out of the bushes, thus alerting him to her peeping ways. This was ironic, as her purpose for following him was to berate him for invading her privacy.

There was also the issue of the throbbing between her legs as she watched with hungry fascination as he brought himself closer and closer to release. She kept her hand over her mouth lest she moan out loud. He was beautifully built, and watching such a powerful man pleasure himself so roughly and with abandon made her desire things she had not desired in a long time.

She sat transfixed as his breathing grew louder, and his body seemed to tense around his shuttling hand. She could tell he was close; his breaths came out in panting groans, growing higher and louder. His hand worked harder, faster, a blur over his bruise-colored cock, jutting proudly from his body like a sword. Olwen froze where she was, breath held. Just watching him had her ready to release her own heat. Her fingers slowly made their way down her body.

Hrafn swore, then roared as his release spurted from his cock in hot flashes of liquid to the forest floor. He pumped himself for a few more seconds, letting the last of his essence leak from his body, before stuffing his cock back into his trousers, tying them up, and heading back up the hill without a backward glance.

Olwen sat in the bushes, stunned. Her mouth was a perfect round 'O' of shock. She had watched Hrafn pleasure himself, and at his moment of release, she heard as he had called out her name.

3

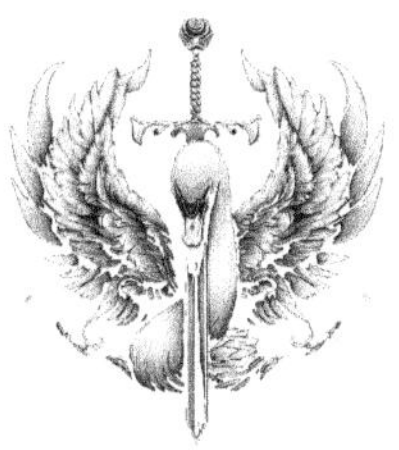

Hrafn

The bath in the river had felt amazing. He had scrubbed himself clean and felt renewed. He had wanted to breathe deep and relax, but the tension remained. Uncharacteristically, his conscience tore at him. Normally he was not given to sentimentality, but he could not seem to get out of his own head.

He admitted to himself he had not needed to be so cruel with Olwen; it was unfair to throw her past at her when it had been out of her control. She was a strong woman, and she was right when she said she had not needed a husband. He wanted to acknowledge it and move on, but the knowledge festered in his mind until he could not relax. It was damned inconvenient.

He knew some of his surliness came from traveling for extended periods, now with her soft body pressed into his, and without sexual release for himself. But that was no excuse to take it out on her. The easiest solution would be to simply avail himself of his new wife to relieve his suffering, thereby alleviating two problems, but that would create other issues. He was going to be stuck with her for a while; there was no point in muddying the waters between them by introducing a sexual relationship.

Add to his misery that she seemed to love to torment and tease him. She seemed to revel in pressing her ass into his cock as they rode. There was no way she could not have been aware that his manhood stood like an iron poker at her back gate. She had acted surprised, insulted even, when he had called her attention to it. But he had seen how she looked at him at the camp with hungry eyes earlier. He could smell her arousal. She may deny it, but she wanted a taste of him as much as he wanted to devour her, and this was a problem. It was especially grievous as it only made him more frustrated and more likely to lash out, even while she played the coquette in denial.

They would have to make a truce between them if he was going to avoid violence or severe emotional repercussions. In the end, he convinced himself to find her and apologize for his cruel remarks. If they were going to be traveling together, they were going to have to get along. He could be the bigger person and extend the banner of truce first. He simply did not want to deal with an emotional woman for the duration of his quest.

When he found the horse by itself, he pulled out a change of clothing. Seeing that Olwen hadn't returned yet, he peeled off his pants and shirt and quickly changed into fresh clean trousers and a riding shirt. Hrafn rounded the horse and listened, then followed the sounds of her splashing and laughing. He should have known better.

"*Faen*," he swore under his breath.

He stood in the trees while she twirled and splashed in the water like a mermaid. She was laughing and playing, completely carefree. She was also completely naked, and it wasn't lost on Hrafn that her small plum nipples were hardened into tiny pebbles. He stood transfixed as she glided into and out of the water, and he could only imagine himself gliding so effortlessly inside of her. His cock ached at the mental picture.

He knew he should leave. He shouldn't be doing the very thing he teased her about. And while he was not normally one to care about rules or breaking them, he knew she would see this as a violation. Still, he couldn't make his feet pull himself away. She pulled herself up onto a rock, and he froze, convinced she would turn and look right at him; he wasn't even hidden. But instead, she laid herself out over the rock and sunned herself, her beautiful globe breasts ripe and luscious.

He couldn't take it any longer. He turned and ran as quickly as he could through the trees and back up the hill, shoving tree limbs aside as he went. But the vision of her laid out naked before him was too much. His cock was screaming for release, and he knew he'd never be able to sit on that horse for another several hours with her ass riding the seam of his pants over his cock. He ran up the hill, putting distance between them. Then, he stopped where he was, unlaced his trousers, and pulled his cock out to slake his need.

He certainly would have rather had some hot female body to empty into, but desperate times called for desperate measures. It didn't take long for him to reach release, with the vision of her wet pussy still laid before his mind's eye. All he had to do was see himself climbing over her and claiming her with his throbbing cock, making her scream and moan in ecstasy. As his balls pulled tight and his cock spasmed in his hand, he pictured her reaching her orgasm and clamping down hard on him as she screamed his name. He whispered her name before he roared, shooting his seed onto the ground.

It took him a few moments to catch his breath again. He did not intend to keep her for the long run, and he didn't want her to do what normal, emotional women did and assume that this 'marriage' between them was going to last. He did not need her clingy and dependent. While she had claimed she wanted to be rid of him, she had also acted as if she had no interest in him; clearly, that was untrue. With his lust under control, his mind was clearer. He simply had to find a swordsmith, get what he needed, and take her home: then he could cut her loose, and she would no longer be his problem.

How the hell he was going to last until that time was beyond him. He would need to come up with a strategy; either that, or she would have to warm to the idea of servicing him like a traditional wife. While his cock liked the later idea, his mind knew it wasn't really in his best interest. It would be a mistake to bed her, knowing they still had a long journey ahead of them before he could relinquish her, and she was bound to have hurt feelings.

And then there was the issue of her Fae heritage. That mortal life-span he had been relying on might pose a problem if it turned out she had Fae longevity. No, thank you. He didn't want to be married at all, never mind for his entire life. He didn't need to risk that she would change her mind and want to stay married to him.

No, he would find a warm body to fuck at their next town. Until then, he had his hand. Better to use it on himself than on her. While he was no longer craving her warm body, his attitude had again taken a dark turn. He climbed the hill to the horse, hoping she was ready to leave.

Olwen

Olwen sat in shocked silence for a few minutes until she could hear Hrafn calling her from the top of the hill. She stood slowly, pulling leaves out of her hair and trying to right her clothing. Looking down, she realized she had pulled her dress on without putting on under-garments, and she felt very naked suddenly. She looked at the ball of clothing in her hands, wondering how she could find some privacy, when Hrafn crested the top of the hill above her, his jet-black hair floating on a breeze.

"There you are! Come along, *Wife*, we have a schedule to keep." He seemed broody as usual; his mouth twisted down with displeasure.

She was not about to announce she wasn't wearing undergarments.

Instead, she picked her head up and moved up the hill to join him. The sway of her breasts was distracting, and she could feel the blush creeping up her face. She looked down, pretending to be choosing her footing carefully, as she made her way to where he was and then passed him quickly.

"Oh good, I see you've bathed as well. Just put your things in the bag. We need to get on the road if we expect to make it to Akvar by nightfall."

Olwen avoided making eye contact with Hrafn. She highly suspected he already knew she had bathed, as he had probably witnessed it, but she couldn't say anything. There was no way she could hold a conversation with him after she had seen him explode with pleasure while he uttered her name. She put her things into the saddle bag and drew it closed tight, sneaking a peak at him out of the corner of her eye. He seemed intent on whatever he was doing, thank the Goddess.

She had just tied the bag down when she felt his firm hands grabbing her waist and lifting her up and over the horse. His hands slid up her rib cage, and the back of his hands brushed against the undersides of her breasts without her shift to hold them in place. She sucked in a breath and looked away quickly. She hoped he hadn't been aware, that he had moved so quickly that he didn't notice.

In seconds he was on the horse behind her, pulling her hips tightly to his, and she felt every inch of the steel bar in his trousers against the seam of her ass. He hadn't missed it at all, and now she was going to be feeling his arousal pressing into her for the rest of the trip.

How could she have been so stupid? Why didn't she stop to dress herself properly? He had already expressed his interest in her and then demonstrated it, even if he was unaware he had an audience. Her face flamed warm as the blush rose over her features. The ride would be torture with her feeling so exposed while simultaneously being aware of his arousal.

There was a part of her that wondered if she shouldn't just give in to the desire. He was endowed; she already knew that. He may be a perfectly good lover. Lord knows she had enough bad sex with Henrick, so why not indulge in something she wanted? Then, when his quest was complete, and he was home safely, she could go on her way and live her life. It was tempting. She could feel the liquid heat building in her core as she considered it, and she squirmed, which caused Hrafn to haul her ass back against his cock again.

No, it was a bad idea. He said he didn't want a wife, but he was stuck with one. Once she opened that option to him, what if he wanted to keep her around to service his sexual needs? What if he decided he didn't want to release her as he said he would? She never had that issue with Henrick; he could never perform, so he chose to ignore her. But Hrafn? Hrafn was virile and clearly lustful. It would be better if he didn't think of her sexually at all. She decided she would have to do all she could to make herself unappealing to him.

It would be different if she was never going to see him after one night, but she was tied to him for the foreseeable future, and she didn't need to become his wife in truth, versus his wife through bargain. She would have to keep herself in check until he released her. She was a practical woman, and she would not risk her freedom for a quick roll with this broody foreigner, no matter how well-endowed he was. Still, she bit back a groan as she felt him snug against her ass as the horse moved out of the trees and picked up its pace.

Hrafn

"Faen!"

The ride was long, and Hrafn's balls were aching by the time they reached the inn at the outskirts of Akvar. He was beyond frustrated; he was livid. It was clear; there was no way she was not tormenting him on purpose. She had come back to camp with only a flimsy dress over her body, the rest of her clothing balled in her hands. There could be no accident there. She was seducing him.

When he lifted her onto the horse, his hands had slid up her ribcage with no undergarments to catch on. The soft weight of her breasts had caught the backs of his hands, sending his cock into spasms. Then as he climbed up behind her, he noticed that he could see right down into her dress, which was untied at the neck. He had a clear view of her beautiful breasts and could even make out her soft mound. The ride was torture as he watched her breasts bounce, and there was nothing he could do about it.

He made her pay. He pulled her back against his cock and rode the seam of her ass the whole trip. A part of him wanted to undo his trousers and take her right there on the horse, but he wasn't going to succumb to her game; no, two could tease. He pressed the tip of his cock against her puckered hole and had the horse trot for most of the ride. It was magnificent feeling her cheeks squeezing him the whole way while his cock head beat her back entrance. Several hours later, however, he was feeling the strain of needing the release he had been denied.

"*Faen i helvete,*" he swore under his breath.

He pulled the horse to a quick stop and jumped out of the saddle, nearly falling over from the ache in his groin. Straightening himself with effort, he turned.

"Stay here, *Wife,*" he growled over his shoulder as he stormed over to the door of the inn. Maybe he would be lucky, and someone would kidnap her while he secured their rooms. A few minutes later, he emerged from the inn with room keys in hand to see her standing behind the horse nervously.

She damned well should be nervous after her little performance, he thought to himself as he grabbed the bags off of the horse. "Come, *Wife,*" he barked as he turned back to the inn.

Hrafn made his way up the back staircase with his bags in hand. Out of the corner of his eye, he could see her trailing timidly behind him. It made his anger flair hotter. Why would she be so brazen as to display herself for him to see and feel and then play the victim when he reached out to take it? No, he wasn't going to play her game. He had a better understanding now of why Henrick was so keen to be rid of her. He could feel the vein throbbing in his neck.

He unlocked a door and threw it open for her.

"This will be your room. My room is right next to yours. I am going to have dinner brought up for you, and I am going to get you some new clothing to travel in. DO NOT leave your room tonight. Remember our bargain."

Before she could say anything, Hrafn turned and walked to the next door, turning the key and opening the door, stepping inside, and slamming the door behind him.

He blew out a breath and dropped his bags onto the floor. His cock ached with need. He knew he could get some attention here and some food, but a part of him was still furious with Olwen for thinking she could get away with tormenting him after telling him she only wanted her freedom. Was this her way of pushing him to release her? Or was this payback to Henrick and him for using her as bargaining fodder? Did she think he would not be able to persuade her to tend to him if it was what he really wanted? Legally, he was her husband, and he could demand that she see to his needs, not that he would do that. He was a man of logic and action, not melodrama and emotion, so the entire situation only left him frustrated and angry.

He liked her a lot better before she was a conniving *fitte*.

If he continued with this train of thought, he would need to find a fight or a good fuck, or both, to get back into the right mindset. Taking a deep breath to clear his head, he chose to focus on a logical and rational solution.

While he was married to her by contract, they had no agreement between them, nor had they had any ceremony. As she did not care to service him sexually, he should feel no guilt whatsoever in getting his needs met elsewhere. He had made it clear to her that he would meet her needs, so she had no excuse to look elsewhere. Yet again, he was being generous while she was choosing to be petty about their situation.

What was it with women hoarding their sexuality? It was not as if she was a virgin; she had admitted as much. Did she think her pussy was so valuable that it was above sharing for the pleasure of others? Especially for her husband. She had done so for that cretin Henrick, so why not him? She clearly wanted him to pleasure her, so why would she deny it? His anger rose in his chest again, and he blew out a breath with a huff. This line of thinking was getting him nowhere. Fine. If that was her decision, so be it. She could let her vagina shrivel to dust for all he cared; there were plenty more to be had.

Her taunting him, however, was unacceptable. He would give her one last opportunity to divulge her sordid plan. If she would confess to him that she was purposefully teasing him, he would not feel the need to punish her. However, if she denied that she was engaging in this behavior with him on purpose, he had no recourse left but to do what he needed to do, whether she liked it or not.

He was nothing if not fair.

With the decision made, he changed into clean clothing, a tight pair of leather trousers, and a loose blouse that showed a significant amount of his chest muscle. He had not been lying when he told Olwen he didn't need to lure women to him. He needed only to sit and wait, and like moths to the flame, they flitted around him eagerly. He eyed himself in the mirror one last time before pocketing the key and exiting the room. One way or another, he would find satisfaction this night.

He stopped at the next door and knocked loudly. Olwen pulled the door open, a look of surprise on her face.

"May I come in, *Wife*?" he asked as he stepped into her room without waiting.

A look of annoyance washed over her features, but she remained silent.

"I have a question for you." He turned to face her, his nose inches from hers. "Why would you return from bathing partially undressed? Did you forget to put on your underthings?" He smirked at her condescendingly, his eyes downcast, waiting for her story.

"Indeed I did, *Husband*. I was drying on a rock when I heard something in the woods. I thought that perhaps someone was spying on me, so I threw my dress on hastily and ran as quickly as I could."

Hrafn stopped to consider. She couldn't lie, even if she was not ready to admit it yet, so she had heard him in the woods when he was watching her. But she never said she saw him. He had quite a lead on her, and she still arrived much later than he did... What was she doing?

"It took you a while to return to camp. I am surprised you did not stop to dress yourself."

"In truth, I got lost." Her cheeks flushed pink, and she looked away as she said it.

"So, you did not return half-dressed simply to torment my cock in retaliation for my comments earlier?" he asked her point blank.

Her mouth fell open in shock and outrage.

"You ignorant, stubborn, misogynistic ass! I returned half-dressed because I was convinced someone was violating my privacy by watching me bathe, and I was trying to catch whoever it was to give them a piece of my mind. Then you found me when I could not find my way back. I want NOTHING to do with tormenting your cock. I am fairly certain that my backside is bruised from you rutting into me like an unskilled adolescent on horseback all afternoon. Would you kindly take your cock and get out of my room?"

The rejection stung, and anger rose to replace it. No one had ever spoken to him like that. Hrafn turned to leave, stopped, and turned to face her again.

"You know, *Wife*, I wonder why it is that you would give yourself so willingly to that oaf Henrick simply because you were married to him, but you parade around half-dressed with me and act as if I am a villain for responding to your wanton ways. Are you not *my* wife now? Would that not imply certain duties on your behalf? You certainly fulfilled them with your last husband. I am just curious." While he tried to sound nonchalant, there was an undertone of anger and hurt in his voice.

"You would force me to bed you?" she asked with a snarl, her fingers pulling into fists like claws.

Hrafn took several strides forward, forcing Olwen to back up until he was in her face, nose to nose. His glare was pure menace, and his words were slow and deliberate.

"Let me be clear, as this is the second time you have made this assumption, *Wife*. I have NEVER had to lure, trick, or force any woman to seek pleasure in my bed. I do not intend to start now. I will not have you slander me thus again. I would advise that you consider your attitude toward me; otherwise, when you do come begging, and you will, I am likely to turn you away, wife or no."

"Do not hold your breath waiting for that day, *Husband.*" There was fear in her eyes, but she held her ground as she returned his glare.

Hrafn pushed through the door, and it slammed behind him no sooner than he cleared it. He did not know what to make of her taunting behavior, but her rejection and insults left him angry at her regardless. He was done being nice.

A small smile pushed to his face. She had all but told him to get his pleasure elsewhere, and so he would.

Olwen

As the hour grew later, the noise outside Olwen's tiny room got louder. She opened the door a crack and looked out over the great room below. The tables were all full of people eating and drinking, laughing, and carousing. It was a rowdy crew. There were bawdy songs sung in the key of drunk and a fist fight taking up a corner. Bar wenches cackled and revealed too much skin, to the delight of the male patrons who dropped coins into their blouses for favors.

Earlier, a boy had brought her up a tray with a simple meal, and she had devoured it. He had brought a mug of ale as well. She normally did not drink ale, owing to the taste, but she was thirsty. Now she sat in her room, warmed from the ale, peeking out over the room below and watching as the patrons got sloppy and drunk. She could imagine her former husband being just like these men. Is this how he had spent all their coin?

She was about to close the door when something caught her eye at the bar. Olwen's brows drew together in anger, and her jaw clenched, as she watched Hrafn sitting on a stool with his back against the bar, surrounded by ladies and barmaids alike. He sat back like the lion of the pride while the women all fought to touch him, stroke him, and in one instance, get a hand down his tight pants right in the middle of the room! Was there no decency?!

"Don't leave this room," indeed! Now she understood why. Apparently, her new husband was a sex fiend. So why did he have to insult her and belittle her if all he wanted was some attention for his cock? He certainly wasn't insulting any of the harlots draped over him.

Perhaps that was the key. Perhaps he preferred unthinking women. Maybe that was a necessity for men, docile and silly women, to help bolster their confidence and help them perform. It would explain why so many childish and dull girls in her village had been popular with the men. Maybe that's why Henrick could never perform with her; perhaps he was too intimidated by her, and men's cocks simply could not deliver when faced with an intelligent woman. If that was the case, she was doomed to a disappointing sex life.

Regardless, she didn't need Hrafn, or his cock, if it came with that massive ego. She watched him for another few minutes lounging like a king. He was making no effort at all. None. The women fell over themselves to fetch him drinks or rub his shoulders... and other places. Having seen enough, Olwen shut the door on his display. She couldn't imagine degrading herself thusly for a man who seemed to feel entitled to the attention.

She turned and opened a door, looking for the washroom, and found that it opened into a small hallway connecting her room to Hrafn's room. Gingerly, she tried the knob to the door on his side and was surprised when it opened freely. She could see where he had dumped his bag on the floor earlier and his change of clothing thrown in a pile. She also noticed her underwear had been laid out on his bed. The thought turned her stomach. She returned to her room, shutting the doors behind her.

Opening another door, and found the washroom she had been looking for. After relieving herself, she washed, undressed, and climbed into bed for the night. It was early, but what else was there to do?

She was standing in a doorway on a balcony with a handsome man in front of her. She couldn't see his face, but his chest was magnificent. His muscles rippled in the moonlight. She had her arms wrapped around him, touching his back with only her fingertips beneath his open shirt. She could feel the indent between each rib and the hard muscle that defined him. It was as if the contact on his skin was lightning; wherever her fingertips touched him, she connected with him like magnets drawn together. He kissed her deeply, and she could feel his pulse through her points of touch, gently pulling him closer to connect with her more deeply. Heat surged between her legs.

A high-pitched laugh tore through Olwen's dreams.

Olwen groaned and sat up. Another woman's laugh ripped through the silence of the room. It sounded like there was a party under her bed. There was giggling and then another female shriek. She got out of bed and wandered to the other side of her small room, closer to the door that connected her to– Surely he wouldn't?

A squeal and more giggles filled the air.

Olwen gripped the doorknob and slowly rotated it. It made no noise, and the door swung silently open into the tiny hallway. The womens' laughter was louder, and she could hear Hrafn.

"Another drink, my pretty!"

"Only if I can drink it from your body!"

Olwen crept closer to the door connecting his room and was surprised to see that it wasn't fully closed. She was sure she had closed it earlier. Had he opened it? The ladies' giggles and cackling laughter grated on her nerves.

"Drink up, my pretty!"

Olwen watched through the narrow opening of the door; Hrafn poured the ale down his naked chest and belly as he kneeled on the bed. One of the barmaids, who was also naked, was perched in front of him, trying to lap up the river of ale as it splashed down his abs and over his–

Olwen covered her mouth before she could gasp.

The barmaid was bobbing her head over his cock and groaning while she wiggled her ass in the air. Then the other woman stepped into sight. She prowled behind Hrafn and seemed to be spreading his ass cheeks. Then she started to lick him from top to bottom in the back while her friend took care of the front. Hrafn just groaned, holding the head of the woman in front of him as he thrust his hips into her eager mouth.

"That's it, my pretty. Take it all like a good girl. That's it. Suck me dry. Oooh, you do have a talented mouth, don't you, Pretty?"

Olwen sat horrified for the second time that day. She, again, found herself witnessing Hrafn's sexual pleasurement, but this time he had two women with him. She was mortified, outraged, and scandalized. She had never seen anything sexual outside of her own few experiences. Yes, she had heard the gossip of the bar wenches and the prostitutes of her village, but she had never seen with her own eyes a man brazen in chasing his pleasure; by his own hand or with not one, but two, ladies. She was not sure which was more shocking, his attitude or their behavior. Her own experiences were dull and lifeless compared to the writhing and groaning pile of limbs gorging themselves on Hrafn before her eyes. It ignited something deep within her. She had never been so eager to have a man's cock near her, never mind...

She couldn't look away as the brunette pushed her fingers into Hrafn's ass. She could never imagine doing that! And yet, her body reacted viscerally to what she was seeing. While her mind screamed in horror, her body exploded with desire. Her pulse was pounding in her ears, and her breathing came in short, breathy pants. She squeezed her knees together as she felt liquid electricity buzzing between her legs. It made no sense!

Hrafn cooed and groaned before pulling his cock out of the barmaid's mouth. She grumbled, but he shushed her. "You have to share, my pretty."

With that, he turned to the girl behind him, turning her and bending her over, so she was on her knees in front of him.

"You want this cock, my pretty?" he teased as he pulled it through her moist slit. She mewled into the blanket and wriggled beneath him, pressing her ass back.

"Yes, you've been a good girl; you deserve this cock, don't you?" he cooed. The barmaid was now trying to lick his balls between his legs from behind while he lined himself up with the woman in front of him.

"Alright, pretties, ready yourselves!" Hrafn slammed his hips forward, driving his cock into the brunette in front of him. Immediately she started moaning and bucking. Hrafn didn't even seem to notice her. Instead, he brought one knee up to change his angle, and then he proceeded to pound the shit out of her pussy with his hardness.

He was violent, masculine, and dominant: all of the things Olwen had never wanted from a man in her life. At least, she hadn't thought she did. But seeing Hrafn drive his cock into this girl like a predator had her rethinking. The girl was clearly loving it as she screamed and wailed. It seemed mere moments before her back was arching, and she was releasing a long keening scream as her orgasm hit her. Still, Hrafn slammed himself at her, plunging her deeply from behind.

After a while, the brunette just seemed to wilt, and Hrafn pulled out of her and turned to the blonde, who gladly fell back and spread her legs wide. Olwen could see everything. She watched as his huge cock disappeared into her wet core, only to reappear again. He pulled her ankles up over his shoulders, and much like with the brunette, he launched his cock into her like a piston. She, too, screamed and wailed, thrashing her head side to side and grabbing at the blankets while he impaled her repeatedly and roughly. His eyes were closed, focused only on his own pleasure.

Soon she was spent, and he moved back to the brunette, but the brunette didn't have as much energy the second time around. Olwen watched as he went back and forth between them until both of them looked as if they would fall asleep where they were from exhaustion; still, he worked his cock in them, focused on his release.

While she still had the cover of their sex noise, reluctantly, Olwen decided it was probably time to creep back into her own room before she was caught. Her face flushed with guilt. It was the second time she had violated his privacy and watched him doing something intimate. She herself would have been outraged if she knew he watched her doing something so personal. But that was the pity... she never did anything worth watching. Yes, he may have seen her nude, but that was all she had to offer by way of titillating excitement.

It made her sad to think that regardless of her education, or perhaps because of it, she may never experience the raw hedonism she had just witnessed, not if men could not be sexual with someone equally intelligent. Right then, she wanted that experience in her life. She wanted a man to use her body for his pleasure and to give her so much that she screamed her release. Her face was still flushed, partly from guilt, partly from arousal. Hrafn was the most erotic man she had ever seen. Just his body made her hot and needy, but seeing him chasing his pleasure left her undone.

She knew she would never be able to go back to sleep, not with the throbbing between her legs. She cast one last look at the door dividing the rooms, and a thought occurred to her. She made her way to the washroom and filled the bathing tub with warm water. It wasn't as hot as she would like, but it would have to do. Once it was full, she climbed in and allowed herself to relax into the warmth with a moan. Her old house hadn't had a bathing tub; it was a luxury she almost never got to appreciate.

With a quick nervous glance at the door, she slowly moved her fingers down to the juncture of her legs, to where her need was greatest. She allowed her fingers to delve and play in the folds, swiping through her wetness; until, at last, she reached for the tiny bundle of nerves that lit her up. She rolled it between her fingers and gasped at the sensation, her body swaying in the tub and sloshing the water. She continued to work it, moving two fingers inside of herself and out, imagining it was Hrafn's cock plunging her depths, calling her name. Not surprisingly, her walls began to tremble, and her body began to spasm as her release took her over, causing her to arch her back and moan as her body convulsed with the sensations. She allowed the waves of pleasure to pass through her like earthquakes of ecstasy.

Finally sated, she lounged in the water, allowing the heat to relax her muscles until she was sleepy again.

Unbeknownst to Olwen, the door connecting their rooms closed quietly as Hrafn made his way back into his own room.

4

Hrafn

Hrafn growled as he stuffed his supplies back into his bag in the early hours of the morning. He had stayed up most of the night fucking two of the women he had met in the tavern non-stop until they just couldn't perform any longer, and he began to chafe. His frustration knew no limits. Instead of giving him many divine releases and relaxing him, they had only served to frustrate him further. No matter how long or how hard he fucked them, they did not bring him satisfaction. He wanted to scream.

He was sure it was all Olwen's fault. She had taunted him all the previous day. He had never before experienced the inability to spill his seed whenever he desired to do so. After he had pushed the ladies out of his room, he had gone into Olwen's room to demand she do something about his state, as she had caused it. He was unprepared for what he found: she had not been in her bed, and he heard the water in her washroom. He headed for the door and stopped in his tracks when he saw her.

She was laid out like a goddess in the water. Moonlight streamed through the window and over her features, glistening in the droplets of water adorning her face and breasts like gems. Her head was thrown back in a mask of bliss as she responded to the exquisite pleasure of her tiny fingers as they fluttered under the water, in and out of her swollen lips. She gasped breaths and moaned gently as her body undulated against her hands. It was the most pure and erotic sight he had ever witnessed, and he was transfixed. This was no wanton sex show performed to arouse an audience; this was a sanctified act of reaching into the depths of what it means to be a woman and wrapping herself in the sensuality and ecstasy that was hers to bestow. This was raw vital sexual power on display before him, delivered in the innocent softness of a velvet rose petal.

Standing before her with his jaw fallen, Hrafn suddenly found his release. Without even touching himself, his system was overloaded with sensory information that seemed to electrify his whole being, and his cock lurched as his balls drew up tightly and unloaded with a massive wave of convulsions that left him blinded momentarily.

He had rushed from the room like a boy caught masturbating, thankful that he had managed to remain silent when he had wanted to scream at the release of the pressure he had felt. He closed the adjoining door silently and fell against it as sweat beaded on his forehead and chest. His breathing was ragged, and his heart raced. His cock, however, was finally flaccid and ready for sleep. Not even waiting to see if Olwen had been aware of his presence and followed him to his room, he fell into his soggy bed and was asleep before his head hit the pillow.

After only two hours of sleep, he had to get up and face the prospect of riding with Olwen all day, after what he had witnessed her do the night before, after what had happened to *him* after witnessing her. He stuffed his clothing in the bag roughly and swore.

He decided that he may need to consider changing the nature of their bargain and just releasing her sooner. He had never been so obsessed with sexual release before. He would not endure months on the road with her like this; he would require an endless stream of female company to tame his cock and make life bearable. It would be easier just to get rid of her; then, he could focus on his mission.

He had too much at stake to deal with this distraction.

He gathered up the bags and the small pile of clothing he had gotten for Olwen, as he had promised her. He would buy her a whole damned wardrobe of clothing if she would leave him in peace. He moved into the hallway joining their rooms and stepped into hers.

Olwen

"Wake up, Wife. We leave in thirty minutes."

Olwen groaned, and her face pouted as she pulled herself out of her dream. When she realized someone was shaking her by the shoulder, she screamed and jumped to sitting; only to scream again when she realized she was naked and pulled the thin blanket up to her chin. Hrafn stood before her with his shirt unlaced and open and his traveling trousers half-laced. He was trying, unsuccessfully, to hide the laugh that was tugging at his chest.

"HRAFN! What are you doing in my room unannounced?! This is inappropriate!" Olwen shouted, her cheeks flaring red as she pulled the blanket close to her body like a shield.

"I have announced myself, Wife. I would say this is completely appropriate. How else should I wake you? I have several ideas–"

"GET OUT!"

"By the Old Gods, woman, will you calm yourself? You've nothing I have not seen before. I have clothing... *and underclothing*," he looked at her pointedly as he said it, "for you to wear, so you do not have to wear that one thin dress. I'll just leave them here for you. Dress quickly. I'll be in the tavern with breakfast, but I won't be made to wait long."

Without another word, he turned on his heel and strode to the door, opening it wide as he left and slamming it behind him. Olwen noticed he was less broody and gruff. Perhaps his sexual escapades the night before had calmed him. She remembered the wives in the town gossiping about how they would fuck their husbands to get back into their good graces, as it soothed them and relieved their stress.

Olwen's heart beat a frenzied pace as she slowly willed herself to calm. She didn't know if he had startled her or seeing him half-dressed had incited her, but either way, she needed a moment to compose herself. She looked at the small collection of clothing he had draped over the end of her bed. With a lingering look at the door, she climbed out of the blankets and picked up each piece, and inspected them.

The clothing was all expensive and well-crafted. The fabrics were rich in color, thick for warmth, but so nicely constructed that they were buttery soft to the touch. They were luxurious, even for the daughter of Cygnus the Swordsmith. The blouse and skirt had beautifully embroidered edging with fine detail. He had included a cape of her own, cut to her length. The final detail was the new pair of leather boots sitting on the floor near the end of the bed. They were the softest leather she had ever felt, and they glowed with a shine. She was not surprised when she tried everything on, and every last stitch fit her as if they had been tailored to her; in fact, they may have been.

Tears sprang to her eyes at the thoughtfulness of the gifts. It would take her a long time to reimburse him for the coin he had spent, even with her sword-making skill. Shaking her head to clear the tears, she gathered her few things and headed to the tavern to deal with her surly and yet generous sex fiend of a husband.

Hrafn was drinking his coffee and finishing the last of his hot breakfast when Olwen arrived at his table. He didn't stand for her, as a gentleman would do, and she shrugged her shoulder. After his generous gift of clothing, she would not create drama over his slight. He noticed her old dress, folded in her hands, and reached to take it from her, stuffing it into the bag carelessly. Again, she remained silent, choosing prudence.

A plate of food was set in front of her: hot eggs, warm bread, bacon, beans, and hot vegetables. Her breath caught for a moment as she fought back tears of gratitude. It was clear that while Hrafn could be a deviant, he at least did not expect her to starve as her previous husband had.

Hrafn must have seen something on her face.

"What is the matter, *Wife*? Is the food not to your liking?" he asked flatly, but with none of the heat he had shown her the night before.

She shook her head, willing herself to speak without her voice cracking. "No, Husband, the food is very nice. In fact, I do not know that I can eat it all, nor that I have ever been fed so well. I find myself in your debt yet again."

Her candor seemed to take him off guard. "Debt? What debt do you speak of?"

She held the edges of the cloak out. "You have bought me expensive clothing, Husband. You know I have no coin to compensate you, but I swear that I will make good on your investment in my well-being. Likewise for the room and board, although it may take me some time."

She looked down at her plate humbly. She had been raised by the greatest swordsmith on the continent and had never lacked funding. She had worked to provide her keep for the family after her mother's death, and her father had been generous with her. Now, only a few years after his passing, she found herself reliant on the generosity of a stranger who technically owned her. At least with Henrick, she could sell "her father's" swords without his knowledge, bringing in the coin they needed to stave off his ever-growing debt. But without the forge and on the road, she had nothing... well, nothing that she was willing to give.

She picked up her fork, but as she raised her eyes and caught Hrafn's look, she stopped.

"Our customs are different, *Wife*, so I will give you the benefit of the doubt that your intentions and words are honorable. Let me educate you so that we may not find ourselves in this situation, as I will not have you shame me publicly again. You are my *WIFE*; whether by bargain or by oath, I am responsible for you. I understand that your last husband was not a man at all, that he would allow his wife to wear threadbare clothing and remain underfed, but I will not have you hold me to his nonexistent standard. You owe me *nothing*, and it is insulting to me that you should feel indebted to me for a basic standard of provision. I will not take your coin, so do not bother collecting it to give to me, as I would only consider it an offense. Eat your fill, and then we leave."

Hrafn got up from the table quickly, not meeting Olwen's eyes; grabbing the bags, he strode to the door and out quickly. Olwen sat shocked for a moment and then quickly began to eat. She would not waste whatever food she could get, as she wasn't sure when Hrafn would feed her next. At least, she felt certain he would feed her, and that gave her a level of comfort she had not experienced for years.

Hrafn

Hrafn strapped the bags onto the horse tightly, causing the mare to nicker and swing her head at him in protest. He stopped and blew out a breath in frustration; he didn't want to take out his anger on the poor horse.

Every time Henrick came up in conversation, he only wanted to murder the man more. It was now becoming a mental game for Hrafn to consider how he would torture him first, to prolong his suffering, before granting him death. It was not just that Henrick had been a selfish ass; he had met many of them... hell, he could count himself as one. He was angry that Henrick had set him up for this never-ending drama with Olwen through his own neglect of her, and he had done it completely unintentionally.

But he had also done it in such a way as to prevent Hrafn from being able to do the same to her, not that Hrafn would. As much of a scoundrel as he was, he would never have the lack of decency to let Olwen suffer without basic necessities. So Henrick had forced her to endure years of abuse, and now Hrafn would have to bear the brunt of her disdain for the lack of compassion she had been shown in the past, even as he, himself, went out of his way to show her compassion.

Henrick was going to suffer; he was going to beg for death.

Hrafn had just finished cinching the last bag in place when he heard Olwen approaching.

"I'm glad you chose the breeches today; it will make riding easier for you," he stated simply as she turned to the horse and pulled himself up into the saddle. He tried not to notice the way the sunlight glistened on her soft blonde waves like frosted gold. She was actually a beautiful girl when she wasn't scowling.

Olwen stared up at him with big eyes, unaccustomed to having him mount first. He held his arm down to her.

"Place your left foot in the stirrup, there. Grab my hand. You will ride behind me today so that we can make better time. I have a meeting to attend."

Olwen did as she was told without comment and settled herself behind him in the saddle. He had thought having her behind him, instead of pressing into his groin, would make the ride easier, but feeling her thighs snugged tightly to his was also distracting. There would be no avoiding it.

"Who are you meeting?" she inquired quietly as he reigned the horse away from the inn and onto the road out of town.

"An informant. This man travels these areas and knows of the merchants and smiths within a few weeks traveling distance. He will know if there is a swordsmith who can do what I need doing."

"And what do you need done?"

Hrafn didn't turn to look at her as he answered. "That is not your concern, Wife. Just hold on tightly."

With a flash of his arms and a kick of his heels, Hrafn urged the horse into a run, and Olwen was forced to drop her line of questioning and grab onto his torso, wrapping her arms around him tightly and squeezing her thighs around his, to his mutual delight and chagrin.

They had only been riding for a few hours when Hrafn brought the horse to a stop at a crossroad in a forest clearing. Both roads were broad and appeared to be well-traveled, although there were no other travelers present. The trees still had most of their leaves, as the autumn season had not fallen fully. Sunlight streamed down lazily through the dense foliage overhead.

"My associate will be here shortly. Why don't you take this opportunity to see to your needs before he arrives?"

Hrafn climbed off of the horse and reached up to help Olwen down, his hands bracing the tight corset under her clothing that he had gifted her. Immediately his blood flowed straight to his cock as he felt the boning that spanned her gentle waist and rib cage through the fabric, and he swore to himself as he placed her down hastily and stepped away.

None the wiser, Olwen moved into the tree line to find a place of privacy in the foliage to relieve herself. He knew she didn't want to be too far from him, but she didn't want him to witness her call of nature, either. Hrafn made his way to a tree nearby, undaunted by the prospect of public nudity, and proceeded to relieve himself in the open.

He heard a whistle in the air by his ear a split second before the wire wrapped around his throat, cutting into it as the weighted ends swung around him snugly, cutting off his air. He could feel blood welling below the tight cord in his skin, and he struggled with cutting his fingers trying to pry the cord from his neck.

"So good to see you again, Lord Hrafn."

Hrafn turned, still struggling to remove the cord which had secured itself around his throat. The highwayman he was to meet stood a foot from him, a big smile on his face.

"Imagine the bounty I will receive when I tell the Magestan General that I have removed Hrafn from the playing field," the man said smugly with a broad smile on his face. Hrafn noticed the dagger in the man's hand, poised and ready to strike. Hrafn realized that his own weapon was strapped to the horse, and his vision was starting to go dark from lack of air.

"W-why?" he choked out with difficulty, his head swimming.

"Oh, it's not personal, Hrafn. They simply offered me a better bargain than you did, and you did not ensure that I would not work against you in our deal, so there was nothing to stop me from making the better deal. No hard feelings, I hope?" He snickered as he stood by, waiting for the bolo to strangle Hrafn into unconsciousness.

Just as the world started to go dark, and the ground felt like it would spin out from under his feet, Hrafn felt the highwayman press into him, a look of shock on his face as he pushed him to the ground with his body. It was then that Hrafn felt the blade enter his chest, but only shallowly. The last thing he saw was Olwen pulling the blade out of the highwayman's back as she stood over them both.

The smoke of a cooking fire danced in Hrafn's nostrils, making him sneeze and then wince with pain. His eyes flashed open as he registered the searing burn in the skin of his neck and the sharp ache in his chest. He looked up to find Olwen sitting over him with a look of concern on her face.

"How are you feeling?" She looked as if she might cry, and she wrung her hands restlessly in her lap.

"Like dritt," he answered dryly. As his memory washed over him. He looked up at her suddenly. "You killed him." It was a statement, not a question.

She looked down swiftly, avoiding his eyes as her cheeks burned hot. "Yes, and I nearly killed you too. I did not gauge his distance from you well and stabbed you through him. It will take a while to heal."

Hrafn looked down and noticed the square of fabric set on his chest with dried blood soaked into it.

"So you can use a sword as well; good to know." He let his head fall back. "It is not the worst I have endured, Wife. I will recover. Fae heal more quickly than humans."

Her head snapped up, her eyes wide and her mouth open in shock.

"So you admit it?" she whispered.

"I was not hiding it, Wife. I am what I am, and I am not ashamed of what I am. Do you still think all Fae are monsters?" The corner of his mouth quirked up.

"That all depends," she countered slowly, watching him warily, "Is it true Fae cannot lie?"

"Unfortunately, that is true."

"So, when you were trying to convince me that I, too, am Fae..." She left the sentence unfinished.

He looked up into her eyes. "It is because you are. Whether you like your circumstances or not, you must accept the truth of them."

Olwen nodded miserably and returned to looking down into her lap.

A question suddenly occurred to Hrafn, and he cleared his throat to get her attention again. "Where did you get the sword? The one you killed the highwayman with? It is not mine."

"Oh." Olwen looked up and blushed fiercely. "I took it from his friend, who tried to kill me with it."

Hrafn pulled himself up to sitting and groaned as pain lanced through him. "Explain, Wife."

"I had just finished... relieving myself, when a man was upon me with a sword to my throat. He said he was meant to kill me, but he may instead keep me for his pleasure."

"So, how did you come to have his sword?"

"I pulled his wrist as if I was trying to pry him away from me and sang his blade back rapidly to strike his own throat. Once he was dead, I sang the sword right again and came to your aid."

Hrafn looked both horrified and fascinated as he took in the details.

"How quickly can you change a sword and change it back?"

"It depends on the sword. If it is an ordinary sword, I can change it rather quickly, but it will require work and time to form it back into a useful blade and not just a sharp piece of metal. However, if it is one of my father's swords, as his was, they respond to me instantly. It is quickly back to being a functional sword again, although I would still like to spend the time to bring it back to its original beauty as my father would have wanted."

"Show me," Hrafn demanded, suddenly serious.

Olwen shrugged and retrieved the sword from a nearby pack. She sat down and presented it to him. He took it from her hands and could feel the energy humming within it. He turned it over in his hands, taking in the razor-sharp edge. He noticed that it was missing the beautiful engravings that adorned Cygnus's sword blades, and while the hilt was fancy, it was not as lovely as they were known to be. He could see the maker's mark at the base of the blade, or half of it; the other half was missing as if it had been erased.

"Do you need a forge to put this to rights?" he asked in awe.

"Not at all," she answered as she gently and lovingly scooped the sword out of his hands.

She cradled it in her lap and hovered her hands over the blade. The faintest song trickled from her lips, the melody winding from her like a thin trail of smoke and light. Hrafn watched with awe as the engraving slowly took shape on the blade like a slow-growing vine springing to life and spreading. The hilt wound and curled on itself to create filigree and fine detail, as well as a superior grip. Lastly, the maker's mark, the swan taking flight, pulled itself into being out of the metal and proudly imprinted itself at the base of the blade. As her melody ended, the light faded, and the sword sat proudly in her lap, a work of art.

"You said Henrick did not have your father's seal to use; that is because you have it. That is because you use it." Hrafn eyed her with a new appreciation.

"Yes, Husband. My father is not making swords from beyond the veil. I am. I have made many in an effort to keep my ... to keep Henrick's debt from my doorstep. To no avail." She frowned and then looked down lovingly at the sword in her lap.

"Why didn't you tell me?" There was a hint of anger in his words, a subtle accusation.

"Why would I tell you? You were a stranger to me; you abducted me. More to the point, you refused to tell me why you needed the swords."

"But you're telling me now?"

"Well, yes. Because we have a bargain. Once I have retrieved the rest of my swords, and you have seen yourself safely home, then you will release me from our marriage." She smiled up at him joyfully.

"You have MORE swords?"

Olwen laughed, and her voice was like chimes in the wind. "Yes, I have a stash of swords, and of the metals I need to make more. When my father died and Henrick inherited the forge, I hid away all of his sword-making materials. Henrick couldn't use them anyway, and I didn't want to chance him selling the metal. I would sneak into the forge at night to work on new swords if his debt grew too steep. Whenever someone came to the village looking for my father, I would tell them that he had passed and that there were only a very few rare swords left with his seal. This would guarantee a higher price."

"And Henrick never caught on?"

"Never. I would simply 'find' another of my father's swords in his mess of scrap when we needed a sale."

"But you told them you had swords of your father's work: that was a lie."

"No, it was not. His work was actually MINE in truth. Every sword he fashioned and sold was sung by my mother first and then by me when she passed, but they all carried his seal. I only said there were a few with his seal."

"So, where are the swords that you have hidden?"

Hrafn's eyes grew wide with excitement. He had the answer with him the entire time. He had access to the enchanted swords and the swordsmith who created them in his grasp, and he had that moron Henrick to thank. He needs only to get them and return to his country to avoid the impending war.

"They are buried behind the forge of my former husband."

"Well then, I suggest we pay him a visit and retrieve them."

5

Olwen

Hrafn woke her before the sun was even up. The day was cold and dreary, with the threat of rain to further darken his mood. But Olwen could not be unhappy. They were headed back to Espar and the home of her traitorous former husband. As they rode, she envisioned scenario after scenario in her head.

She saw Henrick at home, penniless and alone, begging her to return to him. She envisioned him penniless and lonely, sitting in his cold home, wishing he had someone to look after him. She envisioned herself laughing mercilessly in his face as she took what was hers and rode away into the afternoon, a free woman at last.

Well, she wouldn't be free just then... but she was well on her way to freedom.

"We shall need to acquire a cart and maybe another horse," she said aloud as she considered the logistics.

Hrafn turned to her. "You have that many swords to take?"

Olwen nodded to him, and he furrowed his brow in thought.

"I can get us a cart, but I don't dare spend what coin I have getting a second horse, not when we do not know how much longer we will be on the road. I can't risk it. There is a town over the ridge; we will stop there."

They rode on in silence until the town came into view. Hrafn pulled the horse into the tree line.

"I will leave you here, Wife. I cannot risk anyone recognizing you for your own safety. I will wear Henrick's face until I return with the cart.

Olwen was not pleased about having to wait in the murky and wet forest alone, but his argument was sound. She did not need to be harassed or arrested for being a faithless wife to a man who had sold her. Surely her village must know that she was gone by now, so she couldn't very well show up in a neighboring town with 'Henrick' either. As Hrafn was a foreigner, she did not know if they would weigh his story at all. She would have to wait.

With no way to pass the time, it seemed forever until Olwen heard the creaking of the cart as Hrafn's horse pulled it along the path and back to her. She climbed onto the bench beside Hrafn without a word, and they continued on. It wasn't long before the surroundings became very familiar to Olwen, and she directed Hrafn to steer the horse off the road and onto a narrow path that led into the woods. She explained that they would not be able to go through the middle of the town, and as the forge was at the edge of the town anyway, they could approach it from the back, take her swords, and be gone, with the villagers none the wiser.

She was glad for the rain, which fell loudly around them and camouflaged their creaking cart and sloshing of the horse's hooves. Finally, Olwen called Hrafn to stop after they passed the familiar chimney at the back of her former tiny hovel. Sliding off of the bench quickly, she made her way to the back of the forge, out of view of her home. Crouching low, she snuck from tree to tree, looking for signs that the forge was in use; there was no smoke coming from the chimney, no lantern light in the windows. Her luck was holding.

She dashed into the yard and pulled up a small door of rotting wooden planks covered in moss, which were completely hidden against the moss of the yard. She shoved it aside and climbed down into the hole it left exposed.

Hrafn was right beside her as she began grabbing armfuls of blades, bunched and wrapped in blankets and tarps, and hauling them out of the hole. He ordered her out, and he continued to feed bundles up to her while she stacked them beside the hole quickly.

"What are you DOING?!" The shrill voice cut through the relentless noise of the falling rain.

Olwen spun with alarm to see Sofi, the fishmonger's daughter, standing in the rain, soaking wet with a very pregnant belly starting to swell under her dress.

"YOU?!" she screeched, "What are YOU doing back? First, you abandon your husband, and now you come back to rob him? Is your new lover not taking care of you as well as Henrick? You should have considered that before you abandoned him. You're too late now, Olwen; he's MINE. He'll never take you back; I'm giving him a baby, something you never did in all of your years with him." She shouted until her voice was hoarse.

Olwen just stared in utter shock. She had not even been gone a week, and Henrick had moved on. Judging by the size of Sofi's belly, he may have moved on long ago, unbeknownst to her. Is that where all of his coin had gone, right into her pussy? Rage burned hot in Olwen's veins. Hrafn chose that moment to make himself known. Wearing Henrick's face and body, Hrafn pulled himself out of the empty hole and stood beside Olwen.

"Actually," he began, using Henrick's indifferent tone, "I'm pretty sure that baby isn't even mine; I know that most of the men in this town have left plenty of seed in your garden over the last few years. You might as well hear it from me: Olwen didn't abandon me as I told everyone she did; I sent her away. She refused to support me any longer, and I don't want to have to work for my living, so I needed a new patron wife. As you're in need of a father for your baby, and I know your father will make sure that you, and of course your husband, are taken care of; I pushed Olwen to leave so I could stake my claim on you instead. Even if your father refuses to fund us, I can always sell that sweet pussy once the baby is born, as you're used to giving it away, anyway. You head back to the house now and get my dinner ready for me. I may or may not be home tonight. Some of your girlfriends are working at the Alehouse, and you know how I love the attention."

It was Sofi's turn to stand in shock, her jaw hanging open. She tried to call to 'Henrick', but he waved her off with a growl, as he had often done to Olwen. Olwen had to remind herself that it was not really Henrick at all but Hrafn wearing his likeness. Sofi sobbed loudly and ran from the yard, and Hrafn wasted no time in grabbing the bundles they had laid out and running to the cart with them. It took four trips, running the whole time, but they managed to get every last blade loaded without any further interference.

Without a word, they both jumped into the wagon, and Hrafn cracked the reins; the horse shot forward. Olwen clung to the bench, her knuckles white, as she cast looks over her shoulder to see if they were being pursued. The Goddess must have been with her that day because there was no sign that anyone was following them as they got further and further from the tiny village that had been her home for so many years.

Once clear of the village and several nearby, they returned to the main road and continued a brisk clip toward what Olwen assumed was Hrafn's home. She allowed herself to breathe deeply. After they had ridden for many hours, and the horse was nearing exhaustion, Hrafn finally pulled to a stop in a shady cluster of trees deep in the woods where the foliage would hide the cart.

Olwen could see a river nearby, and although she was chilled from the light rain that had persisted all day, she wanted nothing more than to wash the mud off of her clothing. Hrafn set about taking care of the horse and ensuring that the blades were covered. Olwen did her part and got the tent set up and ready, but it would be difficult to get a fire going with no dry wood. She wanted to bathe, but she didn't want to remain wet and cold all night. She stared at the ground, trying to decide what to do.

"Bring me some wood, and I will dry it, so it will burn," Hrafn finally said, catching her attention. She stared at him incredulously, but he only indicated with his hand that she should fetch the wood.

Without second-guessing, Olwen turned and gathered several armfuls of sticks and small logs. She knew they would all burn quickly, as she couldn't carry anything too heavy, but it was something. Hrafn joined her, and once she put the wood on the ground, he waved his hands over and around the pile. Olwen could hear hissing and gentle pops as the wood dried before her eyes. Hrafn then started a small fire in a stone ring before placing the rest of the wood under the wagon to keep it dry until it was needed.

Satisfied that they were settled, Olwen announced she was going to bathe and headed for the river. It could be seen from the campsite, but the view was obstructed, and Olwen hoped that if she moved a little further downstream, he would not be able to see her at all. Her modesty battled with her need to get out of her filthy clothes and rest her sore muscles. She made her way to the river's edge.

Checking one last time to be sure she was alone, she pulled her clothing off and headed into the water. She took her dirty clothing with her, hoping to wash the mud out, even though she knew she would have to sit in wet clothing by the fire when she got back. Maybe Hrafn would give her the tent again, and she could hang her clothing to dry?

She had just gotten the last of the mud and soil out of her breeches when she heard Hrafn's voice.

"How is the water, Wife?"

Olwen turned to see him standing behind her on the river bank, several feet away, and she turned her back quickly. She was trapped in the water, naked.

"What are you doing, Hrafn?" she sighed in exhaustion. She didn't have the energy to get upset and demand he leave. She was getting tired of having this battle with him. She only wanted to be clean and sleep.

"I have come to join you, of course, Wife." he answered happily.

Olwen froze where she stood. "I don't think that is a good idea,

Husband. Why don't you give me a few more moments of privacy, and I will leave you to have the river all to yourself?"

Out of the corner of her eye, Olwen could see Hrafn already pulling off his clothing and throwing them into the shallow water. She groaned with defeat.

"Nonsense, Wife. As I said this morning, you've nothing I've not seen before. Let me come and keep you company, and be sure that there are no miscreants about who would spy on your beautiful body while you bathe."

She turned only her head with a skeptical eye and saw him smiling broadly at her before her eyes began to scan down his form, and she had to whip her head away from him again. She could feel her cheeks flaming with color.

"What's the matter, Wife? Surely you have seen a man's anatomy before. Don't be so shy. I only want to bathe, nothing more."

Olwen considered that he supposedly could not lie and weighed her response before suddenly coming to a realization.

"Husband, I have a question for you." She kept her back to him as she heard him splashing water over himself behind her. She could almost feel the heat of his skin, and his proximity both electrified and terrified her. "When you were acting as Henrick, you told Sofi all of those things... I thought Fae cannot lie. How did you tell her those things, then?"

The splashing stopped. "Well caught, Wife of mine. You are indeed clever. I simply took advantage of an ambiguity in the intention of the natural law. You see, technically, it is a lie for me to speak and say that I am Henrick at all, except that he had given me express permission to use his likeness and name. Therefore, as I was Henrick, for all intents and purposes, my truth would have to be Henrick's truth. I had already surmised what his plan was before I ever went to retrieve you that night. I may have embellished somewhat, but it is not outside of what he would be capable or probable of doing. I was originally going to go back and kill him on your behalf; however, now I may let him live a while longer and suffer the consequences of his poor decisions. I think this is the best possible outcome." Hrafn laughed loudly and resumed splashing water over himself.

Olwen stood in stunned silence, processing everything Hrafn had said to her. A tear slipped out of the corner of her eye as she considered that Henrick had truly thrown her away without regret and replaced her without losing a wink of sleep. She had been nothing to him at all; she was property to be bartered and abandoned. She did not love him, so she was not heartbroken that he did not love her. Her sadness came from the realization that he could not even see her as an object *worth* loving or valuing. While she had honored her oaths to him, even though she hated them, he had never once considered her happiness in his life; her only value was what she could provide for him in the moment.

She released a ragged breath and sniffed. Better that he was gone then. Now she could truly begin HER life. She was the daughter of Ignar Cygnus; she was the Swan of the Sword.

Hrafn

"Hand me your clothing."

Hrafn turned his head in her direction, his eyebrows raised in surprise. He saw she still had her back to him, protecting her modesty and preventing him from getting a full look at her goods, but her arm was stretched back to him, her hand open expectantly.

"Wife?"

"Hand me your clothing, and I will clean them," she said, still facing away.

Hrafn eyed her appraisingly as he considered her request. She had no reason to do anything for him, and it was the first time she had really offered. While he wanted to make a lighthearted remark, some part of him recognized that this was her banner of truce, and he would be a fool to trample it. Without saying a word, he retrieved his clothing and placed it into her waiting hand.

She took his clothing and moved further into the water, away from him, to wring it and scrub it well. She didn't seem as concerned with hiding herself away from his eyes as she focused instead on her task, occasionally pulling fabric from the water high, her breasts rising and swinging with her movement. Hrafn had to turn his head away; it seemed rude to take advantage of her while she was doing him a kindness. Not that he wasn't tempted.

Olwen moved around a large boulder in the water, putting it between them. She hefted his wet clothing up onto the rock.

"Your clothing is clean; you will just need to hang it." She spoke quietly, and there was a haunted sadness lingering in her eyes.

Hrafn gathered his things and headed for the shore. "Wait here, Wife; I will return shortly." He pulled himself out of the water, not caring if she was ogling his naked ass as he went. He grabbed the cloth he had left on the shore and wrapped it around his waist before heading back to the campsite.

From the saddle bag, he pulled some rope, which he ran between trees around the fire pit. He hung his clothing to dry and grabbed a blanket to bring back down to Olwen. He found her where he had left her, lost in thoughts, submerged to her shoulders in the river.

"Come, Wife; I have brought you something warm to wrap yourself while the clothing is drying."

Her face snapped in his direction, but she hesitated to move. Hrafn rolled his eyes and turned his body away so that he could not see her approach. He heard her sloshing her way toward the shore behind him and held the blanket out for her, but was surprised when she stepped in front of him, dripping and naked, to take the blanket from his hand and wrap herself. Before he could even look away, she turned and walked back to the camp ahead of him.

While Olwen hung her clothing, Hrafn pulled out supplies and prepared a meal for them. He watched her in his peripheral vision. She seemed heavier in her spirit; where only a few days before she had laughed and splashed in a river, today she was sullen and serious. He knew she had not loved her former husband, but he had not anticipated that his betrayal would sting her so deeply. Had he known, he would not have spoken those hurtful truths in her presence. He was beginning to understand that she was more sensitive than he had originally estimated.

They ate their dinner in silence. Hrafn watched while Olwen seemed to be miles away in her thoughts. She kept the blanket pulled around her, but the top loosened as she ate, and the curve of her breasts was visible. She didn't seem to notice at all. He wanted to sit and enjoy the view, but again his conscience suddenly made itself known.

He did not know what it was about Olwen that had him so conflicted. He was royalty where he came from. He would inherit the throne one day and was used to getting whatever he wanted, whenever he wanted it. What was it about this prudish little wife and her misguided modesty that made him want to treat her with kid gloves? If it were any other lady, he would have put them in their place, but he couldn't bring himself to be harsh with her any longer. Even after she had tormented him. She was no virgin, but she was definitely innocent.

He lived a life of privilege, where his needs were met first and foremost. He had never had anyone rely on him for their well-being, other than being told to suck it up and make do with what they were dealt. So why did she affect him?

She made his pulse race. He was like a teenage boy, thirsting to catch a glimpse of her form, to steal a look at the forbidden fruit. He had seen her pleasure, and he wanted to own it. It frustrated him to no end that these humans had indoctrinated her into a life of shame for her own sex, that she felt she had to guard her chastity as if it were finite. It would take weeks of work to crack that frozen barrier and warm her to the possibilities if he were to pursue that with her. And he wanted to pursue that with her.

He also knew he shouldn't.

She was his new swordsmith, although she didn't know it yet. If her last husband abandoning her had cut her so deeply, how would she react if he couldn't bring himself to release her as he had promised to do? If she was his swordsmith, he could never let her go. He would need her to help give his army the advantage in the face of the oncoming war;

she would be the difference between victory and defeat, life and death. It would be foolish to simply throw away that advantage. It would be irresponsible to his people.

But she may never forgive him.

Olwen

As the hour grew later and the shadows ran long, Hrafn pulled a change of clothing out of his saddle bag for sleeping. He also pulled out a dressing gown he had gotten for Olwen when he bought her clothing. Olwen took the nightgown and blushed furiously as she remembered him waking her in the inn where she slept with nothing on. The slight smirk on his face told her he had not forgotten that morning either.

She wrapped the blanket around herself and headed into the tent to dress. She didn't know what had come over her earlier that had made her walk up to him without a care for her naked body. She could only say that she was exhausted; not physically, she had been emotionally exhausted. Her whole life had been turned upside down, and she had left everything that she knew behind; being naked in front of her new 'husband' hardly seemed the largest of her concerns. It simply took too much effort to constantly guard against an unwanted view, and to what end? They were traveling together.

She had already ridden with him in nothing but a shift dress pressed against his erection all day. She had seen him in the throes of pleasure. Truly, she had violated him far more than he had violated her, and she needed to let go of the unnecessarily rigid discipline that she had always held herself to. In the end, how had it served her? Her husband had left her for a pregnant woman after failing to satisfy her for years. If she was truly to be a free woman, then she had to free her body and mind of the societal constraints that she had allowed herself to conform to. She wanted the wanton sex she had witnessed for herself.

Having put her sleeping gown on, she opened the tent flap to check her wet clothing but stopped. Hrafn stood with his back to her, completely naked by the fire, warming himself. She did not know why he had not dressed, but seeing his strong back and thick thighs in the dancing firelight, she did not care one whit. He truly was magnificent, his muscles sculpted from hard work and training. His back and chest were massive, leading down to a tapered waist. She remained motionless as he shifted from foot to foot, deep in thought. He turned and paced a few steps, only to turn again and pace back. Olwen stood wideeyed, watching his enormous cock swinging between his strong thighs as he moved. Her mouth went dry.

She stood like a doe in the woods, eyes open wide, frozen and immobile, his sheer masculinity seeming to confuse her senses. At last, she noticed that he had stopped pacing and that he no longer had his back to her. A sense of mortification bloomed cold in her gut, and the color drained from her face as she slowly raised her eyes from where they had been glued to his crotch. When her eyes reached his face, she gulped loudly. His eyes were on her, his stare intense, with just the slightest uptick at the end of his lips to show his thoughts on the subject of her staring at his cock. She had no idea how long she had been there, and now that he had her locked in his sights like a predator, she found she could not move again. She wished that she could just vanish into the earth from embarrassment.

"Do you like the sleeping gown, Wife?" he asked nonchalantly, a small smile licking at his lips.

Olwen could only groan a mumbled response and nod, forcing her eyes to remain locked on his. She felt the heat of the blush that was burning her cheeks in flames of humiliation. They stayed locked like that for a few moments, as she did not know how to get herself out of the situation. Finally, she dropped her eyes to the ground, and turning quickly, she said her goodnights and rushed back into the tent, pulling the flap closed behind her in retreat.

She did not know what it was about Hrafn that turned her into a lovesick young girl. She had pleasured Henrick, or at least she had tried to. She had also had two dalliances with other young men a few years before she met Henrick. They were young and inexperienced and approached it as an experiment. It had been awkward and unsatisfactory. Her experiences were nothing like the stories the women of the village told each other when there were no men around. She had heard tales that had scandalized her, and she had seen uninhibited behavior with her own eyes when she had seen Hrafn with his two lovers.

Perhaps it was her lack of knowledge and experience that made her feel so awkward and vulnerable. Hrafn could strut around naked with his cock on full display and not mind one bit while she covered every inch of flesh: why? When he suggested lewd things he could do to her body, she rejected him reflexively, but her body craved to feel his touch. Why was she holding herself apart?

How was she going to be free and independent if she did not know how to feel the pleasure of a man? And was it even possible, given her intelligence and her theory about male performance? She needed answers, answers she would only get through experience. Maybe she should reconsider accepting Hrafn's offers. If he was honest and was going to release her at the end of his journey, then she had nothing to lose. She could experiment with him and gather experience that would help her to attract a better lover in the future.

But he had been so arrogant with her after the day she had not worn her undergarments. He had told her she would come begging him and that he may turn her away. What would she do then? How much more humiliating would it be to go to him and ask only to have him laugh at her? She didn't know if she could bear that.

Olwen curled on the sleeping mat and pulled the thin blanket over her. She would have to think of a way to make her interest known and to see how he reacted. If it looked like he would be cruel again, she would not open herself to that rejection. She tucked her chin into the warmth of the blanket and soon drifted into a dream-filled sleep.

She woke up with a start. She felt a warm breath on her neck and heard a soft moan as she became aware of the heat of the body wrapped at her back and the hard length again pushed against the cleft in her ass. Her pulse skyrocketed, and her breathing became fast and shallow. She felt Hrafn's hand crest her hip, smoothing over her belly before it landed over her breast and massaged it gently.

She froze. She didn't know what to do. She didn't know how to react. Should she scream? Should she kick? Should she fight? Or should she pretend she was still sleeping and just enjoy the experience?

Behind her, Hrafn moaned again and buried his nose into her hair as he pulled her body closer to him, his hips thrusting against her ass. His breathing was ragged.

She couldn't believe that he would pleasure himself with her body without her permission.

"Hrafn..." she whispered, "Are you awake?"

He didn't answer. His hand still massaged her breast, distracting her with the sweetest sensation that shot directly down to her now throbbing pussy.

"Hrafn?"

He groaned slightly more loudly.

"Hrafn?" She spoke a little louder as he seemed to be getting more excited by the minute.

Suddenly his hand jerked to her hip, holding her tightly as he thrust his cock against her ass.

"Faen! Olwen..." he groaned into her ear. She could feel him convulsing gently behind him, and there was a warm wetness spreading around her ass. "Olwennn..."

"Hrafn?" She tried again, but there was no answer, only his breaths becoming deeper and slower behind her.

She lay in the silence of the tent, confused and conflicted. A week ago, she would have shaken him and demanded he leave the tent at once. But today?... Today she was enjoying his warmth in the otherwise cold tent, and she couldn't help but smile to think that he must want her if he called to her in his sleep.

There was hope for her yet.

6

Hrafn

There was no hope for him.

Hrafn woke up in the early morning hours to find himself wound around Olwen's tiny warm body. He had climbed into the tent the night before to keep them both warm when they ran out of dry wood to burn. His hand was resting over the mound of her breast, and his leg was thrown over hers possessively. She was small enough that she fit in the protective curve of his chest and hips. It was pleasant, and he moaned with satisfaction until he realized that there was evidence of his release all over the back of her sleeping gown. He had spilled all over her ass while she slept.

Faen! He hoped she had slept; what if she had been awake for that?

No, she would have woken him. She would not have allowed him to take advantage of her. At least, he thought she wouldn't... but after last night and the way she had stared at his cock like a starving woman, he couldn't be sure any longer.

This was bad.

He mentally reprimanded himself. He had decided that he would not pursue her for her body; it would not be fair if... if things did not go the way she had hoped they would. And here he was, rutting against her ass again. How was he going to get himself out of this situation? How was he going to explain himself?

Olwen stretched and yawned within his protective grip.

"Good morning, Husband," she whispered sleepily.

She didn't turn to kiss him; she simply pulled the blanket tighter around them.

"Good morning, Wife." His voice was low and deep.

Perhaps he would not have to explain anything at all. Perhaps the less he said, the better. One thing was for sure. He was going to need to find some sexual attention in the next town to prevent himself from seeking her out every night. He needed to put some distance between them because she felt far too comfortable with his cock, which he realized was hard again, sandwiched in her ass.

Gently, he unwound himself from her form and tucked the blanket around her back to preserve the warmth for her. He then hastily made his way out of the tent to relieve the sudden pressure building again. He was spending far too much time lately with his cock in his hand.

The day was overcast, but warmer, as they rode on. Hrafn was grateful for the cart, as it saved him from having her lush body pressed against his all day, but the downside was that he had to watch the sway of her hips and breasts as the cart bumped and pitched down the road. The corset he had bought her forced her breasts up as if they would burst from her blouse, and he worried that each bump they hit might be the one to finally set them free.

They traveled all day, stopping only to relieve themselves, rest the horse, or eat. Even so, it was late when they finally reached their destination, the Blushing Bear Inn. A wooden sign over the door displayed a large bear with rosy cheeks and a mug of ale in its paw. As usual, Hrafn secured their rooms, and they shuttled their bundles of blades with them up the stairs to keep them from being stolen out of the cart while they slept. It took longer than he would have liked, but there was no helping it. He would not feel safe until he was in his homeland, and that was still over a day's ride away. He was tired, and his muscles were sore and tight, but his priority was getting the release he needed so that he could finally relax and sleep.

He settled Olwen into her room as he had in the past, ensuring a tray would be sent up to her with food and ale, and then he washed and changed to hunt for his nightly entertainment. The tavern was full of rowdy guests, and the ale flowed. Hrafn found an empty stool at the end of the bar and sat. It wouldn't be long.

A barmaid approached him, leaning in to display the low cut of her blouse and her ample cleavage.

"What will you have, My Lord?" She eyed him suggestively.

"What are you offering?" He gave her cleavage an appreciative look and wet his lip with his tongue.

"Well, My Lord, I have anything you could desire. I keep it wet and ready for a weary traveler looking to relax."

"I love it wet. I am parched after my long ride, although I still have it in me to ride all night for the right reasons." He smiled at her with his wicked smile, and she smiled back.

"Will you take your refreshment in the tavern room, or do you prefer to enjoy it in your own room, My Lord?"

"You know, I think I would prefer to enjoy myself in the privacy of my own room, where I could truly get comfortable."

"I can arrange that, My Lord, for the right coin; I can ensure that you will be truly comfortable and relaxed." She ran a fingertip up his forearm as she spoke.

"Coin is no problem. I just need to know that I can drink my fill all night if that is what I desire to do. I am not looking for a quick shot."

"I have just what you need, My Lord. Why don't you have a bit of dinner while we finish our supper rush? Within the hour, Lyddia will bring your refreshment up to your room for you. Is that to your liking?" The barmaid pointed to a buxom bleached blond server in the corner who was being pulled into a rowdy customer's lap. "Lyddia has a lot of energy and enjoys her work enthusiastically. I think she can give you what you're looking for."

Hrafn pulled his coin purse out and handed the barmaid a significant amount of coins to secure his entertainment. Then he relaxed and enjoyed a quick meal while he waited.

Olwen

The inns were all alike in style, a main tavern room with a lofted balcony overlooking it with rooms to let for the night or, in some places, by the hour. Olwen watched through the door, only opened a crack. She saw the serving staff being pawed by the patrons, and she also saw the significant amount of coin they dropped into their blouses and onto their trays. She couldn't decide if the staff were victims and being exploited or if they were the ones exploiting the drunk men. Both seemed to enjoy themselves.

She had watched Hrafn talking with the barmaid, who had leaned over so far that her breasts were resting on the bar in front of him. She had taken many liberties with touching him and eyeing him suggestively. Olwen also noticed that several of the servers stopped to pay him attention, even though he had his meal and drink already. It was like he was an irresistible dog that every woman had to pet. Olwen closed the door.

As before, she found the washroom, cleaned up and prepared for bed. Her new nightgown was soiled, so she couldn't wear it; she would have to sleep in the nude again. Hopefully, Hrafn wouldn't come into her room to wake her. In fact, she should ensure that he wouldn't be able to! She walked to the door which adjoined their rooms, just like the last inn. There was a door on her side, a short hallway, and a door on his side. She turned the mechanism on the knob on her side so that it would lock him out. Smiling at her own ingenuity, she headed to bed.

A woman's strangled scream tore Olwen from her deep sleep. She jumped, almost falling out of bed with fright. Another scream sounded, low and howling. The manic rhythmic pounding of the furniture against the wall let her know what had woken her.

Olwen was furious. It was hard enough sleeping on a mat on the ground, but any time she finally got a bed to sleep in, Hrafn had to ruin it by bringing wild animals into the adjoining room with him. She shot to the door and stormed into the hallway. Again, when she got to his door, it was already open almost halfway. Now she was sure he must have tried to get into her room, as she was positive she had shut it behind her. She was going to give him a piece of her mind! This was unacceptable! This was–

She stopped mid-brain rant as she realized that she was standing in his doorway, naked, watching him fucking the buxom bleached blond into the mattress. All of the furniture jumped with his thrusts. She had been so angry that she hadn't even considered she was interrupting him or her own state of undress. Luckily, his back was to her, and he was too engrossed to have noticed. The woman howled loudly as he continued to impale her from behind.

Olwen quietly took one step backward, and then another, and another, until she was safely in the hallway. Breathing a sigh of relief, she rushed to her door, only to find it closed tight and locked. Quiet dread filled her. There was no way out but through his room, and she had no clothing. Again, she didn't know what to do. She didn't want to interrupt them, but she didn't want to wait to be discovered either. She stood impotently in the hallway, listening to the woman screaming in bliss as Hrafn regaled her with his cock.

It was only then that she noticed he talked quite a bit during his pleasure. She had noted that with the last two women as well. Henrick had never talked to her, only grunted.

"*Faen*! That's it! Take that cock! Take it all. Harder. You can go harder. Scream for me, Pretty!"

She responded, wailing and writhing, arching her back into him while her breasts bounced with each violent thrust of his hips.

"Yes! Yes! That's it! Scream for me, Pretty! Make your pussy weep for my cock!"

Again she screamed, and he threw his head back and roared while thrusting into her and holding her hips still so he could shoot his release deep within her. A few moments later, he was pumping her again, draining himself, groaning with a smile of relief on his face.

"My Lord, your cock is amazing!" The maid blew out an exhausted breath, wiggling her ass. He pulled out of her, falling back to sitting on his bed, and she wearily got up to get her clothing.

"Where do you think you're going?" He smirked at her.

"My Lord, you want more?" She seemed genuinely surprised.

"Come here and suck me; prepare me, and I will ride you into the dawn, my Pretty."

The maid smiled, but it didn't reach her eyes. Olwen recognized the look and could tell that she was ready for the party to be over, but he was a paying customer. Hrafn arranged himself against the headboard, and the busty server prowled the bed until she reached his cock. She took him into her mouth with fervor, moaning and pumping him as she sucked him into her throat. It was clear she was acting over-eager, hoping to get him off quickly and move on, but Hrafn seemed to be in no hurry. He closed his eyes, moving his hands to fist in her hair and pulling her mouth over his cock. He growled his approval. The woman worked him and worked him, pumping, sucking, and licking; her wet slurping noises filled the quiet of the room.

Olwen watched from the recesses of the closet and grew more fascinated as she studied the woman taking Hrafn into her mouth. She had never done this to a man before, and she was trying to commit the act to memory. She watched as the woman pumped the base of his cock, while her mouth took in the head. Occasionally she would pull off of him and simply pump him with her hand, or run her tongue up his length, or around his head. Other times she would take his balls into her mouth and suck them. He seemed to like it all as he groaned loudly, tugged her hair, and gave her dirty commands to fulfill. Just like the lion of the pride, he laid back and let her worship his cock.

Olwen assumed he was getting close again because he started thrusting into her mouth with his hips. His eyes were pressed closed in rapture, but his mouth was an endless stream of obscenities.

"That's it, Pretty! Suck my cock! Suck it dry! You feel so good on my cock, my Pretty! You make me want to fuck your tight ass. Would you like that? Would you like my big cock in your tight ass? Say it! Tell me to fuck your ass, Pretty."

Olwen blushed a deep scarlet. She had heard Hrafn say some obscene things, but he was getting more and more graphic. While she was completely horrified by the things he was suggesting, her body was throbbing, aching to see him do it. She wanted to feel his cock in her mouth, to see what it felt like to suck him, to suck his balls. She wanted his cock pounding into her. She wanted to know if it really felt that good or if these women were just pretending for the money, as some of the prostitutes back home had gossiped. She could feel the wet heat gathering between her own legs, and she wished that she had the privacy of her washroom to take care of it.

She continued to watch, her eyes glued to the woman sucking Hrafn's cock, enraptured by the whole experience, until she looked up to see that his eyes were no longer closed, and he was looking right at her. Her blood turned to ice under his gaze. She must have moved out of the safety of the back of the hallway at some point. He continued to stare at her intently, a small smirk on his lips, even as he dragged the woman's head over his cock, never stopping. Their eyes were locked over the oblivious woman servicing him.

"You like that, don't you?" he growled out, his eyes never leaving Olwen's. "You like pleasing that cock, don't you? You're going to make me shoot my load right down your throat, My Pretty. Get ready!" His hands pulled her head more roughly, and he thrust his cock deeper down her throat, still staring at Olwen. "That's it!" he exclaimed loudly, his voice becoming breathy and coming in heaving pants, "That's what you want, isn't it?! You want that cock, don't you?! Take it! Take it all! AAAAAArrrrggggh..."

Hrafn threw his head back and roared his release, his body convulsing with the force of it. He held the woman down on his cock, lodged deep in her throat, as he shot his seed into her. More spasms wracked his body, and he groaned as he pulled back, only to pump his cock into her mouth again and again, his eyes again locked on Olwen while he worked every last drop out. When he was finally finished, he fell back onto the bed.

The woman fell over as well, breathing hard. Hrafn was up quickly, grabbing her skirt and blouse and hauling her off of the bed. She whined in protest, but he pushed her out of the room, stuffing her clothing into her hands as she went before slamming the door behind her.

Olwen scampered as far into the hallway as she could go. Her door was still locked, but she tried the knob again anyway, knowing it was pointless.

"Did you like what you saw, *Wife*?"

Olwen froze and then spun in place, her back to the door.

"My, my, Wife, for someone who was so obsessed with never being seen naked, I find it ironic to catch you watching me take my pleasure, and with no clothing on, no less. Tch, Tch, Tch... One might think that you were looking to join me. Were you looking to join me, Wife?" His voice was deep and rich, and he smirked as he leaned one arm on either side of her head, trapping her against the door behind her.

"N-no, of course not!" she stuttered, trying to compose herself.

"So, you did not enjoy what you saw, Wife?" Again, he smirked down at her as her face flushed, and she blustered for a response.

"I- I-" She couldn't form a cohesive sentence.

He snaked one hand down and swiped his fingers through her moisture. She gasped and tried to move her hips away from him, but he only chuckled, bringing his fingers up to his mouth and sucking them dry with a moan as he stared into her eyes intently.

"No, you enjoyed it. You enjoyed it very much. Did you wish it was you on my cock? You want my cock, don't you?" he asked, more seriously.

"That's NOT why I came in here!" she finally managed to squeak.

"Then why DID you come in here? And why are you naked, Wife?" He slowly brought his face down to hers, his nose by her ear, his warm breath on her neck.

"My... my nightgown was soiled. I couldn't wear it," she whimpered.

"Yes, that was my fault. I'm sorry," he whispered as he nuzzled her earlobe with his nose.

"I was sl-sleeping... but you woke me..." she was trying desperately to explain, but he took her earlobe into his lips and nibbled with his teeth, sending an electric shock straight to her groin. She gasped out loud.

"I woke you, Wife. Was I too loud? Could you hear me fucking her roughly, Wife? Did you hear my cock pounding into her from behind? Or was it her screaming her pleasure that woke you?" He ran the tip of his tongue from her earlobe down her jawline.

"I- I can't think. I can't... you need to stop that. I'm locked out of my room." she was desperate, although she didn't know if it was for him to stop or for him to do more.

"Then don't think," he whispered into her ear.

Hrafn

He brought his mouth over hers and claimed it, his tongue demanding entrance. Involuntarily her mouth opened to him, her tongue hesitantly meeting his confident strokes. She moaned deeply into his mouth. He loved that she was quaking as he kissed her: his delicate swan.

He had been shocked, to say the least, to open his eyes and find Olwen staring from the recesses of the doorway while the girl he had hired for the night sucked his cock. The fact that she was naked and clearly aroused had pushed him over the edge, forcing his release. He had planned to fuck that girl all night, but seeing Olwen wet and waiting changed his plans instantly. No matter what he had decided earlier, his cock only wanted Olwen.

He used one hand on her throat under her chin to tilt her head the way he wanted so that he could dominate her mouth. His hand was firm, not choking her but holding her. She moaned again, and he groaned in response, rumbling through his chest. With his other hand, he reached down and massaged one of her perfect breasts, paying special attention to the pearled nipple. He brought the pad of his thumb up to his mouth, breaking the kiss long enough to wet it and send it back down to tease her nipple again. She gasped into his mouth, her knees going weak so that he had to catch her against the door.

She was going to be so easy. He was willing to bet she was already wet and open for him. He pulled his mouth away and blew a cold steam of air over her wet nipple, causing gooseflesh to rise on her skin.

"Hrafn..." she groaned, "Hrafn... We should... we should stop... Hrafn..." She was panting, trying to heave in breaths.

"Do you want to stop?" he asked with a smirk as he pinched her nipple gingerly, making her moan loudly. "Tell me what you want, Wife of mine, and I will give it to you. Anything you want. I can relieve your suffering. I can show you pleasure you have never known. Simply tell me what it is you want."

Hrafn brought his mouth down over her breast and began to lave the nipple with his tongue, nipping with his teeth occasionally. Olwen's hands went to his head, pulling him in tight as she moaned.

"Hrafn!"

"Tell me," he hissed, pulling his head away, despite her trying to pull her back. "Tell me the truth, Olwen."

She raised her half-lidded eyes to look into his, and they suddenly became clearer. She stood a little taller, raising her chin.

"The truth? I don't want you... fucking... these women. I don't want you to give them all of your attention and your kindness. I don't want you giving your pleasure to them. It arouses me to have seen it, but it makes me feel..." Olwen dropped her eyes, suddenly unable to continue.

"It makes you feel what, Wife?" he asked gently, stroking her golden strands of hair away from her face so he could see her eyes.

"It makes me feel ignorant. It reminds me I am unloved, neglected."

With a sharp cry, Hrafn was on his knees on the floor, grasping at his chest; a hiss of alarm escaped with each breath as he worked through the pain assaulting him.

"HRAFN!" Olwen dropped to her knees, trying to find the source of his pain, grasping his face in her hands. "What's happening? What's hurting you?" She pulled his long raven locks away from his face, searching his eyes which were filled with pain.

Hrafn was still clutching his chest, but he was gulping in deep breaths, trying to calm his body into submission. Olwen could do nothing but sit by him, holding him. They both perched immobile on the floor of the closet for several long minutes before Hrafn could speak again.

"The terms... of the bargain," he croaked in his deep bass voice.

"What?"

"My bargain with Henrick... I must not neglect you. If I do... " He winced as another shockwave of pain coursed through his chest.

"Are you suffering because I said–"

"DON'T!" He shot her a warning glare.

"No, No, No! That's not what I meant! I meant that I feel foolish and inexperienced, not that you had done anything to me!" Olwen's eyes were wide, and tears formed on her lashes. "I would never have said that if I knew it would hurt you!"

"Nonetheless, said is said, and it is clear that the magic will have its way. Come, Wife, help me to stand."

Olwen helped to pull Hrafn until he could stand. He took her hand in his and pulled her back into his room with a staggering gait, shutting the hall door behind them. This was a new predicament he had not planned on, to add to the list of predicaments he was finding himself in daily.

Hrafn sat on the bed and closed his eyes, waiting for the last of the pain to pass. He was in deep dritt. He should have kept his hands off her, as he said he would. He should have left her alone. Now he had violated the terms of the bargain, and he would have to fix it or risk losing his end of it, or worse, much worse. The pain was excruciating, and he had no desire to ever experience it again.

He would have to find a way to fix the terms of the bargain. He could not allow himself to be this incapacitated this easily. There was a war on the horizon, and his people looked to him to lead them. He could not allow himself to be weakened by a wife he never wanted to begin with! Anger sizzled just under the surface of his skin.

"Hrafn, I'm so–"

"DO NOT APOLOGIZE TO ME, WIFE."

Olwen curled into herself on the floor and wept. Hrafn knew she was tired and frustrated. He was sure this was all new to her. The pain started to surge in his chest again.

"Stop crying," he ordered her.

She tried to sniffle and hold it in, but the tears streamed down her cheeks, and her chest pulsed with sobs trying to force their way out. Another wave of pain grabbed him.

"STOP CRYING!"

At that outburst, she simply lost all control and devolved into a sobbing mess. He tried to reach for her, but she was inconsolable. Through the waves of pain, he forced himself onto the floor beside her and pulled her into his lap. He pulled her head into his chest and held her close, even as another wave of pain stabbed at him. It was not as severe as the one before it. He rubbed circles on her back with his hand as she cried herself out. His pain began to subside again, slowly fading. He held her in his arms, talking softly to her and consoling her until her crying died down and her breathing became normal and steady. By then, his pain was completely gone.

Within minutes Olwen was sound asleep in his arms, her face pressed against his chest. Hrafn reached up onto the bed and pulled down the pillows and blankets, wrapping them both up and laying them both down where they were. In the morning, they would have to find out exactly how she was feeling neglected and change that for her. He had a sneaky suspicion it would not be easy or quick.

Olwen

Olwen woke to the sun streaming through the small window. The first thing she noticed was that she was sleeping on the floor. The next thing she noticed was that she was draped over Hrafn, and they were both naked beneath a blanket. The third thing she noticed was that although Hrafn was asleep, his cock was hard and stood completely erect as it pressed into her soft belly.

Her mind was assaulted with emotions: indecision, arousal, fear, anger, and disappointment flitted through her awareness. She was tiring of finding herself in this position, overwhelmed with new experiences and having no way of dealing with them. How should she react? Should she act as if nothing had happened? Should she berate him, as she had planned, for his insensitivity at waking her with his loud sexual exploits? Should she insist on having a conversation about everything that had transpired between them? Or should she just grab his cock and see how he would react to that?

And how should she react to her own shocking behavior? She had wantonly offered herself up to him, suggesting not the slightest bit of resistance to his advances, even while he still had the scent of his last sexual conquest on his skin. Should she be disgusted with herself? Was she so desperate that she would take him wet and willing, his release still dripping from someone else's attention? Had she no shame? Had she no pride? Or had he just shown her something that had never existed for her before, and now she simply *had* to experience it?

She lay with her head on his muscular chest, listening to the rhythmic drumming of his heart, completely overwhelmed. She felt completely raw and vulnerable as if everything that was in her was on display for all to see. She no longer knew who she really was or how she should act; it was as if she no longer existed as the woman who was married to Henrick. Now she was the wife of Hrafn, and she didn't know who that woman was or how to be her.

Hrafn's breathing hiccoughed, and he stretched underneath her.

"Good morning, Wife." His voice rumbled into her ear through his chest.

"Good morning, Husband," she replied quietly.

"I should see to unlocking your door for you so that you can wash properly; then we can dress and eat. What say you to that?"

"I would like that."

Olwen felt like she was outside of herself, watching herself answering Hrafn as if her body was not stretched willingly over his. She felt his keen desire, but he made no word or move to act on it.

"You will need to let me up, Wife," he said gently, and Olwen jumped away from him, blushing with embarrassment.

Hrafn chuckled softly but didn't dwell on their circumstances. Pulling himself up to standing, he first walked into his own washing room and pulled the door closed. A few minutes later, he reappeared and walked to his bag to pull out some clothing. At no point did he seem nervous or uncomfortable being in her presence with no clothing on; he acted the same as he would if he was fully clothed.

Olwen wished she could be so comfortable with her own body, even as she pulled the blanket tighter around herself. While Henrick's wife was insecure, maybe Hrafn's wife was comfortable with her own nudity, or at least she could learn to be.

"I shall be back momentarily. Feel free to use the washroom here or simply wait for me to get the door to your room open. It's your choice."

Hrafn disappeared out the door and into the tavern, shutting it tightly behind him.

Olwen sat up with the blanket still wrapped around her. She needed to relieve herself, but she was uncomfortable with the thought of washing in his room. Then again, she had no idea how long he would be, and she was trapped, nude, with nothing to do anyway. Perhaps Hrafn's wife would be comfortable bathing in his room, as he had offered it.

Leaving the blanket on the bed, she made her way to his washroom and closed the door. She took care of her urgent bodily needs first, and then she eyed his washing tub. She smiled to herself. She liked this new version of herself. She felt brave and confident. Perhaps one day, she would be wanton and have the kind of pleasurable exploits she had witnessed.

She filled the tub with hot water, grabbing a bar of Hrafn's soap nearby. It smelled woody and clean, and it reminded her of how he smelled when he had leaned into her the night before. She quickly put that thought out of her mind and stepped into his tub. The water felt divine and soothed the sore muscles on the side of her body that must have slept on the hardness of the floor. She soaped quickly and then rested her head back to enjoy the heat. She sighed, content.

With her eyes closed and her body limp, Olwen was aware that she was too warm. She must have fallen asleep in the water. She cracked her eyes open just a fraction so as not to be blinded by the sunlight from the window, but instead of sunlight, she saw Hrafn through her eyelashes.

He stood in the doorway of the washroom, staring at her body in the tub. There was a look on his face that she could not quite place: was it awe? Was it determination? His eyes were wide, but his jaw was tight. She kept her eyes opened only enough to watch Hrafn watching her, wondering what he was thinking. She could feel her arousal rising, knowing that he stared at her body and knowing he desired her.

It was an unfortunate time for a yawn.

She stretched with the yawn reflexively, and when she opened her eyes, the door to the washroom was closed, and Hrafn was no longer there. Then there was the knock.

"I have unlocked your door, Wife. Once you're dressed, we can eat and be on our way. We have a full day of travel ahead of us," he spoke through the door calmly, as if he had not just been staring at her naked form.

Well, she had no room to criticize, given her record. She smiled to herself. Maybe she would sneak in and watch him again; maybe this new version of her would be brazen and adventurous. She liked that thought, and her smile took over her face. Releasing the water from the tub, she dried herself quickly and then opened the door to Hrafn's room and walked in boldly with nothing on.

"I've laid out– *FAEN!*" Hrafn whipped his head away from her when he realized she had stopped to listen to him without any clothing on. "I've laid out some clothing in your room, Wife. I'll meet you in the tavern."

Hrafn quickly grabbed his bags and rushed out the door without looking back. Olwen smirked to herself, proud of her bravery, and made her way into her own room to dress. By the time she had everything on and had packed up her few personal things, doubt had already crept into her mind.

Yes, she was proud that she had managed to walk into the room with Hrafn as he would have, without fear of being seen; so why did he look away so quickly and rush to leave her presence? Did he no longer find her appealing now that she seemed willing? Was she only a challenge to be conquered, and he had tired of her already? Should she have refused him the night before? Had she seemed too eager? Was she too late finding her bravery?

7

Olwen

The day was deceptively bright and sunny. It seemed for all the world as if there should be joy and laughter to accompany the bright light that shone down on the colorful wildflowers growing on either side of the road in the fields they passed. But Olwen was not feeling joy. She didn't know what Hrafn was feeling, but it was clearly not joy also.

Olwen's bravery was long forgotten. She had arrived at breakfast with her former self whispering words of insecurity in her ears. It had not helped that Hrafn seemed preoccupied and did not look at her or engage her in conversation beyond a single-word answer. And so they had ridden most of the day in stark and absolute silence: the kind of silence which screamed in Olwen's head, the kind of silence on which her doubts feasted.

Her former self was clearly not gone, nor was she willing to give up her claim to Olwen's life, as she presented every humiliating, embarrassing, and debasing scenario she could imagine. Olwen was simultaneously the prude, the old maid, the wanton whore, the pervert, the tease, and the naive fool. Her former self had laid out arguments and cited examples for each. And with no real conversation and nothing to distract herself, Olwen felt herself slowly devolving into her vulnerable insecure shell once more.

She didn't eat when they stopped for food, and Hrafn didn't seem to notice. Olwen's stomach was too churned up to think about putting food into it. She wondered if she could nap in the back of the cart, among the sword blades, as staying awake seemed to take just too much energy on her part. She didn't know why, but she was afraid to ask Hrafn. She didn't know what it was that seemed to have all of his attention, but she worried that if she broke his spell, things would suddenly be worse for her. She knew it was irrational, but it was just a gut sensation that warned her. Instead, she tried to stay awake but found herself slipping more and more into sleep.

"Why don't you lie in the back and rest, Wife? We still have a long road ahead of us, and we won't be stopping until we get there."

His words were quiet and gentle, but his hard gaze never left the road. Olwen nodded and climbed over the bench and into the back. The bundles of metal weren't exactly comfortable, but she had slept on the floor in her father's forge many times; there was something very familiar about the gentle clanging of the metal as they moved on. Although her mind would not stop tormenting her, she finally fell into sleep with troubled dreams.

Hrafn

The closer they got to his home, the more the reality of their situation settled onto Hrafn. His carefree days of being a playboy prince were behind him. There was a very real threat of war on the horizon, and his father expected him to stand up and take the throne to lead his people to victory. He had successfully accomplished an almost impossible mission, finding a fae swordsmith capable of making the enchanted swords his army would need to win, but he had also gotten himself married in the process.

He had never wanted to be the king and rule the land; he had never wanted that responsibility. And he had never wanted to be married; he had never wanted that responsibility either. But the Gods didn't care what he wanted. The time had come to pay for all of his sins, all of his years spent chasing his pleasure, accountable to no one. Yes, there was hard work and training involved; one does not become the king without having been trained in endless courses of etiquette, foreign policy, economy, strategy, and any other number of dull topics. But largely, he had been pampered and spoiled.

There was a small part of him that wished that he could simply run from it all, that he could disappear and create a new name and life for himself far away where he would never be discovered. But he knew that was not realistic, and his citizens would pay for his laziness and inability to do what must be done. No, this had always been the plan for his life, and it was time for him to accept it.

He rode all day, lost in his thoughts and memories. His father had sent him on this impossible quest, expecting him to fail. His father always expected him to fail. He wondered how he would be received at home. He wondered how Olwen would be received.

Olwen! What was he going to do about her? As if his anxiety was not already consuming him whole, he now had even more to worry about. If he told his father they were married, he would insist on a huge royal wedding so that she would be Queen to his King, and her position as the royal broodmare would be established. He would not be able to release her if the country accepted her as their Queen. He would have to find a way to hide his relationship with her. And he could not let his father know that he had a vulnerability because of her, as that would put them both in danger. With the terms of his bargain for her already strained, he could not afford to upset her either.

"*Faen!*"

The sun had long set by the time the walls of the outer fortress came into view. Hrafn was exhausted. Soon. He would be able to go to bed soon. With only a short ride to the gate, he would have to wake Olwen and prepare her. Ready or not, they were both going to meet their destiny.

Olwen

"Olwen. Olwen... Wake up. I need you to wake up." Hrafn tugged her shoulder roughly, his words urgent.

Olwen jumped with a small screech, startled. He had called her by her name... He hadn't called her by her name since they first met. He had always referred to her as "wife." She looked up at him, and her heart dropped. Hrafn's normally confident or cocky facade was replaced by an uncharacteristic seriousness, and his eyes were too wide. He was concerned, and if he was concerned, she should be as well.

"What is it, Husband?" she asked quietly.

She watched as his eyes shuttered closed briefly.

"Before we get to the gate, I have a few things I need to discuss with you. I am going to need your help and participation. It is very important that you understand and agree." He stopped and looked at her, waiting for her to acknowledge that she understood. When she nodded, he continued.

"Olwen, here in Mikill Sumar I am a prince. I was sent to get the enchanted swords and a swordsmith if I could find them, which I have done. But I have also acquired a lovely wife." He smiled a small smile that did not touch his eyes. "I know you do not wish to remain married to me, and I have promised you your release once this mission is accomplished. If my father, the Konungr, or King, knows we are husband and wife, he will insist on a royal wedding, tying you to me and this country for your life. So I must ask you to play another role while you are here so that others will not know the nature of our relationship."

Olwen could see sweat beading on Hrafn's forehead as he spoke. He was nervous. There was more he was not saying.

"But, Husband–"

"Hrafn."

"Hrafn, I cannot lie. What will I tell people to explain why I travel with you?"

"Do not lie, Olwen. Tell them you are the best *helvete* swordsmith the continent has ever seen." His beautiful smile finally broke through.

But it didn't make her feel better. "Why have you never told me that you were a prince? I feel so foolish now. If I had known–" Olwen blushed pink with the knowledge of all she had done in his presence.

"That is why I never told you. I wanted for you to treat me like Hrafn, your husband, not like a royal."

Olwen sighed. "If that is what you need of me, Hu- ... Hrafn... I will do it," she said, exhaling loudly.

She watched as Hrafn visibly relaxed. His shoulders fell a little less stiffly, and he seemed to breathe deeper. He pointed to the gate, still a way ahead of them.

"Once we reach the gate I will have to address my men. I will have them bring you to the palace. I will not be able to go with you; it would be inappropriate. You will be safe. I will have them prepare rooms for you, and I will come and collect you once I have checked in and I am dismissed from my duties."

Yet again, Olwen did not know what to say or do. She absolutely did not want to be separated from Hrafn, but she didn't see that she had much choice. She was terrified of being in a strange new place alone. She would have no choice but to trust that Hrafn would look out for her well-being.

"I am unhappy about this, Hrafn. Do not mistake my acquiescence for agreement. But I will not make this harder for you. Just, please... do not forget me."

Olwen watched as Hrafn's eyes squeezed with emotion. He looked as if he wanted to say more, and his hand clenched helplessly at his side.

She looked up as a group of riders rode down to them, quickly covering ground. In mere minutes, their small cart was surrounded by riders in dark navy tunics with silver markings. One of the riders jumped down from his horse and dropped to one knee with his head bowed before them, speaking their native language, one Olwen didn't speak. They seemed to be rejoicing the return of their prince.

She sat silently, waiting to see what would happen to her. Hrafn pointed to her, speaking rapidly to the men, but the only word she understood was her name. Several of the men dismounted and walked to the back of the cart to look at the swords, and there were many appreciative stares at the blades and at her. She pushed herself closer to Hrafn.

Hrafn stood suddenly, stepping off the cart and standing with a few of his men in conversation. Another one climbed onto the bench; she assumed to move the blades to their armory. She stood, preparing to step out herself, when one of the men stepped closer and offered a hand. She didn't want to appear rude, so she took his hand and allowed him to help her down. As soon as her feet touched the ground, he pulled her waist close and leaned in to kiss her. She brought the pommel of the sword she had pulled with her up, hitting him under the jaw with a crack.

There were shouts, and blades were drawn as the men surrounded her before Hrafn pushed them aside and stood in front of her, shouting them down. The men grumbled but backed away. The man she had hit was bleeding from his mouth and glared at her as he moved to join the others. Olwen held the sword with both hands, unwilling to release it, as Hrafn leaned into her and spoke quietly.

"I'm sorry about that. They have strict instructions to treat you with the highest respect. I am having my most trusted men bring you to the palace. I promise you will be safe. Olwen, let go of the sword."

She looked up at him, fighting back the tears that wanted to spring from her eyes. If she did this, if she handed him her only weapon, she would be completely defenseless: no husband, no father, no one to defend her. In a new land with a new husband who didn't want her, it seemed just too much to ask.

His eyes pleaded with her, and she slowly released her grip on the hilt. She watched as the muscles around his eyes tightened again. He brought his arms up, and she stiffened. He realized what he was doing and stiffly moved them as if he had intended to pick up the sword and put it back in the cart. He turned to her one last time, trying to convey some message with his eyes, but she had no idea what he was trying to say. She didn't know why, but it felt like "goodbye."

Hrafn escorted her to the horse left riderless by the driver of the cart and lifted her onto its saddle. He handed the reins to the rider sitting next to her and gave him his last instructions. The horses started to move away from the group.

"I will collect you shortly. Do not worry."

She looked over her shoulder, but Hrafn was already mounting a horse in motion, the group heading in another direction. She was on her own.

Olwen looked out of the window. Her room was on the third floor of the palace, which resembled a fortified stone keep, and she had never been in a building so high. She had seen palaces and castles in her travels that had been beautiful and inspiring. This one was neither and felt like a dungeon above ground. It was constructed with thick blocks of stone, leaving it cold in appearance and temperature. It was gloomy and, in some places, dank. And while it was decorated with rich accents and beautiful furniture, the overall oppressive feeling of the imposing dark walls could not be erased or overcome.

She was glad for the view. She watched as people below scurried to their tasks in the courtyard, surprised they worked so late into the night. They were her only entertainment. She had been brought right to the palace as Hrafn had ordered, and while his guard had been very efficient and professional, several other men they passed had ogled her openly and made lewd gestures as well as comments that she could not understand. Once in her room, he had closed the door, leaving her alone with her thoughts.

The room she was in was as large as her entire house had been with Henrick, and there was also a sleeping chamber and a washing chamber attached. She felt tiny and imagined that this is what mice must feel like in people's rooms as she looked up at the ceiling high overhead.

She did not know how long she had been waiting, but she only grew more nervous as time ticked by. If Hrafn abandoned her here, what would she do?

Suddenly the door pushed open with a loud bang, and a handsome man moved swiftly into the room with a devilish smile. He reminded her of Hrafn, tall and muscular, but his hair was not oil-stained black but a dark chestnut. His clothing was exquisite and fashionable, the embroidery was detailed, and the colors popped. He stopped in the middle of the room, looked at Olwen, then proceeded to search the room as if looking for someone else. He started speaking the language that Hrafn had used with the guards.

"I'm sorry. I don't speak that language," she said quietly, standing perfectly still and afraid to move.

"Ah, that is alright, as I speak your language as well, My Pretty!" The man sidled up to Olwen and presented his hand, giving her a charming smile. "My name is Jeger, and I am entirely at your service, Pretty Lady."

"Olwen. Pleased to meet you." As she took his hand, he lifted it to his mouth and kissed the back of it before turning her hand over and kissing the inside of her wrist with just a tease of the tip of his tongue.

"Olwen, a lovely name for a lovely lady. I cannot tell you how delighted I am to see you here. I was told that Hrafn had returned with a swordsmith, and I was most excited to make his acquaintance. Instead, I find you here, and I have to be honest, I am definitely far more excited to meet you at this moment than a stuffy swordmaker."

Jeger pulled her in with his arm around her waist, and the bulge in his trousers pushing into her demonstrated that he was, in fact, very excited to meet her. Surprisingly, Olwen didn't feel the need to push him off. She found him amusing and harmless. The fact that he was incredibly handsome and sexy didn't hurt, but largely she was getting used to being close to Hrafn, so she wasn't so reactive to it any longer. She didn't feel threatened.

"What if *I* am the swordmaker?" she asked with a smirk.

"*You?*" His eyes lit up, and he smiled a mischievous smile, "Well, if you were the swordmaker, then I would say that my prayers have been answered! Then I would tell you that I have a most amazing sword that needs to be worked on. We can work in here or in the back."

With that, he bent Olwen back before she could move, claiming her mouth with his: one of his arms was still snaked around her waist, holding her up, and his free hand was working its way into her corset and groping her breast.

"JEGER!" Hrafn's deep bass voice echoed through the room like a cannonball strike.

Jeger only turned his head over his shoulder to say, "Pussy first; the swordmaker can wait."

Hrafn was on him in an instant, pulling him away from Olwen and causing him to drop her in the process. Both Olwen and Jeger landed on their asses on the floor. Jeger burst out laughing while Olwen was furiously trying to cover her chest and put her clothing right. Her face expressed her shock and flushed crimson.

Jeger started crawling toward her. "No, No, My Pretty! Don't put them away! We haven't even played yet!"

Hrafn jumped into his path, kicking him onto his back.

"YOU WILL LEAVE MY WIFE ALONE!"

Jeger looked up, his mouth open and his eyes wide in horror.

"What did you say? *WHAT* did you just say?!" he whispered. Jeger climbed to his feet; his features spoke of shock and disbelief as he searched Hrafn's face for a joke or a lie.

Hrafn pinched the bridge of his nose between his thumb and fore-finger as he clenched his eyes shut.

"Did you say she is your *WIFE*?!" Jeger demanded loudly, his facial expression morphing into rage. When Hrafn didn't answer him, Jeger stalked to him, getting right into his face nose to nose. "And you didn't think to *TELL ME*? It didn't occur to you to send word? *FAEN*, Hrafn!"

Jeger threw his hands up in the air in disgust, then with his hands on his hips, he turned away from Hrafn, unable to look him in the eye. Olwen caught his eye, and his face softened. He walked to her and extended a hand to help her up. Once she was standing, he addressed her.

"My apologies, Olwen. Please may we start over? It's a pleasure to meet you. I am Jeger, Hrafn's consort. I'm the one he fucks when he's home."

Olwen let out a gasp; her eyes shot from Jeger to Hrafn to confirm the claim.

"*FAEN I HELVETE*, Jeger! You don't have to be so crass to her!" Hravn bellowed as he glared at Jeger.

"No, I imagine that's your job, isn't it?" Jeger shot back. "I'm not the one sticking my cock in her ass nightly." While there was anger in his words, Olwen could hear the hurt in his voice as well.

"If it gives you any comfort, it came as a surprise to me as well," she volunteered to Jeger, who turned to look at her in shock, her hand still in his. "Being his wife... er... not having a cock in my ass nightly... although... never mind." Her blush burned her cheeks. Why could she never think of the right thing to say? Why was she always humiliated?

"Jeger, I didn't tell you because NO ONE is supposed to know. The Konungr must NOT find out. I didn't mean to shout it, but you were upsetting her," Hrafn explained.

Jeger released Olwen's hand and turned to him with narrowed eyes filled with hurt. "Yes, Hrafn, I can imagine you would never want to upset your *wife*."

"You are out of line, Jeger!" Hrafn said, pointing his finger at him. "You forget your place!"

"Please forgive me, *Your Majesty*!" Jeger cried mockingly, "May I please suck your cock to earn my forgiveness?" He swept his arms wide and fell to his knees on the floor in front of Hrafn as if he would make good on his offer.

"Why are you making this so difficult?" Hrafn hissed. "Why do you have to be so dramatic? I am just trying to explain. You are the only one making a scene about this."

"Yes, I can see how it is ME that is the problem, Hrafn. You'd do well to stay on good terms with your *wife*, or you'll have no one to suck your cock for you anymore."

"Oh no," Olwen interjected as the two men stared daggers at each other, suddenly drawing both of their attention, "No. No. No. You may keep THAT job." She crossed her arms over her chest. "Tell me, does he strut around here naked like a peacock as well?"

"I think I'm going to like you," Jeger said with a smile as he turned to her and winked.

"Fantastic," Hrafn said flatly, "Now that we're all good chums, can we discuss this, please? I need a drink." Hrafn fell into the nearest chair, cradling his forehead in his hand.

Hrafn spent the next hour reviewing the events of the previous few weeks with Jeger and Olwen. She was embarrassed by the way Hrafn would talk so openly about what had happened between the two of them, including catching her watching him with the server in bed. He spared no details and, in fact, seemed to add many when he portrayed Olwen as the siren-temptress, stripping out of her underthings and pressing her ass into him as they rode together to torment him. His version of their history was much more exciting and raunchy than hers, and she noted he gave her credit for being a masterful temptress.

Jeger was shocked when he found out that Olwen truly was the swordsmith Hrafn had brought, and his cheeks flushed pink for a moment as he apologized for his earlier behavior. He seemed to struggle, but Olwen understood. After all, how does one discreetly say to your consort's wife, "I am sorry I mistook you for a prostitute?"

It was yet another awkward and uncomfortable moment for Olwen.

Jeger listened to everything, seeming to soak it all in and consider, but he did not look pleased. He would cast glances at Olwen, but she couldn't decipher the emotion in his eyes. Was he angry with her? Was he curious? He seemed very sullen, and although he was never rude to her, there was a chill in his attitude. She could understand it; she imagined she would be none too happy if her husband came home with a new wife.

However, she hadn't asked for the situation, either.

It was late into the morning hours before they were done talking. The conversation waned uncomfortably, and Jeger kept eyeing Hrafn. It occurred to Olwen that he probably wanted some time to reunite with his consort alone. Her heart tugged; was it sadness or jealousy? Putting on her bravest face, she stood abruptly and announced that she was tired and was retiring to bed. She was about to walk away, but Hrafn jumped up and stopped her. He pulled her in tightly for a hug, kissing her on her forehead before saying goodnight. She registered it with shock and scurried into her bedroom before they could see the pink in her cheeks. In moments she heard the door to her suite close behind the men as they left.

Olwen stripped out of her clothing and drew a bath. Her heart ached. Why hadn't Hrafn told her he had a consort? Not that she felt that he was her true husband in more ways than ownership, but she still felt foolish knowing he had been attached the whole time they were together, with her unaware. What if she had acted on her lustful desires? Clearly Jeger assumed she was his rival, even after Hrafn explained the situation. He must know what a man-whore Hrafn was and simply assumed he'd sampled her as well.

She felt terrible for Jeger, in part because she understood his situation. How betrayed had she felt when she saw that Henrick had replaced her not even a week after she had left? Jeger had never asked for this, but neither had she.

But she wasn't replacing Jeger, was she? Hrafn and Jeger still had a relationship, and she could see the passion between them in their stolen looks and touches. It was obvious what the two of them had left to do tonight while she lay alone in her chaste bed. Or were they? Perhaps they would argue further.

She cringed with guilt when she considered what had almost happened between her and Hrafn only the night before. She did not want to be Hrafn's nightly entertainment when he was away from Jeger. A part of her was sad that she would never get to know that passion with him, but another part was glad that she had not taken what was Jeger's. She was not mistress material.

Was Jeger the real reason that Hrafn didn't want anyone else to know that she was his wife? She supposed that if he planned to release her eventually anyway, it would be easier for him and Jeger to simply continue their relationship as it was, without her interference. If no one knew, then it would be as if she truly wasn't married to him. It would be easier for everyone when she left.

Would it be easier for her? Perhaps. Perhaps it would be more convenient than staying and watching the passion between the two men, the passion she couldn't have.

Tears sank down her cheeks as she sat in the hot water, allowing her sadness to the surface and releasing it. She realized that she was indulging in self-pity, but she would give herself this night to mourn what might have been and what would never be, and tomorrow she would be a new woman...

But who?

Not Henrick's wife... And now, not Hrafn's wife... Perhaps it was time she was no man's wife, and she was simply Olwen. Wasn't that what she had dreamt of?

The thought made her smile.

A sudden pounding on her suite doors startled her, and she jumped, sloshing the hot water out of the tub. She reached up and grabbed a cloth as she heard first the outer doors, and then her bedroom doors, fly open. She could hear Jeger shouting her name. Wrapping herself in the cloth, she ran into the bedroom to find Hrafn naked on the bed clutching his chest in agony. Jeger looked panic-stricken, and there were tears forming in his eyes.

"I don't know what happened!" Jeger shouted. "He was fine. He was fine, and then he was screaming! He told me to bring him to you! What is happening to him?!" Jeger's movements were panicked as he partially paced and partially watched Hrafn with terror in his eyes.

Olwen stared helplessly down at Hrafn. He was forcing himself to take deep breaths, and his eyes were clenched in pain. She did the only thing she could think of; she tried to recreate the scene from the previous night.

She climbed down onto the bed next to him and curled into a ball so that her head rested above his lap and near his chest. She pulled him close and slid her arm up his back to rub circles there. She spoke soothing words to him and promised him it would get better. Soon Jeger joined her on Hrafn's other side and mimicked what she was doing.

Hrafn's eyes finally opened, and he looked from Olwen to Jeger. There was fear in his eyes, but there was so much love. Olwen could see the way Hrafn looked at Jeger like he was his world. She didn't understand how he could share his body with others and feel that way, but that was between them, and she would not judge it.

Hrafn pulled his head down to hers and whispered in her ear. "Thank you." He pulled one of his hands to rub her back, even while she was rubbing his. She could hear his heartbeat normalizing, becoming less erratic and strained under her ear. He started taking deep breaths with less effort, and soon he could straighten to sit straight again. The spell had passed.

Hrafn fell back onto the bed exhausted, his cock on full display, of course. Jeger took his hand.

"Come on, let's get some sleep."

Hrafn looked at Jeger and then at Olwen.

"I don't think I should leave here tonight, Jeg. What if it happens again?" There was real fear in his eyes.

Jeger considered it for a moment, but Olwen saw the wetness gathering on his lashes.

"Why don't you both stay in here tonight," Olwen said quietly, "I can sleep on a sofa in the next room. I'll be nearby if you need me."

Jeger looked at her with deep gratitude and hope, but Hrafn's eyes still held a sadness as he watched her walk out of the room.

Olwen settled herself with a blanket and pillow on the plush sofa. It was far more comfortable than any of the beds in the inns she had slept in, so she wasn't complaining. She had left the room with only a towel, so yet again she was completely naked. It must be because she spent so much time with Hrafn. She was just about asleep when she heard her bedroom door creak open, and a small bit of candlelight shone into her space.

She watched as a large masculine silhouette made its way into the room, and when she looked up, she saw Jeger kneeling by her side.

"You saved him for me, and I will always love you for that," he said simply before he pulled her up by the arms and hugged her desperately to his chest.

She felt like a fraud. She hadn't saved Hrafn; she didn't even know what afflicted him. But she relished the warmth and sincerity Jeger shared with her, making her feel welcome by someone, at last.

He finally released her, stood wordlessly, and headed back into the bedroom. Olwen noticed he did not shut the door all the way. She got herself comfortable once again and considered what all of this would mean for her. She expected to hear the two men in the next room, but if they ever did make any noise, she was already lost to sleep.

8

Hrafn

Hrafn felt like *dritt* in the morning. Jeger was still sound asleep, his head resting on Hrafn's chest, his face angelic. He was a handsome man, no matter when one looked at him, but in sleep, Hrafn found him otherworldly. Just looking at Jeger made his cock hard again, or was that just because he had only just woken up? Either way, it didn't help.

Hrafn took a moment to look around the room, the room Olwen was supposed to be sleeping in. It was her first night here in her new home, and he had ousted her with another attack. He decided he had to prioritize finding out how not to violate the terms of the bargain, as sooner or later, the attacks might prove too much for him. As it was, they were already the most painful experiences he had ever endured. And if his understanding of the magic of bargains was true, it could kill him.

Next, he would have to find some way to bring peace to his situation with Jeger and Olwen. He knew Jeger was furious with him. Jeger had always wanted to marry, and he had refused him. Hrafn had told him he would never marry: not him, not anyone. He had given him the title of consort to appease him; it was the only compromise he would make with him. Jeger was his 'partner,' but not a husband. Hrafn never had, and still didn't, want a spouse, male or female.

It occurred to him when he saw the gates of the outer stronghold that he would have to tell Jeger about his wife. It had never crossed his mind before that as he was away from home, and he didn't really consider her a wife. She was a... bonus... if you will, to a bargain he desperately needed to make. In truth, he didn't think of the long-term consequences of the bargain at all. He only considered getting out of the town intact. So now he found himself facing the ramifications with a very pissed-off consort and a put-out wife. It looked like none of them were happy with this arrangement.

The easy solution was to release her. He could let her go, set her up with a forge of her own, and go back to his life. But he couldn't do that in reality, not while she held the key to victory for his people. It looked like the three of them were going to be unhappy for a very long time: four of them, if he included his cock, which was going to get no attention from anyone now that his wife and consort were both upset with him.

"*Faen.*"

He gently pulled himself from beneath Jeger and found a dressing gown in the bathing room. He made his way through the sitting room where Olwen was still fast asleep and let himself out into the corridor and back to his own suite of rooms. He needed to get dressed and prepare for the day ahead. He knew his father would be calling on him soon to detail his mission, and he wanted to have her set up with a forge space before that, so he had some swords to present as an example of her work. He had no intention to disclose that their new swordsmith was a 'she' and not a 'he,' as would be expected. Let them assume she was a man.

As he pulled his formal trousers on, he considered what he would say and how he would present it. His father... the Konungr, he corrected himself, was one of the reasons he had never wanted to marry. He was a cruel, demanding man, for whom the ends always justified the means. He had Hrafn's own mother removed from the court when Hrafn was young to prevent her from "softening" him as he grew older. He wasn't even allowed to address his sire as "father," but instead "Your Highness" or "Konungr" like any other loyal subject. It was as if he had no father at all, only a mentor meant to bend and beat him into submission so that he would rule the country in the way the current Konungr wanted it run. He was expendable, with plenty of other bastard heirs to replace him if he should fail to please.

Hrafn would never get married and take the chance that there could be children, not while the Konungr lived. It would be too easy to make himself disposable with another royal child available for the shaping; he would never allow a child of his to fall into the hands of that man. So marrying a woman had been out of the question, even though he enjoyed them well enough.

The Konungr would never have blessed a union between him and a man, as it would ensure that there would not be heirs available for the plucking, and Hrafn believed that if he had announced his intention to do so, it would only serve to put a target on his intended's back. Experience had taught him that anyone blocking the path of the Konungr would disappear or die under mysterious circumstances. Hrafn had never told the king that Jeger was his consort; in the court, Jeger was his advisor, with enough battle experience to justify it. If anyone thought there was more to their relationship, they smartly kept their opinions to themselves.

So Olwen being a woman and a Fae swordsmith with a gift of metal presented a potential problem. If the Konungr saw a union between Olwen and Hrafn as a means of securing 'peace' for the land, he could demand a wedding, more so if he knew that they were already husband and wife by bargain. What better way to tie her to the country and secure an endless supply of enchanted weapons? And while the Konungr held the ascension to the throne over Hrafn's head like a prize to be sought, the truth was that he would likely never voluntarily surrender his own rule. No one else would sit on that throne so long as the current ruler lived.

Hrafn shook his head with concern. He had never wanted to put

Olwen in danger. He had never even thought about what would happen when he brought her home. But he hadn't known she was a swordsmith when he agreed to the terms of the bargain, so it wasn't a consideration. At the time, he assumed she was a short-lived human. Her being Fae and the swordsmith was both a blessing and a curse. And now she was his responsibility, and he had all he could do to manage his own safety. Worse; if he negl– if he failed her, it could kill him.

Satisfied with his reflection in the mirror, Hrafn made his way down the corridors and dark stairwells to the kitchen. It was inappropriate for the royals to be in the kitchen itself, it was considered beneath them, but he loved the atmosphere. He greeted the cook and let the staff know that he had a guest and needed breakfast for himself, his advisor, and his guest sent up to the room as soon as possible. He avoided the royal dining room, as he wasn't ready to face the Konungr just yet. He had to play his hand carefully.

Olwen

Olwen woke with the sunlight streaming brightly on her face; even the blanket she had pulled over her head did not keep the golden glow out of her eyes. There would be no more sleep. Stretching, she pulled herself up off of the sofa and wrapped the blanket around her. Through her open bedroom door, she could see that Jeger was still in her bed, alone, sound asleep. Where was Hrafn? He had left again?

Silently, she crept into the room. The armoire was filled with clothing, and she found a pair of leather breeches and a shirt that she hoped would fit her. She wanted functional clothing, not fancy dresses in which she couldn't defend herself if needed. After finding the necessary clothing, she crept into the washroom and closed the door as quietly as she could. She would have to hope Jeger didn't wake and need to relieve himself.

She had been in the tub of hot water for only a short while when she heard the door to the washroom open. Luckily, the privacy screen hid her from view. She froze, trying to be silent, hoping Jeger would leave. Unfortunately, he did not. She could hear him relieving himself.

"Hraf, have you fallen asleep in the water? Do you need me to stir you to life again?" he asked suggestively. "I shouldn't touch you after what you've done. I should make that wife of yours service your needs until you apologize to me properly, but I might be convinced to tease you a little just to make your cock miss me more."

Olwen looked around wildly, realizing she'd left her drying cloth too far away to grab without being seen.

"Don't give me the silent treatment, Hraf, not unless you want me to make you moan uncontrollably. Honestly, now that you have married, you have no excuse not to marry me as well." He rounded the corner, around the screen, and shouted. "*FAEN!* You're not Hrafn!" He instantly turned and walked back beyond the screen, giving her privacy.

"No, I'm not," she agreed, yet again not knowing how she should respond or react. She was tired of being caught naked and unprepared. She might never get undressed again.

"I apologize. I thought..." His words trailed off. "I'll let myself out."

She heard his footsteps on the stone floor and the door shutting behind him. What had he meant when he said Hrafn "didn't have an excuse not to marry him?" Wasn't he his consort?

She washed and dressed quickly, and as she was pulling her wet hair up and plaiting it, she could hear the men's heated voices coming from her sitting room. Hrafn had returned, it seemed. She tied her hair and opened the doors to the room. The men's conversation died instantly.

"Good morning, Wife," Hrafn said pleasantly with his most charming smile, "Will you join us for breakfast?" Hrafn smiled like a man who was stifling his displeasure.

She looked at Jeger, but he was purposefully looking away, clearly angry.

"I don't want to intrude," she said quietly but kept her head high.

"It's no intrusion, *is it*, Jeger?" Hrafn looked at him pointedly.

Jeger's eyes found Hrafn with a glare before he turned and looked at Olwen.

"No, of course not, My Lady," he said flatly.

Hrafn guided her to the table before she could retreat, his hand at the small of her back gently. He pulled her chair out for her and then pushed it in once she was seated. Then both men took their seats, as well. The table was laid out with a small feast of hot and cold foods, and there was a large carafe with coffee. Olwen started to panic when she realized that she did not know the etiquette for an informal breakfast with a prince, but as soon as the men started filling their plates, she breathed a sigh of relief. She filled her own plate and began to eat.

"I will have to meet with the Konungr, probably later this morning. Olwen, do you have any of the enchanted swords that are finished and battle-ready?"

She nodded as she chewed some bacon.

"Good. I only need a handful. I need to have something to show the Konungr so that he is reassured that we have what we need."

"What *do* you need?" Olwen asked with her entire focus on him. This had been what he had been withholding the entire trip, the 'why.'

Hrafn looked down and then at Jeger, who gave him no help whatsoever, before he answered.

"There is a country to the Northeast of us, and the king has said they are very aggressive and greedy. He claims they have been trying to push our borders back and claim our land for generations. Now, however, their King has died, and the oldest Prince, Kriger, has set his sights on war with us. He thinks he can invade and overcome us."

"Why didn't you simply tell me this before? Why was it such a secret?" Olwen wondered aloud.

"Largely because I was the prince and traveling abroad. There was also the issue of spies and assassins on the road. For me to voice my concerns gives away who I am to anyone who overhears. And I couldn't travel with bodyguards, as that would put a target on my back as well. No one can discuss it if no one but me knows it. It was part self-preservation."

Olwen mulled this over for a few minutes and said nothing as she returned to her breakfast.

"When we are finished here, will you both come with me to the armory? Wife, I will have you pick the best of the swords for me to present."

"And what do you need me to do, *Your Majesty*?" Jeger's words were laced with venom.

Hrafn pinched the bridge of his nose again in frustration and blew out a breath. "Jeger, stop that. I understand you are angry with me, but it is not her fault. We can discuss our issues in private. Please try to make her feel comfortable while she is here. I am going to ask you to be her handler. If the Konungr thinks I have any interest in her at all, it could be disastrous for all of us. I need you to be my intermediary."

Jeger shot to his feet, his chair dragging on the stone with a screech. "You must be out of your MIND," he said with a growl, his eyes narrowed, and his hands fisted tightly. "You wish for ME to babysit your WIFE?"

"JEGER," Hrafn shot him a warning look, "She does not require babysitting. She requires someone to get her set up with a forge, and an assistant and a guard who both never see her. I would like to keep her gender under wraps if we can. I expect you to be kind to her."

Jeger was visibly shaking with anger. "You ask too much." was all he said.

"I only ask for what is needed to avoid a royal wedding and spectacle. Unless you want to see me forced into a public marriage with her, I need your HELP!" Hrafn stood and leaned over the table, his knuckles supporting his arms.

Jeger leaned over the table from his side, mimicking Hrafn's posture. The two men glared intensely at each other, seeming to have forgotten Olwen altogether.

"One of these days, I am going to have had enough. One of these days, you will push me too far. On that day, I will leave, and I will not look back."

Jeger pulled his chair back to the table and sat down, not meeting Hrafn or Olwen's eyes. Hrafn pulled his hand down over his face but took his seat as well, while Olwen just looked back and forth between them.

She wished she was noble or brave. She wished she could demand that they stop talking about her while she was present with them and that she could give some input on her own future instead of having everyone else handle it. She did none of those things. Instead, she stared at the two men, wishing she could evaporate.

One thing was certain: she needed to get him his swords so that he could complete his bargain with her and release her. The sooner she left, the better. Life would be difficult for her on her own, but it was no pleasure being stuck between these two broody men.

"Can you disguise yourself as a man?" Hrafn's voice pulled her out of her thoughts. This time, his words were aimed at her.

Hrafn

Olwen had picked out seven of the best swords from the cache. She assured Hrafn that most of the swords they had brought were very close to being complete, and only another small percentage were still at the beginning stages of work. The ones she had chosen were exquisite, and he could feel the power thrum through them with each flick of the wrist, each swing of the blade. These were divine weapons that would destroy his enemies.

He had left Olwen with a very pissy Jeger to set up her forge and see to her needs. After all, that is what he would have done if the sword-smith *had* been a man. He would delegate that task. It would draw unwanted attention if he, himself, had to see to the new swordsmith. However, he didn't trust anyone with her secret, so the only candidate acceptable was Jeger, who probably hated her.

Perhaps that was unfair. He may not hate Olwen, but he certainly DID hate Hrafn at the moment. He would have to get over it quickly; there was too much at stake to let their feelings interfere. The Konungr had to believe that nothing suspicious was afoot. Both Olwen and Jeger could be used as weapons against him; they were safest together.

It was several hours before the Konungr's messenger sent for Hrafn. He made his way to the royal reception room; the throne room was reserved for high-level meetings and official business. The smaller reception room was just a smaller, less-formal throne room. The Konungr liked to be reminded often, and in many ways, just how important he was.

Hrafn was announced and marched straight into the room. His father was seated on an ostentatious throne of gold on a raised dais while his adoring and loyal court members lined the sides of the room. He was the only one allowed to sit; the rest of the court would be made to stand for the entire preceding, regardless of how long it lasted. At last, Hrafn stopped a few feet short of the stairs leading up to the Konungr, his guard behind him with an armful of swords in ornate sheaths.

Hrafn knew his role. He dropped to one knee and inclined his head. "Oh great Konungr, I have returned from my quest, successful."

The king eyed him suspiciously, letting out a small huff. "Let me see the swords."

Hrafn stood and indicated for his man to step forward and present the swords. Hrafn watched as the king's eyes grew wide as he took in the details. He reached out and picked one up, and Hrafn saw that the Konungr felt the power in them. There was a gleam in his eyes even if he schooled his face to look disinterested.

"How many?" was all he asked.

"I have three hundred, but I have the swordsmith who made them. We will have as many as we need."

At this, the king's eyes finally lit up, and a small smile curled his lips. "Excellent. This is good news, Son. You have done very well. See that we have enough to outfit our Northeastern legions, and then we can move on to arm all of our soldiers with these."

Hrafn didn't allow his facial expression to change at all. He hid the sick terror that was building in his gut. "Of course, Your Majesty. As you wish."

When the king waived him off, dismissing him, he did not let his relief show. He marched from the room just as blandly as he had stood there, as if nothing touched him at all.

But it had touched him. Their Northeastern legions numbered nearly one thousand, and the entire army was closer to three thousand. It would take Olwen the rest of her life to make that many swords. She was going to hate him as much as Jeger did when he had to tell her that he could never release her as he had said he would. His mission would never end, not if the Konungr had anything to say about it.

Olwen

Olwen looked over the fine blade that she held. The engraving was intricate and beautiful, and the blade was deadly sharp. The mark of the swan rose and then settled into place. It was a lethal work of art, just like the others she had made. She put it aside for polishing.

She had her own workroom off of a forge. In the room next to her, where she never went, was another swordsmith. His job was to pound out the rough metal, shaping it to be more sword-shaped to save her time. It also drew attention away from her role, as everyone assumed *he* was the one making them.

Olwen worked hidden in the back, wearing men's clothing in case she was seen, using only her magic to form and complete the swords. Once they were done, they were piled up to go back out front for another assistant to polish. No one asked questions.

It had been five days since Jeger had brought her to this forge. She hadn't seen Hrafn since breakfast that morning. At first she had been delighted to work the metal again, and her heart was filled with joy. In those five days she had finished another fifty-two swords, including the one she had just put down.

Now her body ached from the non-stop use of magic. It was almost easier when she had to pound out the metal, heating it and cooling it in between. It had given her a magical break to focus on the physical.

But here, Hrafn was streamlining the process, and camouflaging her involvement at the same time.

"You should rest."

She looked over her shoulder to see Jeger walking into the room, closing the door behind him. He carried a skin of water in his hands for her.

"He said he wanted as many as he could get, as fast as he could," she replied, taking the skin and then drinking deeply.

"Olwen, the Konungr will never be satisfied. If you did fifty, or five hundred he would want more. Do not kill yourself for him. Pace yourself. Take if from me."

She eyed him wearily. He stopped by often to check on her, make sure she had everything she needed. She knew she was not his favorite person, and that he was only helping her because he had to, but it didn't change the fact that she felt terrible for the position that they were both in.

"May I ask you a personal question," she asked quietly. When he nodded she continued. "How did you come to be Hrafn's consort?"

Jeger chuckled a mirthless laugh and sat on a stool. "I have known Hrafn since we were both boys. My father was a general in the Konungr's army, and I spent a lot of time with him. You could say we grew up together; he is family to me. We did everything together, and I do mean everything. It was inevitable that we would be lovers one day as well as friends, we know each other better than anyone else. I begged him for years to marry me, to make us an official couple, but he insisted that the Konungr would retaliate against me if he knew about us. Hrafn believes the Konungr wants grandchildren, heirs to the throne, so that he can dispose of any current heirs he does not like."

"Would he really do that," she asked on a shocked gasp.

"He already has. There have been other princes before Hrafn. He sends them off on impossible and dangerous missions knowing that if they come back victorious, he gets all of the credit; if they do not come back at all, no great loss. He has more heirs. He invests no emotion in any of them, except in the satisfaction of what they can give him to further his reign."

"That is horrible."

"Indeed. That is the life of a prince in Mikill Sumar. That is why he cannot claim our relationship publicly. So he told me he would consider me his consort, his partner, but not a husband. He said he would never marry, not if it meant giving the Konungr a weapon to use against him, an innocent child."

"So that is why you were so enraged to find out..." she didn't finish her sentence.

"Indeed." He sat staring at his hands.

"I did not know he had a consort; not that it would have mattered, I did not know about the bargain either until it was already too late."

"It would not have mattered if you did, Olwen. He is the prince, and the prince gets what the prince wants. I have watched him chase skirts and cocks alike. Sometimes, I even chased them with him. There is no point in wondering what it would have been like if we were not born into this life, if we could have been together otherwise, because the reality is that we can't. Up until now I have made myself satisfied with how much of him he would give me, but the older I get, the more weary I grow of sharing."

"How... How is he?" Olwen looked up timidly, "I haven't seen him since the morning of our breakfast. How is he?"

Jeger sat up, stiff with shock. "He hasn't been to see you at all? He hasn't visited?"

Olwen just shook her head sadly. She didn't want to appear clingy or needy, but she truly felt like he had come back to his life just to dismiss her. She had servants to clean her room and deliver her meals. She was fed well, and her rooms were better than any she had ever had.

But she was lonely. This was no better than waiting for Henrick to stumble home, except that he *had* stumbled home every night. It had been five days since she had seen Hrafn. Every day that passed pushed her a little further into a depression, with an endless pile of swords to drain her, and nothing else in her life.

"I will speak with him. I was not aware he was not seeing to you. That is not right." Jeger looked genuinely concerned. She knew he didn't hate her as a person, and he had a good heart. He was dealing with his own heartbreak and betrayal, and she had just been there to witness it. She felt for him.

"I don't want you to put yourself out on my behalf, Jeger. I have already put enough strain on your relationship."

"Is that what you think?" he asked incredulously. "No, Olwen, you have not put a strain on our relationship. Hrafn did that all by himself. You cannot injure us more than he has."

"Still, I would feel badly if there was affection withheld between the two of you because of his lack of interaction with me. You should not have to suffer."

At this Jeger threw his head back and laughed out loud. Olwen could only look on, stunned. "He is not withholding affection from me, I can guarantee you that. I have not laid a hand on him since the night of his return, so you are not robbing us of anything. He has tried to initiate with me, but I have not allowed it. He has got to learn that, prince or not, we are people and not property. I will not be used and flaunted. I have been through too much with him."

Olwen blushed deeply, and brought her hand over her mouth to hide her smirk. She would never wish anything bad on Hrafn, but she had to admit that this punishment seemed to fit the offense.

Olwen

Another two days had passed since Olwen had spoken with Jeger from her heart. They had come to a mutual understanding between them, a sort of respect. Neither of them was entirely happy with the situation in which they found themselves, but it was neither of their faults either; in a way, it became a bonding experience.

Jeger always escorted Olwen to and from the forge and personally delivered her meals, often joining her as she ate. He shared many stories about growing up with Hrafn, and she shared her history with the world-famous swordsmith that was her father. She found him easy to talk to, and he was quickly becoming a friend.

The afternoon dragged, and Olwen was more fatigued than usual. Jeger had told her to pace herself, but she secretly hoped she could finish enough swords to be free of her marriage, and so she pushed herself further than she should have. She didn't want to be a burden on the men's relationship any longer than need be. She was almost ready to leave the forge for the day when Jeger burst into the room, a look of panic on his face.

"Come quickly! It's Hrafn!" He grabbed her hand and yanked her out of the room behind him and through the courtyard.

He pushed the heavy oaken door into the palace open, barely giving them time to squeeze through. They ran through hallways and up staircases, only to turn and rush down new corridors. He ran so quickly that Olwen had trouble keeping up; he simply dragged her behind him, not stopping. At last they pushed into a suite of rooms she had never seen before, but the colors and the decor told her they must be Hrafn's; they even smelled like him. Jeger pushed her into his bedroom.

Hrafn was in his bed, his blanket pulled up over him, as he writhed and screamed in agony. He clawed at his naked chest. His eyes were squeezed shut in his suffering.

"Help him," Jeger begged.

Olwen climbed onto the bed with him, curling up in a ball as she had before, but he was moving so violently that it was hard to press against him. She tried to rub circles on his back but he just screamed louder.

"STOP! IT HURTS! MAKE IT STOP!"

Tears sprang from her eyes as she tried to soothe him in any way she could, but the more she did, the worse he seemed to get. She and Jeger both tried anything they could think of, but nothing helped. Olwen was crying openly at the futility of the situation, when Hrafn let out a strangled cry, and then fell unconscious.

At first Olwen and Jeger were terrified and panicked, but seeing him breathing, and not screaming and clawing in pain, allowed them to breathe a hopeful sigh of relief. There was nothing to do but wait it out. They couldn't risk bringing in a healer, Hrafn had made that clear the last time. The Konungr must never know of this affliction. They had no choice but to sit by ineffectually. They laid on either side of Hrafn, each of their cheeks resting on either side of his sleeping chest.

"Can you tell me exactly what happened the first time he had an attack?" Jeger asked. "Maybe we can figure out what is happening to him."

"Well, I had just caught him with the serving girl in his bedroom."

Olwen blushed. "And after he... was done, he sent her away and cornered me in the hallway."

"And what did he say?"

"He... he asked me if I wanted his cock. He was pressing into me, taking my earlobe into his mouth. He asked again if I wanted him. He told me to tell him the truth."

"And what did you say?"

"I told him the truth. I told him I didn't want him having sex with those women any longer. I told him that having to hear it or see it did arouse me, but it also made me feel ignorant and neglected. What I meant by that was how my prior husband had neglected me, and how inexperienced I felt, but it didn't matter. He collapsed on the floor in pain."

"And then what happened?" Jeger rubbed his thumb over the back of her hand as she spoke.

"Then we got him back into the bedroom. I panicked and I was crying. He told me to stop, but I couldn't; it just made me cry harder. When he saw that he climbed down to the floor next to me and just held me while I cried helplessly and he suffered in pain. Eventually, I was all cried out, and his pain must have passed. We both fell asleep there on the floor."

"So you said you felt neglected, that's the word you used?"

"Yes, but I–"

"Because the terms of the bargain stated that he had to take you for a wife and ensure that you are not neglected. That idiot Henrick got one thing right."

"But he wasn't neglecting me! I wasn't asking him for... that." Her face blushed bright pink.

"I disagree. He was neglecting you, just not in the same way your previous husband had. He was giving his attention to other women, and withholding it from you. It was only after he comforted you that night that he seemed to improve, am I right?"

Olwen stopped, eyes wide, as she considered.

"What about the last time? He wasn't comforting me then."

"No, but he did stop and pay you attention. He thanked you and then reciprocated. I noticed he started feeling much better right after that. I think we have our answer."

"He has to pay attention to me?"

"Not just attention; I think he needs to make you feel experienced, confident, all of those things you felt the opposite while he was with those other women."

"You don't mean... No. NO. I absolutely do not want him that way. Especially now that I know about you."

"I don't think it even matters what we want, Ollie; the terms of the bargain were agreed to. He will have to pay you special attention from now on if he wants to avoid this again."

"But if that's the case, what brought on this attack? The fact that he hasn't spoken to me in seven days?"

"That, or the fact that he was trying to fuck one of the chamber-maids downstairs after you told him you didn't want him to."

"He WHA—" Her head whipped up, and Jeger just looked into her eyes with a tiny smirk pulling the corner of his mouth.

"He was fucking her when he just collapsed. Luckily, he told her to find me. She was an incoherent mess after witnessing it. I think our prince is about to learn a few new lessons."

Jeger was chuckling softly.

"This isn't funny, Jeger. No matter what Hrafn told you, I never tried to seduce him. I won't say I wasn't tempted, but I never did. He promised to release me from this marriage once his mission was complete. I don't need this complication right now."

Jeger was suddenly very serious. "He promised to release you?"

"Yes, once his mission was complete."

"And what did he say his mission was?"

"That wasn't entirely clear. He said he had to get a swordsmith who could make and provide enchanted swords; then he just had to get home and complete his mission safely... he never elaborated beyond that. Well, I knew I could make the swords, so I made the bargain with him. I just need to see how many he needs so that I can fulfill my end and be released."

Jeger wore an uncomfortable expression; his eyes looked saddened and worried. Olwen didn't know what to make of it, but she was beyond physically exhausted. He must have seen it on her face.

"Why don't you go clean up and get ready for bed? If it's not too much of an imposition, could I ask you to stay here with us tonight? I worry he will wake in pain, and we will need you for him to make it go away. We can test my theory when he wakes."

Normally she would never agree to sleep with two lovers in their bed, but she was beyond caring at that point; she was mentally, physically, and emotionally drained. She nodded in agreement and went to the washroom to clean up. Several minutes later, she came back into the room with an incredibly soft but incredibly thin night dress. She knew that she might as well be nude, but it was all she could find. Jeger, being the gentleman, pretended not to notice and kept his gaze elsewhere.

She climbed in next to Hrafn, her head on his chest; to her surprise, after Jeger washed up he climbed in behind her, throwing his arm over her and nuzzling into her hair. It wasn't sexual; it felt comforting in a sensual way. She placed her arm over his, securing it over her. They were on the same team at last.

Hrafn

Hrafn ached all over; it felt like he had spent hours training and had been beaten within an inch of his life. He groaned as he slowly flexed and stretched, trying to get his blood into his extremities. He felt the weight of a head on his chest and was surprised that Jeger had shaven; he usually had a little stubble first thing in the morning. His cock jumped at the thought.

He knew he needed to get up and use the washroom, but his cock was begging for attention, and feeling the warmth of the body beside him only pushed him to want more. He had been interrupted with the chambermaid, and Jeger had been a bitch all week refusing to give him what he had needed, but maybe if he was still asleep, he could be worked into it.

Moving only his arm, he brought it across his body to run it over Jeger's hip. It felt a lot softer than he remembered, but it instantly sent a spark to his cock. He reached up and took Jeger's hand off of his chest and moved it down onto his cock, stroking himself with it. Jeger usually loved to wake up that way and was always game when he felt Hrafn's desire. He moaned softly, and he heard Jeger moan in reply; Jeger's hand started moving of its own free will, so he was free to run his hands over Jeger's body beside him.

The first indication that something wasn't right was when his hand landed on a plump, firm breast, far too round to be Jeger's hard pectoral. He moved his hands down over the too-soft belly until he reached the juncture of the legs, and... his hand was met with a wet slit. Jeger's cock wasn't there.

Slowly he turned his head and cracked his eyes open. He strangled the gasp that was working its way out when he saw Olwen's pretty face asleep on his chest, his hand on her mound. Looking down he saw that at least it was Jeger's hand stroking his cock, and it appeared that Jeger was starting to get frisky with Olwen behind her in her sleep.

"*FAEN.*"

He grabbed Jeger's shoulder and shook him gently, trying to wake him up without startling Olwen. Jeger's hand grabbed him harder, stroking more quickly, and his own breathing became rapid and hoarse.

"Jeger! Wake up," he hissed on a whisper.

Already his cock was feeling too good. He had gone a week without enough attention whatsoever, and he was desperate for a release. As he felt the sensations rising, he suddenly had the pain in his chest again, as if he had been stabbed with a long sharp needle. His scream woke both Olwen and Jeger. Both of them were startled, and they both jumped up to sitting when they saw that he was in the throes of an attack.

"Time to test a theory," Jeger announced. He turned to Olwen. "I need you to kiss him."

"WHAT?"

"Just trust me. Kiss him passionately, try to get him to kiss you back. Please."

Olwen did not want to initiate anything with Hrafn, especially while he was in pain and his consort was sitting right there with them, but what other choice was there? It was the only theory they had.

She leaned over and put her mouth over Hrafn's, claiming his mouth as he had done with hers at the inn. He moaned in pain, and tried to push her away, but she persisted. When he wouldn't kiss her back, Jeger took matters into his own hands, literally. He grabbed Hrafn's cock and began to stroke it. Even in pain, Hrafn responded to the pleasure. Olwen pinned him down and kissed him deeply, and this time, he returned the kiss with fervor. Soon, he was reaching up for her, grabbing her by the arms, and devouring her mouth while Jeger pleasured him. His groans were no longer from pain.

Jeger stopped what he was doing, causing Hrafn to cry out in disappointment. He opened his eyes to see Olwen pulling away from him, Jeger sitting behind her. But he noticed that he wasn't in pain any longer.

"What?... What happened?" he asked, eyeing them. "Why did you stop?!"

"We've solved the mystery of your attacks," Jeger informed him. "It appears when you go against her wishes and try to have sex with anyone else to get relief, you will have an attack. If you don't talk to her and ignore her, you will have an attack. And the only way to stop an attack as it happens is to pay her... *special attention*."

"That's ridiculous! You can't expect me to abstain from sex unless it's with her. It's preposterous," Hrafn snapped. "Jeg, you've known me my whole life. You know I do not do monogamy. I will fuck whoever I want, and neither of you are going to stop me."

"Well, that's fine. Just hope that Ollie's close enough when the attack hits and that she's willing to take your messy second attentions to stop them." Jeger narrowed his eyes in disgust.

"Ollie?" Hrafn asked with one eyebrow raised, his arms crossing over his chest.

"Yes, Ollie. She and I have a lot in common, and I find that I quite like her. More than others, I can tell you that. If you are unwilling to satisfy her, then perhaps she and I will–"

"That is enough talk of satisfaction. If anyone is going to be satisfied, it is going to be me! I have been neglected for a week now!" Hrafn sulked like a petulant child.

"Well, it won't be done by me," Jeger said with a snort, getting out of bed.

"Don't look at me," Olwen said as she, too, climbed out of bed in search of her clothing.

"Fine, I can take care of this myself. Just see if either of you gets anything from me after this!"

Jeger shot Olwen a smile as he dressed. If he was right, Hrafn would be giving her all kinds of particular attention in the near future, and he looked like he couldn't wait to be present to watch.

Olwen

The day got off to a late start as Olwen made her way to the backroom behind the forge. She still tingled from having seen Jeger pleasuring Hrafn while she kissed him. She had thought it would be awkward and repulsive to be with two men pleasuring each other, but having just gotten a taste, she was already fantasizing about having more.

Was this the new daring and adventurous Olwen?

When Hrafn had wanted someone to bring him to release, she had been so tempted. She wanted to try the techniques she had seen the server woman perform on him, but again, there was the weirdness of having Jeger in the room as well. And once Jeger said he would not do it, she had to stand in solidarity with him, as much as it left her throbbing and wanting. Hrafn complained about having no sexual attention for a week, while no one had touched her that way for years.

Shaking her head, she focused on her work, pulling the first of the swords out for the day. She lost herself in the magic and the singing, and a few hours later, she had finished her second sword for the day. It was moving quickly, but as she got to the blades which were more basic and closer to the beginning of their journey, she knew that they would start taking longer and longer. She did not relish that. Already the sweat was dripping down her neck and back.

Jeger showed up at midday with their lunch, and she was glad to put her work aside for a while. She took a long swig of water from the skin he offered. He seemed quiet, as if something was troubling him, he fidgeted with nervous energy. Finally he just spit it out, as she sat to eat her meal.

"Ollie, I wanted to apologize. I... I know we had to test the theory, but I should have warned you before I... did what I did. I didn't mean to make you feel awkward, and I hope that you can forgive me for putting you in that position."

It took Olwen a few seconds to figure out what he was talking about.

"Do you mean when you were pleasuring Hrafn?" she asked. Jeger actually blushed as he nodded. "Jeger, you do not need to apologize to me. He's your consort, and we were trying to save him. It worked, and if I'm being fully honest... I enjoyed watching it." It was her turn to blush as Jeger's eyes snapped up to hers.

"Would you be open to doing something like that again, if we needed to? I mean, it appears that the only way I may be able to be intimate with him again is if you are joining us." He said the last part a little sadly.

Olwen suddenly felt horrible. She hadn't realized that in precluding Hrafn from whoring all over the land she was keeping him from his consort as well. Guilt swelled in her chest.

"I would never want to keep you away from him, Jeger."

"I know, Ollie. This was his doing. We just have to figure out a way around it. Until then, would you be open to joining us?"

She bit her lip as she thought about it. It excited her more than she wanted to admit, but she also had to consider the consequences, as she valued her friendship with Jeger.

"I am open to it, but Jeger, are you going to resent me in the future? Am I splitting your relationship? I don't want that."

"No, you're not," he assured her. "The bargain he made has already driven the wedge between us; the way I see it, this is the only way to salvage what we have. I won't ask you to participate in any way which makes you uncomfortable."

"I appreciate that Jeg. I trust you." Walking to him, she placed a hand on his arm to comfort him.

And there it was, the level of comfort she had always sought with a man, but had never achieved. It wasn't horses stampeding, fireworks, or butterflies in her stomach; it was respect, caring, and decency. She had never had a man who had returned those things to her, other than her father, and it was oddly surprising that it was Jeger who was offering them, and not her husband.

Hrafn

"Pull your head out of your ass and focus," Jeger growled as he swung the flat of his sword against Hrafn's backside, knocking him down. Hrafn was breathing heavy and sweat drenched his naked chest and made his trousers stick to him uncomfortably. The air of the late afternoon was starting to cool, the warmth of the sun having passed its summit, and Hrafn's flesh pocked with gooseflesh.

"Enough for today," Hrafn bit out between deep breaths. "I am useless beyond this point."

"And why is that? You usually have more stamina than this. If we were on the battlefield, Hraf, you would be close to death now."

"Jeg, the attacks take a lot out of me. And there is also the fact that I have blue balls because while I have both a consort AND a wife, I cannot seem to get anyone to bring me release." He angrily strode back to his gear and snatched up his shirt.

"We thought you had it well in hand, Hraf," Jeger said before chuckling at Hrafn's discomfort.

"It seems that since I met my *wife* I have only been able to release once, and that was in her presence. Every other time I have tried I have gotten nothing but frustration for my efforts."

"Then perhaps you will listen to reason?"

"NO," Hrafn bellowed. "I will not be pussy whipped by her or by anyone."

"Suit yourself. Just be prepared to suffer with frustration for a long time."

Hrafn stormed off the training field and headed back to his suite to wash up and change. Jeger followed behind, not bothering to hide that he disagreed with Hrafn's decision. Was he jealous? Was that why he was creating such fantastic theories about the sudden attacks? But if that was the case, then why would Jeger be sending him to Olwen's bed, and not his own? It made no sense.

Olwen was a beautiful woman, and her body was very desirable, but she had all but admitted that she was inexperienced in the ways of pleasuring a man. What was the point of going to her for release if he would have to teach her as if she was a virgin? He didn't have time for that. There was nothing arousing about having to walk her through the act like a child bride. And he very much doubted that she would simply lay back and let him take his pleasure the way he liked; in fact, he would probably hurt her, making his situation worse.

When he arrived at his rooms he stripped off his pants, socks, and boots and threw his clothing in a pile on the floor. Jeger moved behind him to gather his gear and weapons and put them away like a good and dutiful consort.

If he was good and dutiful, he would be taking care of Hrafn's cock instead of his sword, though, wouldn't he?

Hrafn pushed his way into the wash room and set the waterfalls to flowing. He didn't want to sit in a tub, not in his current foul mood. He would wash up in the waterfall, and get on with his night. He ducked his head under the rush of water, and almost sucked in a mouthful when he felt Jeger's hands rubbing soap lather onto his chest.

He was desperate. His mind warred with itself, telling him to refuse Jeger and cut him off for his behavior, but he couldn't bear to stop the man's hands from running over him and sending shockwaves through his body and right to his cock. He knew it was completely rigid and standing at full attention; he just prayed that Jeger would weaken in his resolve and give in to give him what he needed.

He stood still, with both arms leaned on the rock wall as Jeger soaped him from top to bottom. Strong hands caressed the muscles of his chest and abdomen, smoothed up and down his arms, and washed his strong thighs. The closer they got to his aching cock, the more he groaned with need. At last, he was rewarded when he felt his consort's hands wrap around his length, stroking him firmly, slowly at first. He could feel Jeger's cock pressed into the seam of his ass, also hard, and feel the heat of his chest as it pressed against his back. They both groaned loudly under the rush of the water, the reverberation through their chests uniting them.

"I... I need you... *please*, Jeg," Hrafn begged on a gasp.

He felt Jeger hesitate, then move to kneel before him. Hrafn's cock leaped with anticipation, and the pressure in his balls became unbearable.

"*Please*," He hissed when Jeger didn't move.

He felt Jeger's warm mouth envelope him and then take him in to the root. He let out a cry of relief as Jeger began to pulse on his cock, taking him in and out, sucking and laving him with his tongue; armed with years of knowing what pleased him best. No one knew his cock like Jeger. Instantly he felt his balls constrict, his release poised and ready. Tears of gratitude began to leak from his eyes as the euphoric feeling thrumming from his cock spread over his body, pulling his muscles taut in preparation. Just as the first spasm began to unfurl, the pain stuck him in the chest and knocked him to the floor, screaming.

He didn't know how long he had lain on the floor, clutching his chest and screaming. The pain was unbearable. He wished he could simply pass out, or die, just to end it. But it persisted. And then he felt the hands, heard the voices. Opening his eyes, he saw Olwen in front of him and Jeger behind her; both were naked. On another day, he would have been overjoyed to be surprised like this, but on this day he just wanted to die.

His eyes were closed to the pain again when he registered that someone, it must be Jeger, had his mouth on his cock again. Anger burned hot within him, and he wanted to scream. For all that he had been begging for a blowjob all week, while he was on the floor dying was not an ideal time for him. Again, his traitorous body would not allow him to stop the miraculous feelings Jeger was giving him, even as his heart felt like it was exploding.

And then there were two soft breasts pressed against his chest and a warm mouth delving into his. Her tongue was small but insistent. He grabbed her shoulders to push her away, but she threw her arms around him, refusing to let go. As another wave of pain tore through his chest, he considered just for a moment what it would mean if Jeger was right.

Experimentally, he kissed Olwen back; it wasn't full of passion, but it was an effort. Immediately the squeezing pressure around his chest was reduced. He kissed her again, this time with a little more interest. Once again, the pain level subsided. The glorious euphoria coming from his cock outweighed what remained of the pain in his chest. As he didn't want them to stop, he made no indication and kept kissing Olwen.

His kisses were genuine, and his need evident as he took domination of the kiss, pulling Olwen to him so he could devour her mouth. One hand snaked up to fondle her breast roughly, and he felt her moan loudly into his mouth. Still, Jeger pumped his cock closer to release. He groaned loudly as he felt the pressure starting to build at last.

And then the pleasure stopped.

He screamed in frustration, pulling away from Olwen and turning to Jeger in a rage.

"DON'T STOP!" His breath came in heaving pants, and his body was shaking with need.

"I will not continue unless you promise that you will give Olwen what she needs," Jeger stated as he looked Hrafn in the eye.

"JEGER!" Hrafn howled, but Jeger wouldn't budge.

Hrafn looked like he wanted to rage, scream, or kill. Finally, he fell back onto the floor with a splash, defeated.

His weak voice rose over his body. "Fine. You win." His hand flopped into the water beside him with a 'plop!'

Jeger launched his mouth over Hrafn's cock and began to work him like a starving man. His groans were as loud as Hrafn's. Olwen seemed unsure about her role but didn't have to think about it too long. Hrafn grabbed her and pulled her down over him, again dominating her mouth and neck while his hands took advantage of her naked breasts. Her groans soon joined theirs.

It wasn't long before Hrafn was throwing his head back and roaring his release while Jeger couldn't seem to get enough of his cock. As Hrafn unloaded down his throat, Jeger grabbed his hips with fingers that would undoubtedly leave bruises. Olwen was still pulled tightly against Hrafn, and as soon as he regained his breath, he launched his mouth onto her nipples, sucking and nipping like they were delicacies.

The three of them remained on the wash room floor, splashing in the puddles, groaning and writhing until Hrafn couldn't take it any longer and called an end to their play.

"Not yet," Jeger reminded him, nodding his head in Olwen's direction.

"And just what is it that you want me to do?" Hrafn asked.

"She needs release as well, Hraf. We saw to you, now you must see to her."

Olwen paled and pulled herself back.

Hrafn lay on the floor, one arm under his head looking up at Jeger.

"So give her a release, Jeger, it's not like you can't."

"It has to come from *YOU*," he hissed.

"I... I should leave," Olwen said quickly, starting to pull herself off of the floor, her face flushed red with embarrassment.

Jeger grabbed her wrist and pulled her closer to them. He stared at Hrafn.

"You promised. We are doing this for your sake. Do not embarrass her or reject her now, after everything she has done for you."

Before Hrafn could answer Olwen spoke up, her voice cracking.

"I do not want his attention, not like this, not as an obligation, and not when it should be yours. I did not ask for this." Tears formed in her eyes, but she kept her chin up.

"There, you see? She doesn't want it," Hrafn pointed out.

Jeger clenched his jaw and a vein in his neck throbbed. "You're an idiot, Hraf. You will *DIE* from these attacks. Are you so proud, or think yourself so much better than her, that it is beneath you to pleasure her for her own sake, even when she has sacrificed her dignity to be here on your behalf? I am disgusted. After all this time, I have never seen this side of you, not to this degree. If you will not give her what she needs then you must release her, Hrafn. Otherwise you will die, and while you deserve that fate right now, she does not deserve to have to be a witness to it. I want nothing more to do with you."

Hrafn sat up quickly and whispered, "You don't mean that Jeg."

"I do mean that. Every word." Jeger's anger was tangible in his look. Hrafn sat in stunned silence, looking from Olwen, who averted her gaze, to Jeger, who glared at him. When he didn't move fast enough, Jeger pushed to standing, pulling Olwen gently with him.

"Come on. Let's get you dressed," he said as he quietly moved to lead her back out of the room.

"Wait!" Hrafn called in a panic. "Wait... can we meet in the bedroom? My skin is starting to prune from the water."

Jeger glared over his shoulder, but Hrafn quickly rushed after them so they could not leave him.

Olwen

Olwen let Jeger dry her gently. She was humiliated, and she knew her face must be crimson. She was tired of never knowing what to do or say. She was tired of feeling embarrassed and having men decide what would happen in her life, especially because it lately involved a lot of nudity. And she was furious that she couldn't just think of something brilliant to say to take charge of her own life the way she wanted to.

Jeger leaned in close to her ear. "You don't have to participate if you don't want to. I understand that you did not agree to this bargain. I just... I don't know what else to do to keep him safe."

She looked up as his muscled body loomed over her. There was no mistaking the sadness that pulled at his eyes. Even though he was furious with Hrafn, he loved him also. It tugged at her heart.

She closed her eyes to consider everything; she didn't want to make a decision out of obligation any more than she wanted them to. On the one hand, she didn't like that she was having to offer up her body for a mistake that Hrafn had made and perpetuated. On the other hand, she didn't want Hrafn to suffer or die, nor for Jeger to suffer unfairly. And she *had* wondered how she would get to experience those pleasures once she was on her own. Wasn't it better to have them here and now, with Jeger present to watch out for her wellbeing? They were all adults, after all.

Steeling her resolve, she opened her eyes and looked back up at Jeger, who stood waiting patiently.

"Jeger, you do not deserve to suffer any more than I do for this bargain. I will participate, but if he is hostile toward me or unkind, then I will end this. There is only so much that I can endure on his behalf." The light came back into Jeger's eyes, and he nodded his agreement.

"So, what are we doing?" Hrafn strolled into the room with a bored expression.

Jeger shot away from Olwen's side and pulled Hrafn out of the bedroom doors, shutting them firmly behind him. "A *word*, Hrafn." Olwen just stared at the doors. She could hear a heated conversation taking place, but thankfully, not what was being said. A few moments later, the doors re-opened, and a very chastised Hrafn returned to the room looking nervous. He stopped in front of Olwen but couldn't seem to look her in the eye as he pulled his hand up the back of his neck nervously.

"I owe you an apology, Wife," he began before turning to Jeger, who nodded for him to continue. "I have been unfair to you..." He stopped, flustered. He looked back at Jeger and then back to Olwen.

"I'm sorry, I cannot say this in anyone else's words but my own. I am sorry that you felt I flaunted my sexual exploits. In truth, I was trying to resist you by sating my hunger with others; it was never meant to be an insult or a punishment for you. I did not think you would want a stranger to expect to bed you just because you were my wife. Also, it was never my intention to make you feel ignorant or... uncared for. I should very much like to correct that with you."

"In what way?" she asked carefully, her eyes traveling between Hrafn and Jeger.

Hrafn gave a small smirk as he approached her and reached to brush a wet lock of hair off of her forehead. "You did say that you felt ignorant and unloved; I would very much like to educate you, Wife. You have a body that begs to be pleasured, and I would be honored to be the one to teach you how to achieve that."

Olwen felt her cheeks burn even hotter. She had understood what would be involved in this, yet as she stood in front of his naked body, his arousal for her already on display, she was instantly afraid.

Hrafn placed his palm over her cheek. "I will not hurt you, Wife. You can tell me to stop if you ever feel that I am rushing you or pushing you. But it would be a shame for this luscious body of yours to have never known the pleasure that I can guarantee I could give to you." He leaned in and claimed her mouth with his, a gentle moan leaving his mouth as his hard cock pushed gently against her soft stomach.

Olwen's eyes were still open with shock and fear. Instantly Jeger was behind her, his cock pressing into her lower back as he held her shoulders gently and kissed the back of her neck softly. "I am here for you, Ollie," he whispered quietly.

She let her eyes fall shut as the heat of both of their naked bodies pressed into hers. The sensations of Hrafn's mouth dominating hers while Jeger's explored her tender neck stimulated her entire body as if a spark had ignited in her blood. It especially pooled between her legs, where a thrumming of need could be felt. She had never felt this need for a man before.

She was surprised when she felt herself being lowered to the bed between four hands; she hadn't been aware they had been moving. Reverently they laid her out on the large bed, Hrafn still draped over her, kissing her deliriously. He pulled back slowly and moved down her body, stopping to worship her breasts again. He took them into his hands and mouth, nipping, sucking, gently pulling, and kneading. His groans flowed into her soft skin.

Olwen moaned deeply. It was all so new to her; no man had paid her this kind of attention before, certainly not for her benefit. She felt like she ought to be doing something for him; she shouldn't just be laying back doing nothing. She had heard stories of bad lovers and wives who just laid listlessly while their husbands and lovers served themselves with their bodies. She didn't want to be a bad lover. Anxiety crept into her belly and disturbed even the amazing sensations Hrafn was giving her.

Jeger was there suddenly, his hands in her hair and his mouth on hers. She didn't have time to say anything before she felt another shift as Hrafn dragged his mouth further down her belly, kissing her belly button and running his fingers over her torso. Finally, his hands landed on her hips, his hot breath directly over her mound.

Her eyes opened wide with fear. No man had ever put his mouth on her... there. But Jeger just whispered softly to her. "It's alright, Ollie; please, let him give you this pleasure. We can stop if you don't like it." He brought his mouth back over hers and kissed her until she was dizzy from it.

She felt the first pull of Hrafn's tongue over her wetness, and she moaned loudly into Jeger's mouth. He moaned back as he deepened his kiss, his hands grasping into her hair. Hrafn moaned as well, and the vibration moved through her sensitive folds and her tiny pleasure bud. She felt her hips rock up against his eager mouth, and soon Hrafn was devouring her. His tongue pulled between her folds, stretching to reach into her as far as he could, and then it was lapping tiny circles over her center and her little bundle of nerves.

She cried out, losing herself in the feeling, as her fingers clawed at Jeger's back while he continued to explore her mouth, throat, and breasts. The sensations were overwhelming, Jeger's warm mouth tugging at her nipples while Hrafn pushed a finger deep into her wetness and began to move it in and out in time with his ministrations to her clit. She cried out again, her body responding to them without her conscious decision. The feelings were too delicious, too good to resist, and she shamelessly pressed herself into them for more. Hrafn seemed to smile around her mound as he added a second finger inside of her, plunging her deeply as he teased and feasted on her.

Olwen was lost in the bliss. She could hear keening wails, and she quickly realized it was her. Her breathing was becoming erratic, and her body was winding tighter and tighter. All she knew was that she needed it... whatever was about to happen, she needed it desperately, and she would do anything to feel it. She shamelessly ground her mound against Hrafn's face and pulled Jeger to her breast tighter, her nails digging into his firm muscles. Hrafn pulled his fingertips as he stroked out of her warmth, hitting some spot deep within her, and Olwen lost all connection with reality.

She screamed out her pleasure as Hrafn massaged this spot with his fingers over and over again, even while his tongue was laving her tiny pleasure pearl. Her head whipped from side to side, and her hands were claw-like vices pulling Jeger onto her body and holding him there. She had never experienced pleasure this intense before! It seemed to light up her entire body, pulling on every muscle, and she was helpless within it. She could do nothing but react, scream, buck, and wail as her body slowly began a tight-spiraling climb toward her release.

"That's it, Ollie, just let go," Jeger whispered into her ear softly.

She threw her head back and screamed as her back arched off of the bed. Spasms overtook her as every muscle first pulled tight and then seemed to unfurl within her. She could feel her core rippling around Hrafn's fingers, which still plunged, hitting that blissful place of pleasure deep within her. She heaved in breaths, still moaning and still bucking against Hrafn's face as he continued to lick up her juices and pump his fingers inside her, sending her into aftershocks.

Finally, he pulled away and rested his head against her thigh, a huge smile on his face. Jeger was beside her, still nuzzling her hair.

"Tell me, Wife, did that oaf Henrick ever bring you such pleasure?" He was smiling a boastful smile.

"Never," she tried to say but only croaked, her voice raw from screaming.

"That is lesson one, Wife. There is a world of pleasure within your own body that you have never explored or been shown. I will make it my duty to make you aware of each and every pleasurable thing I can."

Hrafn pushed himself up and began to drag himself up Olwen's body. When she felt his rock-hard cock pulling through her folds, she froze in terror. Jeger felt it immediately and leaned in to whisper.

"He's not going to do that with you today. He's just getting close.

Don't worry; I will take care of his need later. Just enjoy your time." He kissed her ear tenderly, and she turned to kiss his mouth, her lips still swollen from all of the kisses she had received earlier.

When Hrafen reached her face, he gently pulled her chin away from Jeger and took her mouth with his. She could taste her own sweetness on his mouth. He allowed his weight to slowly sink down onto her, pressing his hardness into her belly while he lost himself in kissing her. Jeger's hands moved through her hair gently as both men paid her homage.

"How was that, my little Swan? Are you well-loved this afternoon?"

She moaned as she smiled a broad smile, looking from Hrafn's eyes up to Jeger's eyes.

"Shall I help you clean and dress?" Jeger offered. Olwen knew that he must be looking to take care of Hrafn, after he had clearly followed Jeger's orders.

"Can I stay?" she asked timidly, "I mean, I could watch... or..." She blushed fiercely as she looked away.

"You'd like to help?" Hrafn asked. His eyes were wide, and his eyebrows raised with surprise. "My little Swan, you never cease to amaze me." At that, he smiled a broad smile full of mischief.

"Only if you'd like to." That came from Jeger, who watched with protective concern. "Same rules apply. You can stop anytime you'd like. You won't be expected to do anything you're not comfortable with."

She knew she was blushing fiercely, but she nodded. She didn't know what to say. She was uncomfortable with the whole situation, but there was only one way to get comfortable with it. And it felt far too good to simply leave, knowing what they would be doing without her.

Hrafn moved up and off of her, and she got up to let him lie down on his back where she had been. Jeger moved up to sitting, taking Hrafn's cock into his hand and gently beginning to pleasure him. She moved around the bed until she was sitting close to Jeger. At first, she was mesmerized, watching his hand working Hrafn's cock, and how Hrafn would moan and react in response.

Then she grew curious. She placed her palm on Jeger's thigh and slowly slid it up toward his own hard cock. He looked down at her with curiosity, but when she met his eyes, he understood her question and simply nodded. She followed his lead, taking his cock into her much tinier hand and doing everything she watched him doing to Hrafn. Jeger groaned, and she felt his cock stiffen in her hand under her touch. She looked up to meet his eyes, and there was heat and longing there. She felt immensely powerful controlling his pleasure with only her tiny hand. She watched as Jeger pulled his eyes away to look back at Hrafn, and her eyes followed, only to find Hrafn staring, transfixed, as she pleasured Jeger in front of him. It seemed to push his arousal higher.

Hrafn licked his lips. "More," he said simply.

Olwen didn't know what more consisted of, but Jeger led the way, pumping Hrafn's cock harder and faster within his fist. From root to tip, he pulled and twisted, paying special attention to the head. Olwen followed his lead, doing the same to his cock, and soon both men were panting and moaning loudly, all of them watching her pleasuring Jeger.

"I'm close..." Hrafn let his head fall back with a groan and then snapped it back up quickly. "I know... Jeg, can you eat her pussy? I want to see you two together."

Jeger looked to Olwen with concern, but she just smiled back at him, eager to try. Once again, everyone shifted until Olwen was again on her back, this time with Jeger's mouth on her mound. Spreading her thighs wide, he gently kissed her thighs and mound, giving her an open-mouthed kiss over her folds and then pulling the flat of his tongue up her center. Her head fell back with a groan instantly. She could see Hrafn watching intently as he stroked his own length.

"Use your fingers in her," he ordered as he continued to pleasure himself, lost in watching them.

Jeger obliged, and Olwen felt him press two thick fingers inside of her. She felt the walls in her core stretching to accommodate him. He groaned and shuddered between her legs. His fingertips found the magical spot inside of her that had made her explode.

"I had no idea how tight you are, Ollie. *Faen!*" Jeger groaned and then took her in his mouth with a mission.

Hrafn was working his own cock harder and faster, his own breaths coming out in rough pants.

"Make her come, Jeg. I want to see her cream on your face."

Hrafn was kneeling right beside Jeger's head, thrusting his cock into his hand as if he would splatter his seed all over Jeger's face and Olwen's mound. He was groaning loudly, his eyes glued to Jeger's mouth as it devoured her glossy pussy. There were only the sounds of their slick pleasuring and Hrafn's dirty commentary.

Looking down and seeing both men so lost in the concentration of pleasure, Olwen let out a strangled cry as her hips thrust forward and her core tightened. Her release ambushed her, and she lost herself in the throes of waves of pleasure as they slammed her body. When she could finally open her eyes again, she saw Hrafn was behind Jeger, preparing to take him.

Hrafn's eyes only left her to line himself up; once he was pressing inside of his lover, he was again watching her intently, even as he groaned.

"My Swan, you are so fucking beautiful when you fall apart under Jeger's mouth. I don't think I have ever seen anything more erotic than your sweet innocence exploding and your fluids running down my consort's face. I could watch that every day and never see enough."

He was grabbing Jeger's hips roughly and slamming his cock into him in an almost violent claiming. At first, Olwen worried he was hurting Jeger, as Jeger's head was down, and he had yet to lift it. When he did lift it, however, there was no doubt whatsoever that he wasn't feeling anything other than the sweet bliss she had just experienced. Jeger groaned, his mouth open and his eyes closed as Hrafn's cock pummeled him. Hrafn continued to slam his hips into him while Jeger could only push back, begging for more, groaning. Olwen could see Jeger pleasuring himself to release between his legs, even as Hrafn slammed into him with one final deep stroke, screaming and swearing as he convulsed over Jeger's backside and then pumped him a few more times as he released deep into his body.

The two men fell to the bed, boneless, but Hrafn did make the effort to pull Jeger back to him so that he could kiss him deeply. The sight made Olwen happy. She hadn't known about their relationship before she arrived, and she didn't want to cause unrest between them. It was clear that they loved each other deeply, even if Hrafn made it seem like it was all about sex. Without opening his eyes, Jeger reached his long arm out and snagged her around the waist, pulling her into their little cuddle pile, and her heart overflowed.

Hrafn

Hrafn's cock hummed with pleasure at the thought of seeing Olwen later in the evening; even taking care of his royal duties around the palace didn't seem so bad. He had assumed she would be annoying in her naivety, but he had been so wrong. He decided he would have to do something very nice for Jeger to thank him for forcing him to consider her as a sexual partner.

She brought a refreshing new spark to their combined pleasure. His cock thickened in his breeches as he envisioned her face in the throws of passion or Jeger's face as he watched her intently. Just watching the two of them getting off was enough to push him over the edge himself. It had been a few weeks since they first had Olwen join them, and now he found he had to stop several times a day to give himself release because he could not stop obsessing over their escapades together.

He had yet to fuck her, but he wasn't really in a hurry. Watching her morph from the shy girlish figure she had been into the woman who was not afraid to grab one of their cocks in the heat of lovemaking was delightful. Still, she was too reserved, and he looked forward to seeing her sucking his cock, or Jeger's, for that matter. He knew she would be a good lay already from her tightness and the way she responded. It was very liberating. He was very much looking forward to fucking that pussy hard all night long until she begged him to stop.

Hrafn was so deep in thought that he didn't hear the footsteps scurrying up behind him until a hand reached out and touched his arm.

He spun, ready to rip the hand off its offending arm when he noticed it was the Konungr's messenger. He was being summoned. His cock went limp immediately.

Without argument, he followed the messenger toward the Receiving Room. As a prince, it was bound to happen sooner or later, no matter how hard he worked to stay out of his father's line of sight. There was no need to worry just yet; it may be nothing. The Konungr did like to hear himself talk; he might just want a fresh audience.

Soon he was standing before the Konungr as he shared his thoughts and opinions with the court and the prince. The king was very dramatic in drawing out all of his news and then showing his well-rehearsed emotions to them. There were more reports about atrocities being committed on the Northeast borders. Hrafn stiffened. A cold tingling began at his lower back and slowly crawled its way up his spine as if in warning. It was then the Konungr revealed his true purpose for the meeting: he was sending the prince, a small delegation, and a large military presence to the Northeast border to quell any further incursions. It wasn't calling for outright war, but it certainly had all the markings of it. The prince was dismissed to make arrangements, while the Konungr moved on to his next topic of entertainment before his loyal court of admirers.

"*FAEN!*" Hrafn swore as he stormed down the hallway toward the office he shared with Jeger. The Konungr had told him years ago that he was too old to rule the country through another war; he had used that as justification for the many missions he had laid on Hrafn "to prepare him to rule as Konungr one day, himself." And yet, here they were, on the brink of war, and the Konungr was holding court like a young man seeking the attention of a young girl. He was, again, sending Hrafn into harm's way while he himself stayed in the relative safety of the palace with his adoring audience.

Hrafn wasn't stupid. He knew that it was only a matter of time before one of these missions would kill him or would prove to be too much, so he returned unsuccessful, which would open the door to ridicule and discipline by the Konungr. Hrafn had seen half-brothers and cousins alike put to death for failing to perform their given tasks. A few years ago, Hrafn would have been fine with simply being removed from the royal hierarchy. But not now.

Now he had to think of Jeger. Now he had to consider Olwen. And if he was being honest, he knew the Konungr had very little to do with the running of the country, so he had to think of the people. The king gave his advisers a lot of leeway to run things as they saw fit so long as nothing made him look bad in the eyes of the people. Hrafn had often had run-ins with the Konungr's advisors over how they ruled the population. He would be removing most, if not all, of them the moment he was crowned Konungr... assuming he was ever truly crowned Konungr.

Hrafn stormed into his office and threw himself into his chair. Jeger looked up from his stack of paperwork, ready to admonish him for being so loud and careless, but the look on Hrafn's face made him bite his tongue. Instead, tempered by years of experience, Jeger got up, made Hrafn a drink, and brought it over to him.

"Want to talk about it?"

Hrafn took the glass and downed the alcohol in one long gulp. He wanted to crush the glass in his hand, but Jeger quickly took it away from him. Letting out a long sigh of frustration, he looked up. He was going to have to tell him, regardless.

"The Konungr wants me to lead a delegation to the Northeast to put a stop to the incursions at the border."

Jeger's face paled. The Konungr had never sent the prince into hostile territory before: it was either a test of some sort, or he simply wished to dispose of the prince in a convenient way.

"When do you leave?"

Alone in their office, Jeger could allow his sensitive side to show. His eyes were wide, filled with fear of losing Hrafn. His breathing was quick. In front of the other advisors or military personnel Jeger would appear cold and heartless, completely devoid of any feelings, but alone with Hrafn, he was close to tears.

"We. We leave in seven days. Ollie is coming with us, as a man, of course." Hrafn looked up to be sure Jeger understood his meaning.

For their safety and for hers, she must appear to be a man in front of anyone who saw her. Hrafn was giving that task to Jeger: to make her pass for one of the men. They would still keep her very close to them, but they would outfit her so that from a distance, she wouldn't stand out. The three would have adjoining tents as well. It was normal to have Jeger's tent adjoining his whenever they did travel together. This time it would be explained that the swordmaker was a priority and would be guarded with the prince and his advisor. If there was back-talk, they would deal with it. He would need her swords on the field, potentially. More to the point, he couldn't leave her alone at the palace, where the Konungr might discover her and her secret.

At least while they traveled, he would have them together and away from the Konungr. Maybe fortune would favor him, and the situation on the border wouldn't be as bad as previously thought. He knew it was wishful thinking, but he had to hold onto it. He couldn't allow anything to happen to those he loved. They would just have to get through this, and then perhaps they would have to start considering plans for the future. Hrafn was no longer willing to be a pawn in the Konungr's game, not while Jeger and Olwen hung in the balance.

Olwen

Olwen turned to the side again with a sigh. She was not at all happy about having to bind her breasts, but the clothing Jeger had brought her did a lot to hide the rest of her womanly curves. She was even encouraged to wear a sword at her hip as the other men did. She smiled a sad smile to herself. As a young lady, she had been allowed to wear trousers and carry a sword as boys did. Her father had taught her the art of swordplay, as well as the art of sword making; he believed you could never be a good smith if you didn't understand the workings and necessities of the finished product. While she was no master sword fighter, she could hold her own; which is much more than any other woman she had met could say for themselves. It was ironic that she was again wearing trousers and a sword. She wondered if her father looked on from Valhalla and sent his blessings.

Jeger stepped behind her and pulled her to himself as she watched him in the mirror. He dropped his nose into the crease of her neck and dropped a lingering kiss there, sending shockwaves of desire through her.

"You are almost as sexy when you dress as a man as you are when you play the lady, Ollie." His hands began to climb under her shirt, pawing at her bound chest.

"Jeger!" she reprimanded, "I don't want to have to tie them again! Stop it!" She giggled as he changed his assault to tickling, causing her to draw herself in and protect herself while she laughed.

Hrafn walked briskly into the room, grabbing the last of his items to pack.

"Come along, you two. We have no time for that before we're off. I want to make haste and be as far away from here by daybreak tomorrow as possible." His face was sour as he shoved clothing into his bag.

Olwen knew he wasn't mad at them. Ever since he had told her that they would be traveling again, he had been different, restless. Even his sexual attentions were more cautious, and she caught him lingering as he stared at her. She didn't know what to make of it, but she knew he had a lot on his mind. They had come to a peaceful understanding between them, and she wanted to comfort him. She made her way across the room to stand behind him as Jeger had done to her, and wrapped her arms around him and squeezed, as she wasn't tall enough to kiss his neck. She laid her cheek against his back and was surprised when he stopped packing to hold his hands over hers for a moment. He was not one for sentimentality; this was his way of acknowledging her comfort. She smiled to herself.

Within the hour, they were mounted on their horses, and their procession made its way away from the palace and toward the mountains in the Northeast and the border with Fimbulvetr. Hrafn had been teaching her to speak their language. Where Hrafn's land was known as the "Great Summer," the enemy country which bordered them was the "Mighty Winter." She could vaguely remember fables about the Summer Court and the Winter Court, but she had always thought them to be just that: fables. Now she wondered.

They rode on in silence for hours, Hrafn on one side of her, Jeger on the other, and an entourage of guards encircling them. She knew she was strong for a woman, and the clothing did a good job of camouflaging her shape. Still, she didn't want to speak too much or send too many glances to the men, lest she appear feminine or weak. Whenever they stopped for food or rest, Jeger always took over as her "personal guard." While the other men did not seem to care and would simply drop their trousers and relieve themselves publicly, Jeger always ensured her privacy as they walked into the treeline together. Not for the first time, Olwen wrinkled her nose at what crude beasts men could be sometimes.

After a long day of pushing the horses hard on the road, Hrafn finally called for the group to stop and make camp. They were still a half-day's ride from the border, but that suited him. He explained he didn't want to be near enough for an attack if there were forces already gathered there.

Olwen, or "Ollie" as she was officially called now, was just glad to be off her damned horse. Her thighs and ass hurt, and she couldn't help but remember her first travels with Hrafn; how much had changed since then. She walked into their shared tent to find Hrafn already there. As she tried to massage herself, she noticed he smirked at her, a devilish glint in his eyes. She knew he was thinking exactly what she had been just a moment before. He walked up to her and bent down to whisper into her ear.

"I can take that ache away from you, My Swan, but I would have to gag you to keep you from screaming out your ecstasy and giving yourself away," he said, chuckling.

"You are just jealous of my horse," she retorted, surprised at herself for having thought of something so quickly. She caught him off guard because he threw his head back and laughed out loud as she limped away.

A small area was set up for her to work on her swords in private while the men attended meetings and had scouts survey the area for enemies. Other than the change of scenery, it was just as dull for Olwen as it had been at the palace. At least she had the fresh air here.

They had dined together, but the men had left again to see to duties. It was late that evening before Jeger returned to their shared tent. Olwen was glad to have him back. She knew it was no different than it had been at the palace, but there was an illogical fear that someone would discover her, as if the fabric of the tent was too thin to shield her from all of the men that surrounded her. In truth, there were more men around the forge back at the palace and a higher risk of discovery, but it left her irrationally insecure nonetheless.

Jeger made his way to the innermost part of the tent and flopped down on the sleeping mat. Bringing his arms up behind his head, he groaned. He did not like riding either; he confided in her. She followed him to the mat and sat beside him. A thought worked its way around her brain, and she considered whether she should ask what she was thinking or stifle it. She worked her bottom lip between her teeth as she debated. They were traveling, so it was not the ideal time to bring up her sexual education. She just couldn't help when ideas came to her.

Jeger studied her face with a slight smirk and knowing eyes. "Ask what you will, Ollie. I can see you chewing on it; spit it out before you choke on it."

She looked down as her cheeks flared red in the subtle lamplight of the tent.

"I was just thinking... there was this... technique... I saw a serving woman doing it with Hrafn... and I wanted... I thought I could..." She twisted her hands together in her lap, and she couldn't help but notice how Jeger was trying not to smile and hurt her feelings as she sought the bravery to say what she wanted.

He sat up, wrapping his arm around her shoulders to bolster her, and with his other hand, he lifted her chin until he could look into her eyes.

"You are a fierce and desirable woman. There is no embarrassment in asking for what you want by name. Ask, and it is yours, Ollie. Let there be no shame between us."

"Fine," she said, blowing out a breath. "I want to suck your cock."

His body stiffened, and she heard him choke back a groan. She also noticed that his trousers tented immediately.

"Are you sure?" he asked tenderly, his cheeks as red as hers. "We could wait for Hrafn if you wanted."

"I do want to do that with Hrafn, but Jeger, I need to know what I'm doing first. I only witnessed it being done once. What if I am awkward or unskilled? What if I am bad at it? He has clearly had women who are proficient in this before; how am I ever to compete?"

He had to pull her chin up again as she sought to hide her humiliation.

"No shame between us, remember?" he asked gently. "If you're sure that you desire that, then I would be happy to help you learn. You need not compete; you are his wife. And any man would be a fool to deny you this, with or without experience, Ollie."

She smiled brightly and then began pulling her shirt off over her head and untying her breeches.

"You mean to do this now?" Jeger chuckled. Seeing her so enthusiastic, he simply followed suit and discarded his clothing. He laid back down on the sleeping mat. "All right, where do you– Nnnnnng"

He couldn't even finish his thought as she dove for his cock, stroking it as he had taught her. He ground his jaw in an effort not to groan.

"A little warning next time, My Swan?"

Olwen simply giggled as she continued working him with her hands. After a few minutes, Jeger opened his eyes to watch her; she seemed fascinated with watching his cock growing harder under her fingers.

"I am happy to do this with you all night as well, but I thought you wanted to learn new things?" he inquired with a smirk.

She looked up at him in surprise, seeming to have been pulled out of her fantasy, and then she blushed fiercely again.

"It... it would help me if you would close your eyes," she said softly.

"I will close them at first, Ollie, but I have to be honest with you; I cannot keep them closed while you do that to me. To see you taking me in your mouth..." He groaned low.

Olwen watched him close his eyes, putting his trust in her. She slowly brought her face down to his cock. It was a magnificent and proud cock, slightly thicker than Hrafn's. She inspected it up close as she continued to stroke him firmly. With one last look at him, she brought his length into her mouth. She felt him groan as he stiffened, and his hands moved to her head gently to guide her. He was hard and solid like a muscle, and yet his skin was velvety smooth and soft.

She allowed him to guide her gently, his grasp in her hair firm but not painful. She experimented with the things she had seen, running her tongue along his underside and flicking it beneath the head of his shaft. Each different thing she tried elicited a new gasp or groan from him, and his hips started rising to meet her. She hollowed her cheeks and sucked, and he responded immediately by tightening his hands in her hair and groaning again.

"Can you take me deeper?" He asked, his voice choppy and breathy.

She looked up to see that his eyes were fixed on her, watching his cock disappear into her mouth and return again. His pupils were blown wide with desire. She could feel him fighting with himself not to be too rough with her; he would grab her hair tightly and jerk, only to release it and try to soothe her right after.

She pulled off of him slowly. "I can try," she answered, "But I want you to treat me as you would Hrafn. I want you to be rougher with me. I will tell you if I cannot handle it."

She felt his cock leap in her hands. He nodded at her slowly. As soon as her mouth was seated all the way down onto his cock he fisted her hair in his hands tightly.

"You have to tell me if it is too much. Tap on my leg if I hurt you, and I will stop," he hissed.

Olwen allowed him to drag her head up and down over his cock, pushing her face into his pubic bone and feeling his balls on her chin. His fingers burned her scalp as he tugged, but for some reason, it only made her more aroused. When she made no move to stop him, he upped his pace, pulling her down more forcefully until she started gagging a little around the size of him as he invaded her throat. She learned quickly when to take a breath and hold it.

The feeling of Jeger, under her mouth, absolutely losing control spurred her on to endure more. She wanted to feel him explode in her mouth. She wanted to swallow his seed as she had seen the serving girl do. She looked up, completely enflamed with arousal, to see him watching her intently, his face a picture of bliss.

"You feel so amazing on my cock, Ollie. *Faen!* You should stop, Ollie; I'm going to come! Ollie... if you don't–"

She only threw herself onto his cock harder, sucking more, working her tongue around him wherever she could in a frenzy. His hands gripped her tightly, pulling her head down onto his cock and holding her there, with his cock lodged deep in her throat. She felt him spasming against her tongue, and then her mouth was full of his hot fluid. Shot after shot, he released into her throat and mouth, pulling back a little to pump into her again as he let out a silent scream of release. Still, his hands didn't release his hold on her, his cock too enthralled to let go.

"HVA FAEN!"

Hrafn stood just inside the door flap of the tent, utter shock on his face as he saw Jeger holding Olwen's mouth over his cock while he pumped in and out of her. Jeger released his hold on her, but she still tried to devour his rapidly deflating cock.

"Is this what you two do all day while I'm working?" Hrafn asked angrily, crossing his arms over his chest.

Olwen finally managed to control herself and pull herself away from Jeger, but his juices were spilling down her face and dripping onto her chest. She tried to look contrite, but she had never been prouder.

"Hraf, you know this is not what we do all day. Are you going to come join us, or are you going to stand there and sulk?"

When Hrafn didn't move a muscle, Jeger got up and strolled over to him, throwing his arms around his neck and kissing him deeply. Olwen noticed his hand reached down and caressed Hrafn's hard cock through his pants.

"I know you like watching. I know you've been standing there for minutes, and said nothing to stop us, so get naked and get your ass on that bed. You've absolutely got to feel her small little mouth on your cock."

"I don't know," Hrafn argued, "This feels like a betrayal." His words had no heat in them at all; even Olwen could see he was posturing.

"Fine," Jeger said at last, still grinding his hand on Hrafn's cock, "I'll just let her suck me off again. You can stay and watch if you like. She's amazing."

Before Jeger could turn to walk away, Hrafn was ripping his clothing off.

Hrafn

Before the sun was even up, the camp was abuzz with activity. The men knew their jobs well and were already preparing for the day's work. Hrafn shook Jeger awake but hesitated a moment as he looked at Olwen curled beside him, sleeping soundly. They had kept her up most of the night, and he had delighted in being responsible for the tiny squeaking noises that had escaped her throat as she had tried to be silent. She was a goddess when she was in the throes of release, her face slack with bliss. Before he could second-guess himself about waking her, Jeger was kissing her awake.

He had wanted to let her sleep, but there was too much risk that someone would wander into their tent looking for the men and instead find a naked woman in their bed. As a woman was not supposed to be there, they would not have given orders not to touch her; it would be disastrous.

Olwen stretched and pouted as she rubbed her eyes to clear them. Hrafn had to admit that she was adorable. He had never remained until morning to see a woman waking, so he couldn't be sure that they all weren't, though. He tried to harden his heart; it would do no good to get attached to her. His eventual betrayal would leave her hating him. He felt his heart clench as he got up quickly and moved to wash up for the day.

Dressing quickly, he left orders with Jeger to set Olwen up with some swords to finish while he went to discuss the mission with his generals. He needed distance between him and Olwen right now, and he needed a clear head to think with: the one on his shoulders. He needed to focus on his mission.

He made his way around the camp, taking in the efficiency of the men as they prepared the horses and the weapons. He grabbed a quick bite to eat at the mess tent and sat with his generals to discuss routes and tactics. Today was exploratory only; their mission was to search the border area for signs of incursion or enemy occupation. Any enemies caught on their territory were to be captured for questioning. They would take ninety percent of the soldiers with them and split them into three large groups to cover the most ground as quickly as possible, leaving the enemy no time to retreat if they were already trespassing. Once they agreed which general would take which group and on which route, the plan was set, and the men were called to order.

Hrafn watched the men gearing up and falling into place. He had a very high training standard, and his men worked seamlessly. The men on horses led, and the foot soldiers and bowmen followed. Each group started in its direction, and only a trace group was left behind for defense. Still, Hrafn had ordered two men to guard his tent with Ollie inside. He had told them only that their swordsmith must be protected at all costs. Without further delay, he joined his group and set out to search the border.

After hours of searching under the hot sun, the area Hrafn's unit was patrolling was suspiciously absent of any signs of trespass or violation. The undergrowth had been untouched, and the soil had not been over-turned in quite some time. There was no evidence that any large group of people had come through at all. This knowledge should have pleased Hrafn, but it had the opposite effect.

If there were no signs of enemy trespass, then why were they really there? The Konungr was known to send him on missions that turned into puzzles to be solved; Hrafn would have to discover his true moti-vations if he was to return successfully. It made him uneasy.

When the men had finished their sweep, he was considering whether he should push them beyond the agreed-upon area, or turn back to camp, when the pounding of horse's hooves approaching drew everyone together defensively. He looked back the way they had come to see a lone rider bearing his standard racing to him.

There was only one reason a single rider would approach at that speed: for reinforcements. Hrafn hauled his horse in the opposite direction, turning back toward the camp, and kicked his horse into a full gallop without waiting to hear the rider's report. If anything had happened to Olwen, he would never forgive himself, and the Konungr would never forgive him for losing their swordsmith.

When he estimated he was halfway back to the camp, he pulled his body in tightly and called on his magic. He allowed his body to shrink into his clothing, taking his raven form. He would normally never attempt it while both clothed with armor and on horseback, but the fear in his gut was unrelenting. Once in bird form, he fought his way out from under the shirt, almost getting trapped under the heavy chainmail. As he pushed out of the clothing, he slid off of the saddle and allowed his large wings to catch air as he wheeled upward and away from the running horse. His men would find his clothing and weapons and return them; he needed to be at camp.

He screamed in the wind as he made his descent upon the camp, where his fears were realized. Small fires burned out of control, and the small group of men he had left to defend the camp was strewn on the ground, dead or wounded. His shrill scream lit the sky as he wheeled and shot into his tent through the flap, pulling on his human form just as his feet hit the ground with speed. He took several running steps and then threw himself into the sword room they had created for Olwen. He found two enemy soldiers dead, but she was gone.

Grabbing a pair of breeches and a shirt, he rushed out of his tent as he dressed. He could see his unit approaching and another of his units from another direction. The defense force had sent riders after the three units when they were overrun, as was protocol.

But how?! How had the enemy forces gotten behind them? They had not passed anyone on the way in; his scouts had reconnoitered far into the woods to be sure. Something was not right about any of this.

His unit pulled into camp at the same time as the second unit arrived, with the third on the horizon. Immediately, wounded men were treated, and the dead were pulled to the side while a force was gathered to search the area for the offenders and try to recover Olwen.

Jeger was enraged, shouting orders and driving soldiers to their tasks in a fury. Hrafn knew he was worried about her; Jeger never lost his cool in front of the men, and he could see the effect it was having on them. If enemy soldiers had captured her– if they found out she was a woman! Hrafn started shouting orders of his own.

He grabbed at his horse's reins, ready to mount and head off on his own to search when shouts were heard from the south side of the camp. Several men were running his way, and he nearly fell to his knees when he saw they had Olwen with them. There was blood on her clothing, but she seemed alright. Hrafn released the horse and ordered his leading general to search the area while he questioned the swordsmith. He and Jeger took Olwen by the arms and pulled her back into their tent, closing the flap securely.

Once inside, Hrafn had all he could do not to collapse with relief. He turned to see Jeger already pulling Ollie in tightly to his body, curling himself around her possessively, his fingers straining to hold her against the fear of what he had almost lost. Hrafn joined them, allowing himself to grab her tightly and hold her, something he would normally never do. Signs of devotion or sentimentality were things he avoided at all costs so as not to send the wrong message, but at that moment, all he could do was breathe her in and say a prayer of gratitude to the Old Gods.

"What happened?" Jeger croaked as he tried to calm the emotion from his voice.

"I don't know," she began. "I was getting ready to begin another blade when I heard shouting. Before I could even get out of the tent, two men were coming in. I don't know if they knew this was your tent or if they were looking for me, but it looked like they expected me. One of them went to grab me, but I got to my sword first and ran him through. The other one unsheathed his sword, and I had to fight with him before

I took him down, but he died quickly. Once they were dispatched, I slipped out under the tent flap in the back and made my way into the trees to hide. I didn't know how many of the enemy there were, but I know I could not take them all on. I only had to hope you would find me first. When I saw it was your standard that had returned, I made my way out of the woods."

Hrafn stared at her in stupified silence.

"You can fight with a sword?" Jeger said with a tone of awe.

"Of course I can fight with a sword," she responded, insulted. "I don't just make them, you know. How can you expect me to understand the art of the design, the balance of the blade, if I don't understand how it's meant to be used? I have never had to use my skills on the battlefield, but I have been trained and tested all my life. I have carried a sword as long as I have been walking."

Jeger just pulled her into a tight hug again; his eyes cast to Valhalla with gratitude.

"Something is not right here," Hrafn said quietly, and Ollie and Jeger turned to look at him. "There should be no way an enemy force got behind us, and we found no evidence of them traveling across the borders; the other generals reported the same. The Konungr is convinced that we are being invaded, yet I see no evidence of it at all. This feels too much like a trap. I want the camp moved. NOW. We will choose a better outpost, one that was not predetermined before we left. Jeger, fetch the generals."

Jeger gave Olwen one last squeeze and then rushed out of the tent to carry out his orders.

"And you, my surprisingly vicious little Swan," he said with a small smile as he turned to Olwen, "I want you to keep yourself hidden. I do not know if we have a spy in our midst or if we are being sacrificed, but I must act as if both are true if I am to keep you safe."

12

Hrafn

The troops had packed up quickly, despite the number of wounded or dead that had to be dealt with. Hrafn would not have them stay a moment longer than they needed to at the current camp, not while he was unsure that it hadn't been an ambush from the very beginning. Not for the first time, he wondered if his father had orchestrated it to be rid of him. In the end, it would not matter; the Konungr would find a way to dispose of him if that was what he wanted to do, and it did not serve Hrafn to become paranoid, looking for invisible assassins around every corner.

Following his map, Hrafn guided his horse up into the foothills, along narrow paths which would make it difficult to follow them with a large force. He was moving along the border to his country and getting closer to more clusters of settlements. If there were invading forces, they would likely invade nearby, where there were towns to plunder. If there were no signs of entry, well, he would have to deal with that when he got there.

He stopped the men when they reached the summit of a slight elevation, which allowed views of the surrounding valley and settlements below. With a wave of his hand, the men dismounted and began setting up a new camp with the efficiency he had grown accustomed to. He pulled Jeger close by the arm.

"I know it does not need to be said, but keep an eye on the generals. I want to know if anyone tries to send word to anyone outside of our location."

"You think the generals betrayed us?" Jeger whispered quietly.

"I do not know who betrayed us, but the generals were the ones who knew where we planned to make camp, so I am not ruling them out."

Both men shared a terse look before moving off to set up their own tent and oversee the camp. If one of their trusted generals was working against them, either for the Konungr or the enemy, they would need to discover it as quickly as possible to avoid another attack. In the meantime, there was nothing to do but set up tents, care for the wounded, and prepare for the evening meal.

Hrafn and Jeger sat at the table in their tent, looking over the map one last time before they retired for the evening. They had all eaten and then retired to discuss strategy. They both knew Ollie was already in bed waiting for them, but they had wanted to go over a few last things. Just as Jeger started to fold the map, the guard called from the tent flap. The two men exchanged looks before Hrafn got up to answer the call. He poked his head outside to see what the guard wanted.

When the guard explained what he needed, Hrafn signaled behind his back to tell Jeger to warn Ollie not to come out of the back of the tent before he allowed the guard to bring someone inside with him. Hrafn took his seat, and Jeger joined him when he returned to the main compartment. A tall thin guard ushered in another guard whose eyes darted around nervously.

Hrafn addressed the first guard. "Explain to me what happened again, in detail."

The tall man never took his hand off the second guard's arm as he launched into his story. "I was told to watch the path we came in on, if you'll remember, Sire, in addition to the guards placed by the generals. I was a little farther down the road than the camp gate. About twenty minutes ago, I heard a noise in the brush and investigated. I found this man making his way back along the road, so I grabbed him and brought him back to you for questioning."

Hrafn turned to the second man, although he was hardly a man. He couldn't have been even twenty turns of the year yet, and he was so frightened that he was shaking visibly. Hrafn could not remember ever seeing a member of his fighting force show such cowardice in his presence. Even the young recruits came in boldly and fiercely. How had this man come to be in his ranks, and more importantly, why had he been trying to escape them?

Hrafn turned his eyes to the youth, who swallowed audibly. "How do you explain your actions?"

The boy paled further and seemed to stutter as he tried to find something to say. He never got the chance because another guard shouted as the tent flap pushed inward roughly. General Lenz pushed into the middle of the room to stand before the shaking young man being questioned. He dropped to his knee and bowed his head as he addressed Hrafn.

"Your Highness, this man is my son, and I will bear the weight of his punishment."

Hrafn didn't need to look to know Jeger was staring at him in shock. They knew Lenz had a son but was he already of age? Hrafn still remembered him as a blond child giggling for his Papa when he returned from training. He couldn't have already grown into the young man they saw standing before them, could he?

"Explain yourself, General," was all Hrafn said.

"Highness, the Konungr has been ordering me to work against you, and I have always managed to find a way to avoid it, but now he has brought my children in to use against me. He enlisted my son into the army against my wishes, and I have no doubt he has ordered him to relay back our location for his own purposes. I saw him trying to leave after we set up our last camp, and I held him off until I knew that you were safely away. It is my fault for not turning him in sooner, but he is my boy, Highness. He is the only son I have left. I would gladly take his punishment in his place. The fault is mine."

Hrafn said nothing in response but looked to Jeger. The general hadn't known Ollie's secret, only that there was a swordsmith in their tent. By waiting for them to be safely away, he had endangered Ollie.

Jeger got up from his chair and approached the still-kneeling general. "So you've known since the attack that your son was responsible, and you said nothing? Not even when it resulted in the death of some of your men?"

The general dropped his head in shame. "I only suspected he was responsible, but even still, I should have turned him over. Their blood is on my hands."

Hrafn finally stood, looking to have had enough drama for one afternoon. "Well, this puts us in quite a predicament, doesn't it? The Konungr will know we have uncovered his plot if the lad doesn't report back. Either way, we can't have the two of you interacting with the rest of the camp without knowing your true motives. And as for YOU," Hrafn snarled, whacking the general's head as he walked by, "I will need a complete understanding of why we have been sent out here in the first place. It's evident that there are no incursions and no enemy forces to fight back. You will tell me everything you know, or both you and the boy will not live to face the Konungr again."

Hrafn sent the guard to take Lenz's son to detention and then sat and listened while General Lenz laid out all the details he knew of the Konungr's actions. Hrafn's heart sank as he heard how the Konungr had been creating this story about enemy hostilities for the last several years. All the generals suspected it to be false, as none had seen any signs of it, and none had sent men to fortify any border.

However, none of them could contradict the Konungr, so they had to sit by idly. Lenz could not explain what the Konungr had expected to gain from pressing this story at court, but it was clear his mind had some purpose. Already, Lenz had seen two of Hrafn's half-brothers sent on missions such as this, only to perish. There were now two fewer contenders for the throne.

When asked if Lenz thought the Konungr had sent them only to dispose of Hrafn in an alleged attack, Lenz shook his head. He explained that, while it might be convenient for Hrafn to die if the Konungr wished him gone, the greater purpose of these missions seemed to be in causing the very hostilities he was claiming already. There had been inquiries from the Court of Fimbulvetr, wanting to know why armed groups were suddenly prowling the boundaries between the countries. Tensions were developing where there had been none.

Hrafn and Jeger questioned the General late into the night before finally sending him away to be detained and heading to bed themselves. Hrafn washed and undressed in silence. Ollie was already asleep and sprawled on their sleeping mat, and Jeger was lost in his thoughts.

He now understood how the fighting force got behind them; it had followed them. They were not enemy soldiers but local soldiers or mercenaries dressed to play the part. So what would they have done with Ollie had they gotten her? Was it the Konungr's orders to get the swordsmith away from them, or was it a coincidence? Perhaps the king didn't feel he needed Hrafn any longer now that they had a fae swordsmith who could make him enchanted swords. But why did he need those swords without a real war on the horizon? Had he lost his mind and decided to create a war?

There were too many questions and not enough answers. Hrafn dragged himself to the sleeping mat and fell quickly into a dreamless sleep.

Olwen

Olwen became more aware of the throbbing need between her legs as she slowly climbed out of her dream to feel the sleeping mat rocking in subtle jerking motions. She could see that it was still dark outside her tent, and the hour still felt early. Her body swayed in time as the mat shifted her with each rocking movement. Next, she became aware of the heavy breaths and low moaning sounds reverberating through the mat. No wonder she had been having such sexual dreams.

She cracked one eye open to confirm her suspicions; Jeger was being dragged by his head over Hrafn's hard cock. Both men had their eyes pinched closed in bliss. She continued to watch as Hrafn used Jeger's mouth to chase his release, their movements rocking the mat underneath them and shaking Olwen with them.

When she couldn't take it any longer, she carefully crept her way to Jeger's body. He was on his knees, his ass in the air, and his mouth working his consort into a heated frenzy. His hand worked his own hardness as his mouth offered Hrafn untold pleasures. Olwen gently reached underneath Jeger and took over his pleasure; Jeger only moaned a little louder, releasing his hand so she could do the work for him.

They continued this way for a few moments of sighs, groans, and tensing hips before Olwen was brave enough to take another step. Pushing Jeger's knees further apart, she crawled between them with her face just under his hard and pulsing cock. Without asking, she took him deep into her throat, her hands grasping at his hips and ass firmly, encouraging him to spill into her.

She was surprised to hear Hrafn's gasp of surprise and his whispered commentary; she had thought him lost to his own bliss. How he had seen her with Jeger attending to his cock was beyond her.

"Oh, my little Swan! That's it! Suck his cock for him! Make him shoot into your throat. Suck him dry. Ooooohhhhhhhh, yeeessssss.... Yes. Yes. YES. YES!"

Olwen felt Jeger's body pull forward tightly and lock down onto Hrafn's cock as Hrafn arched his back and released with a strangled groan. This triggered Jeger to follow him over the edge, as his body began to thrum, and then his own back tightened. Instinctively he dropped his cock further into Olwen's waiting throat, fucking into her roughly. He lost all rhythm as his cock pulsated and shot his seed in thick warm streams. Olwen had all she could do to resist moaning out loud as her nails dug into his thighs for purchase, wanting him deeper.

The two men were still panting when Hrafn pulled Olwen up to sit with her back to his front. He reached around her and caressed her nipples with his fingers as his lips and teeth entertained themselves on her neck. Jeger pushed her thighs apart roughly and launched himself onto her mound, his mouth still slick with Hrafn's release.

It wasn't long before Olwen was reaching her climax, and Hrafn had to take her mouth in his to muffle the cries she released. As her body lay in spasms, the men exchanged positions and brought her to orgasm again and again with their mouths and fingers until she could only push them away because she was too sensitive to bear it any longer.

Olwen lay on her side, panting for breaths as Hrafn smiled down at her smugly. "Are you well satisfied, my little Swan? Did Jeger and I sate your hunger for you?"

He looked far too pleased with himself, and Olwen knew this wasn't doing anything to control his massive ego. Still, she honestly couldn't complain or find fault. Where she had worried she would be interfering in their lovemaking; instead, she had been welcomed with open arms... and other body appendages, even if she hadn't ridden their cocks yet. She didn't feel like they only tolerated her. She felt valued and a part of their lovemaking.

She watched Jeger washing on the other side of the room as sadness filled her as her reality settled into her mind. She enjoyed pretending to be a part of their relationship, but in truth, she wasn't. She was a temporary diversion for them.

Soon, Hrafn would release her as he had agreed to do. He would expect her to leave and move on as she had said she would. He had told her he had no interest in emotional or overdramatic women trying to cling to him. She needed to remind her heart that they were not in love with her; they were fulfilling an obligation. She should not mistake their kindness and enjoyment as a sign that they wanted anything more with her. Hrafn had to pay attention to her, and she made their cocks swell. That was all this was.

She felt very empty and alone suddenly, even though the two men still moved around the tent, finding clothing and weapons as they got ready for their day. She closed her eyes to stop the tears that suddenly wanted to spring to life.

"Why don't you stay and rest a while longer, Ollie? I'll bring you some food from the mess tent for breakfast."

She heard Jeger as he moved out of the room, and she only nodded, her eyes still closed tight.

Olwen stretched and yawned. She noticed it was significantly brighter than when she had woken previously to play with her men. She internally scolded herself, reminding herself that they were not "her men" at all.

She could smell food and just make out conversation from the next room. She languidly pulled herself up to standing. She could still feel the tightness in her core and the stiffness in her muscles from her earlier escapades, and it thrilled her a little. Even if it would not last, she had experienced the wanton desire and pleasure she had heard about. She felt like a woman at last.

She moved quietly so that she wouldn't alert anyone in the next room of her presence, in case Hrafn had guards present. As she approached the washing basin she could hear the whispered conversation more clearly, and she stopped dead.

"But you *promised* her!" That was Jeger.

"Yes, and I meant it when I did. But you know I can't, and you know why."

Jeger's words were heated and full of venom as he responded to Hrafn. "I don't give a *faen* what has changed. You made a bargain in good faith, and she has kept it. She has made the *jævlig* swords!"

"I KNOW!" Hrafn whispered vehemently. "But it will never be enough for the Konungr. The mission will never be done. So long as he is alive, there will be no peace for any of us. He will never allow me to release her, not while he is concocting this imaginary war to hold over my head–”

“You will destroy her!” Jeger whispered with a hiss. “I don't care what the Konungr wants; you have to release her!”

“And then what?” Hrafn demanded quietly. “She's practically a girl, Jeger. Where would she go that the Konungr wouldn't find her and enslave her? How would she support herself without a husband to defend her and bring income? Yes, she is a swordsmith, but she is still a WOMAN. WHO would buy from her? Tell me, who would take her seriously?

“Who would not seek to take her, own her, control her? If not the Konungr, there are many men out there who would think nothing of breaking her spirit and using her for her skills or her pussy, and you know it. Don't be stupid, Jeger. Think with your head and not your cock. She's a lot safer with us, even if she's unhappy about it. That's my last word on the subject; do not bring it up again.”

Olwen heard shuffling in the other room and the sound of the tent flap falling back into place with a woosh. She stood stunned by what she had just heard. It took her mind a moment to wrap around the truth of it all.

Hrafn did not plan to release her.

No matter how hard she worked, no matter how many swords she produced, he did not plan to release her. He was knowingly breaking his promise to her, using the king as a loophole.

Tears welled in her eyes and overflowed down her cheeks. She thought they were friends, more than friends. She knew he didn't want her as a wife, but he had been kind to her; he had made her feel confident and sexy. Now, everything that he had said and done was worthless in the face of the truth. He still thought she was a naive girl, unable to support herself.

And maybe he was right. Perhaps no one would take a female swordsmith seriously, but she doubted it based on how the swords were always received with reverence and awe. She wasn't stupid. And as far as men wanting her only for her body or her skill, well, she would kill any man who tried, or die trying. It would be better to die independent than to live as some man's lap dog for the rest of her life.

Anger burned hot in her throat, but her heart was shattered. This betrayal stung more deeply than Henrick's; at least he had always shown her that he did not value her. He did not pretend to find value in her to get what he needed; he did not pretend to like her or compliment her as if he truly cared.

What Hrafn had done to her was cruel. He had offered her a way out, only to pull it back when it suited him. And he had enjoyed the friendship, and her body, which she offered when she assumed they were all on equal footing. Had she known he would betray her like this, she never would have allowed him...

Fury burned in her, making her clench and unclench her fists and jaw. Her vision went red. She could not stay here, not like this. She could not be a pawn for Hrafn or the Konungr. She needed a way out.

Washing quickly, she dressed in her usual male garb and packed a small bag with travel necessities. She peered into the next room to find it empty, a tray of food on the table for her. She grabbed all of the food and stuffed it into another bag. Then she went to the sword room where she would normally be working today to fetch the final piece she needed.

Deep in one of the chests of blades was a sword that she had been working on to give to Hrafn as a parting gift when he freed her. In truth, prior to that morning, she hadn't wanted to leave him. She had planned to ask to stay on as the royal swordsmith. Now she understood that would never work. She pulled the sword out of its wrappings. It was magnificent; it was one of the finest swords she had ever crafted. There was so much detail and power imbued in it that she could only work on it one small area at a time. It wasn't even finished, and already it thrummed with energy even from a distance.

He would not have this. She would take this with her as her own protection. She would call it "banamaðr" or slayer.

Sheathing the sword at her own hip, she gathered her bags and moved to the back of the tent. She bent down to peer out of the bottom of the flap. When she saw no one around, she first pushed her bags under the flap and outside, and then she laid down and pushed herself through the narrow opening. Once outside, she rushed into the trees.

Olwen fought to control her breathing as she stealthily moved through the trees around the camp. She couldn't afford for anyone to see her and return her to Hrafn. A large group of men moved through the clearing with their weapons, and she ducked low to wait them out. They seemed to be in no hurry as they joked and laughed as they walked. Her impatience grew as one of them even stopped to wait for someone near the back of the group. She forced herself to take a deep breath and calm herself. Haste would work against her.

Suddenly she heard shouting. She froze where she was, sure that someone had spotted her. She watched as the group of men in front of her turned away from her and started running. Beyond them, she could see smoke rising into the sky. Luck was with her; something had distracted them. She wasted no time, getting up and moving swiftly.

She was almost out of the camp when she saw the makeshift jail cell that had been erected. Inside a primitive metal cage sat General Lenz and his young son. Her eyes scanned the area but found no guards. Perhaps they had run to see whatever had distracted the last group of men? She knew she didn't have long to consider, so she went with her gut and rushed to the back of the cage.

"Where are the men you were going to meet?" she demanded of the boy.

"He won't tell you unless you take him with you," the general replied, not looking at her. "Take him with you, and he will show you the way."

The boy tried to argue but the general wouldn't hear it.

"Why should I take him? I can probably find them on my own," she replied.

"Perhaps," the general said, "but he's only seventeen years, and if it's the last thing I accomplish, I will see him survive this treachery of the Konungr and his son. He is innocent. Take him with you, please. I can offer you safe haven away from here if you take him with you."

Olwen scowled. Having a teenage boy with her wasn't smart. She had barely enough food for herself, never mind a growing boy. But if he could get them to allies; or better, if he could get them to safe haven… it would be worth it.

"Fine," she spit, "But I need your guarantee that I will be kept safe and not betrayed to the Konungr or his son at this safe haven you offer."

"If you take my son to the house he knows is safe, you will both be received there and kept safely. Your whereabouts will not be given to the Konungr, any of his representatives, or his sons. You have my word."

Without turning, the general stuck his hand outside the cage. She clasped his hand and shook and was aware of the energetic tug that seemed to sear her skin briefly as the bargain took hold. She had felt this before, but never so acutely as she did now.

"You will have to get the keys back from the guard to get him out," the general said quietly, still not turning his head to look at her.

"No, actually, I won't," she replied.

Olwen called a song to her head, barely breathing the melody in her attempt to remain as quiet as possible. The boy gasped as the metal which formed the cage began to warp and sway, creating a hole he could climb through.

"One more thing," the general said as his son was getting ready to make his escape, "I need you to knock me unconscious. If they question me, I will have to say I was knocked unconscious when my son was taken."

Olwen grumbled under her breath. She did not want to have to hurt anyone and add it to her list of sins, but she didn't have time to argue. The guards might return at any moment. Pulling her sword from its sheath, she lifted the pommel over her head and brought it down hard onto the back of his. With an "oof," he slumped down to the bottom of the cage. She called her melody up and crudely put the cage back together. She didn't want it to be obvious that she had released him, but she couldn't take the chance that she was caught either. Once it looked sufficient, she turned and moved into the trees quickly, the teenager at her heels.

"What is your name?" Olwen whispered as they slipped silently through the trees.

"Mavok. What shall I call you?" he replied respectfully.

"You can call me Ollie," she said as she surveyed their surroundings.

13

Hrafn

"I WARNED YOU!" Jeger roared uncharacteristically. Jeger usually never raised his voice.

Hrafn pulled things apart in her workshop as if he would find her body hiding under a pile of sword forms. His movements were panicked. Although his brows were drawn together in anger, his wide eyes expressed his fear.

"Will you stop searching in here and take to the woods?!" Jeger grabbed Hrafn by his shoulders and physically stopped his manic searching. "She is not in the tent, Hrafn!"

Hrafn's eyes met Jeger's in a daze. Slowly, the shock that had seized him at finding Olwen gone began to recede from his mind, leaving him foggy but more alert by the moment.

"Ready the horses," he said, clarity beginning to show. Jeger rushed outside.

Hrafn stood looking at the piles of swords. He was aware of a sharp pain in his heart, but it wasn't the pain that happened when he broke the terms of his bargain. It was a pain he had not felt in a very long time, hundreds of years, in fact. This was the pain he experienced when the Konungr had removed his mother from the court when he was still very young. This was the pain he experienced when the Konungr berated him in front of the court as a child and told him to address his king as "Konungr" and not "father." This was the pain of loss and betrayal, and it was bitter in his blood.

He was furious. She had agreed she would not run from him; she had broken her bargain. Surely she would suffer as he had when he had broken the terms of his bargain? He had been nothing but kind to her, even offering her pleasure after her idiot husband had managed to trick him into making her his primary sexual partner and wife. But did he complain? No. He had accepted her with open arms, even into his existing relationship.

Had she been planning to escape this whole time? Was she just using her body to distract him? Was she hoping he would develop feelings for her?

He had told her from the beginning he did not want a wife, so if she was upset now that he still felt that way, it was not his responsibility. If he was being honest, he could admit that he had grown... fond... of her, yes. He did enjoy her body very much and had been looking forward to fucking her into oblivion, but that was all he was willing to give to her. By the Old Gods, why did she have to be so difficult? Why now?

Turning on his heel, he pushed out of the tents just as Jeger brought their mounts. He swung up into his saddle without a word, and Jeger did the same. Hrafn knew Jeger would have already sent out scouts in all directions to hunt her down, but he would not rest until she was found. He kicked his horse into a trot and headed to the west side of camp, where General Lenz had been found unconscious and alone.

"You will tell me again," Hrafn repeated flatly.

"Sire... I have told you everything. I heard someone in the woods; they wanted to take my son to find the group he was planning to meet. I was struck from behind, and when I woke, my son and the stranger were gone." General Lenz looked up from the ground where he sat, nursing the large lump on the back of his head.

"And you never saw this mysterious person?" Jeger asked.

"No, Lord Advisor. It happened quickly; I never turned before I was unconscious."

"This stranger, what did he sound like?" Hrafn asked as he stared daggers at the older man.

"I never said it was a man, Sire. In truth, it sounded very much like a woman, and not a local by the accent."

Hrafn's nostrils flared as he took a deep breath, his fists clenching. Without a word, he turned and stormed back to the horses, throwing himself up into the saddle quickly. Jeger followed, but Hrafn was already galloping down the path ahead of them.

Hrafn circled overhead in his raven form, watching Olwen and the boy below him huddling in the bushes. The mercenary scouts were everywhere, strolling about the woods without a care in the world. He was sure the Konungr was paying them well to camp out and wait to take him and his men down. When one of the mercenaries seemed to hear Olwen and start heading her way, Hrafn circled down and made noise on their opposite side, pulling their attention away from Olwen and sending them in the wrong direction. As mad as he was at her, he couldn't have the mercenaries, or the Konungr, claiming his prize.

He shot back into the air to see her leading the boy further into the mountain pass, staying high above the road in the trees. She was smart. It was harder and slower moving higher up the pass, but it also meant she was less likely to run into any mercenaries who were generally lazy and took the easy path. Once he was sure she wasn't heading directly into any more groups of hired thugs, Hrafn wheeled back the way he had come to find Jeger and inform him of her whereabouts. With any luck, they would recover her this night.

This time, there would be punishment, and he looked forward to it.

Olwen

Olwen woke to her shoulder being shaken roughly. She cracked her eyes open and gasped when she saw it was not Hrafn or Jeger who shook her. As her memory ambushed her, she sat up quickly and pulled her cloak around her. Mavok had watched through most of the night and had not run as she feared he might. It was now her turn to watch while he got a few hours of sleep. Olwen could see the beginnings of light on the horizon, so sunrise was not very long off.

A deep pain ached in her chest, bringing tears to her lashes. She still saw Hrafn and Jeger in her mind whenever she closed her eyes. She had been so disappointed when it was not one of them waking her, and she was even more devastated when she remembered why. Anger still burned below the surface, but it seemed this day would be spent dealing with sorrow and mourning. Unfortunately, she had a few hours in near darkness with nothing but her thoughts and her sadness to occupy her. She let the first of the tears slide silently down her cheek.

The day had been long, and the air was crisp and cold with autumn. Olwen pulled the cloak tighter around her as she and Mavok picked through the trees and undergrowth. She was glad that he seemed to know where they were headed because she was a stranger to this country, and even if she hadn't been, they were in the middle of a deep forest with no landmarks that she could see. She would have said they were lost.

Mavok seemed sure of himself as he trudged forward, and Olwen did her best to keep up with his long youthful legs. The ache in her muscles was a blessing and a relief because it pulled her attention away from the ache in her heart. She chose to focus, instead, on the blisters that were forming on her feet and her stiff legs.

Mavok turned to her, "If we continue on, we can reach the safehouse by dark. We will arrive late, but we will have a bed and food tonight."

Olwen wanted nothing more than to stop where she was and curl into a ball of hurt, but seeing the hopeful light in Mavok's eye, she nodded in agreement. Withholding a groan, she continued to push one foot in front of the other.

It was fully dark when the lanterns of the cottage came into view. Olwen's feet were numb, and her legs were heavy and burned. Despite her anger and sorrow, she would have been willing to surrender if Hrafn had shown up even an hour earlier. Two days of walking through the mountains had been more activity than her legs had ever experienced. She could work the forge for hours, her arms and chest muscles burning; but walking? She was glad to see their destination.

Mavok moved forward quickly, astounding Olwen as she had all she could do to continue moving at all. He knocked on the door and then had a quiet conversation with someone hidden behind his body through the cracked-open door. She blew out a breath when she saw the door open fully, the light spilling out ahead of her. Mavok ushered her into the house, and the door closed behind them.

Olwen was led to a chair by a wooden table. She made very unladylike noises as she sat, taking the weight off of her legs and feet. Mavok sat across from her, and their host made his way to the cookstove to heat water. He was an older man, balding and battle-scarred, with dark art marking his forearms in a way that Olwen had only read about.

"I am Bjørn, and you are welcome here. Mavok tells me you have secured his freedom; for that, we are grateful. What of his father?" The man glanced at her as he pulled out cups for them.

"Bjørn, I am Olwen. Thank you for your hospitality. I cannot say what will happen to the General. I wasn't much more than a captive of the prince myself."

"But you were his swordsmith. Did you not work for him willingly?"

"I was tied to him through a bargain," Olwen began cautiously, "But we came to an understanding for my work. When that understanding was no longer in place, I chose to leave." She didn't know these people well enough to lay her truth bare for them, but she needed to give them enough to understand that she was not their enemy.

"And the Konungr?" Bjørn asked.

"What of him? I have never seen him. My agreement was with Prince Hrafn alone."

That seemed to satisfy the man. He pulled a kettle off of the fire and brought tea and cups to the table for his guests. Bjørn served them, and they sipped in silence for a few moments. Mavok yawned, and Bjørn chuckled as he turned to the boy.

"Get to bed, Mav. You know where your room is."

Mavok didn't argue, instead getting up and saying his goodnights. Leaving his mug on the table, he turned and walked down a hallway and into a room.

Olwen took the opportunity to look around the small cabin. It was cozy and rustic, as she would expect to find in the middle of a forest. It was modest, with minimal furniture and decorations. Most of the furnishings were either handmade or foraged. But there were furs for warmth and at least one rug near the mantle. Bjørn's voice pulled her attention back to him.

"I have a room for you as well. You are welcome to stay as long as you'd like, but I need you to vow that you will not let the prince or Konungr know of my home in any way. This is a safe place for all of those escaping cruelty or persecution, and I can't have that compromised."

"I vow not to reveal your location to the prince, the Konungr, or their men." Olwen felt the telltale snapping against her skin as the vow took hold.

"Come, I will show you to your room."

Hrafn

"It's getting worse, isn't it?" Jeger asked from his horse beside Hrafn.

Hrafn clawed absently at his chest, even while he was riding. "It's no better. We need to find her." He pulled his horse in another direction and headed deeper into the trees.

It had been two days since he had seen Olwen from the air. In those two days, it had snowed, and he had lost her again. He had sent for scent-tracking shifters, but it would be another day, at least, until they could catch up with him. There was almost no chance that her trail would even be left for them to follow, but he had to try.

He had diverted most of his manpower and resources to recovering his swordsmith, instructing his men to capture the Konungr's mercenaries wherever they could and kill them if they couldn't. He did not have time to waste with them now. The sun was already setting, and the shadows were growing long; it was too difficult to see to track any longer, and he knew he would have to return to camp empty-handed, again. Begrudgingly he brought his horse to a halt and turned her head back toward camp.

Jeger's eyes were haunted as they searched. Hrafn had never seen his consort so upset in all of their time together, even when he had told Jeger he would never marry him. Olwen had broken something inside of him, and Hrafn had not been able to repair it. He wanted to hate her for it, for destroying something so beautiful as the joy he had seen in Jeger, but he could no longer deny the guilt that sat in his own gut over his role in the whole situation.

While he knew that Jeger loved him, he also knew that Jeger laid the blame on him as well. He had been distant since Olwen left as if his heart was breaking, and that was frightening to Hrafn. Jeger was supposed to love *him*. Had his heart been turned? Did he pine for her? Would he really choose her over him? *Would he leave him?*

The thought made his blood run cold. He could not imagine his life without Jeger in it, no matter what he told himself or Jeger. Even these few days without Olwen had been torture, although he would never admit that to her. His entire adult life, he had tried to keep his heart distant, untouchable, to protect himself from the hurt he had endured as a child. If he invested his love in no one, then no one could ever hurt him.

So why was he hurt now?

And it wasn't just his heart aching from Olwen's betrayal and Jeger's heartache. It was the very real pain of a contract unfulfilled. Every day that Olwen remained neglected, his pain would worsen. He dared not touch Jeger, or anyone, in a sexual way. Considering how much pain he lived with from the moment he woke up until the moment he lay to sleep, that was not an issue. For once, his cock's needs were not first and foremost. Surviving the day was becoming his primary goal.

Later that night, Hrafn lay awake on their sleeping mat with endless thoughts spinning in circles like dervishes, never getting anywhere but making him dizzy nonetheless.

"Jeg, are you awake?"

"Mmm..." was the reply at his back.

"Jeg, I... When we get back, I want to marry you. I still can't let the Konungr know about it; he'll kill you, Jeg. But I want us to be married."

There was a long moment of silence behind him, and then Jeger lifted up to rest on his elbow.

"No."

"What do you mean, 'No?' You've been asking me to marry you for years now."

"No, I won't marry you to appease your guilt over what you did to Olwen. Nor will I tie myself to you after seeing how cruel you were to her, Hraf. You and I have some things we need to work out between us, but first, we have to find Olwen and make sure she's safe."

Hrafn rolled to face Jeger with a huff.

"Are you serious? I am offering you marriage. I am offering you the throne beside me one day."

"*Jeg gir faen i det,*" Jeger replied heatedly. "Because Ollie and I are the same, Hraf. We are people who care about you but whom you choose to take for granted. You have shown me how much you value marriage. If you would do this to her, you would do it to me. Until this issue with Ollie is resolved, I will not even consider marrying you."

"Ollie doesn't give a FAEN about me!" Hrafn hissed. "She abandoned me, Jeger. She's not the hero here. She knew what it would do to me, and she left me to die."

"Because of your own stupidity!" Jeger hissed back. "She adored you. Even though you captured her and took her away from her home, she adored you. I saw how she looked at you. She always wanted your approval. She always wanted to please you. Did it never occur to you to do the RIGHT thing and simply release her and ASK her to stay and be your swordsmith? Did you never think to give her control over her own life, even when you knew that was what she wanted above all else? Or did you just continue to do what every other man in her life has done and lord it over her? She would have gladly stayed forever as your employee and not as your wife if you had simply GIVEN her the choice."

Hrafn stopped in shock. No, the thought had never occurred to him. His face flushed crimson with humiliation and guilt, but he could not stop himself from sputtering words in his own defense, even when he knew they were exaggerations and not enough.

"I took her away?! Have you ever been to Espar? It's a cesspit! She is lucky that someone, anyone, stole her away from that life. Even more so that it was a prince and not some highwayman looking to use her body for financial gains. I gave her opportunities she would never have had–"

"That's right, Hraf. She would never have been her husband's slave in her small town. She would never have been his dirty little secret, among many. She would never have had the chance to become a political prisoner or die for someone else's throne and agenda while in a strange land." There was no mistaking the sarcasm in Jeger's words as he flopped onto his back on the sleeping mat, no longer bothering to look Hrafn in the eye.

"Jeg. I don't want Ollie to come between us. All of our lives, we have been together."

"Then you shouldn't have accepted a wife when you knew how I felt. Don't put this back on me, Hraf. You have always been in control of everything between us. That no longer works for us. You are going to have to share that control."

Hrafn clawed against the sharp pain in his chest before heaving his head onto Jeger's chest in a child-like attempt to mute the pain he felt emotionally and physically. He craved the connection to his lover and a reprieve from the hurt that haunted him. Jeger threw his arm around him but didn't say anything, and so they lay there long into the night silently.

The next morning was worse. Hrafn's pain level was rising, and he was no longer able to get up and walk around easily. Riding was out of the question. Instead, he took a command position within his tent, delegating the search out. When all of his minions had left them alone, Jeger cornered him.

"We cannot keep doing this. It is going to kill you if we cannot find her in time."

"You think I don't know this?" Hrafn hissed, slamming his mug onto the table. "I am open to suggestions if you have better ideas." His hand moved absently over his sternum, something he had been doing unconsciously for days.

"In fact, I do," Jeger said, pushing Hrafn to sit. "Lenz. Let us use him to find her. He said she wanted to meet his son's contacts; he must have some way to get in touch with them, some mutual contact. If we could convince him that she is in danger, he may be willing to help us."

"He will never help us if it endangers his only son," Hrafn countered.

"It doesn't have to involve his son. I will request a parley with her in a neutral place."

"No, I will talk with her."

"NO. You will NOT." Jeger pushed Hrafn back down into the chair he was attempting to climb out of. "I think you have done enough damage to this relationship. She will listen to me. Even still, she may not agree to come back, so YOU must stay as far away from her as possible for the time being."

"And how will you convince her to return?"

"I won't. I will ask her. I will tell her that you will release her as you agreed and offer her the position of royal swordsmith on your behalf. It is what you both wanted anyway. She may be willing to do it, as it will offer her the protection of the crown while allowing her to be a businesswoman."

"And what of the Konungr?" Hrafn growled through gritted teeth.

"One problem at a time."

"It will never work, Jeg. She is stubborn. She won't come back, even for that. She–"

"She has to, Hraf. I can't bear to lose you like this. I will do whatever it takes to bring her back. But you must promise me, PROMISE, that you will be kinder to her. I won't bring her back just to have you chase her away again."

"I can't–"

"PROMISE ME."

The words hovered in the air like a commandment. Jeger loomed over Hrafn in his chair, and to an outsider, it would have appeared that he was the prince and not the consort. His posture and attitude demanded respect and nothing less than full obedience. Hrafn's eyes shuttered miserably before he nodded his assent, his head bowing in defeat.

Olwen

Olwen sat in front of the fire, wrapped in a blanket. It had been seven days since she had arrived at Bjørn's home, and she was feeling restless with nothing to do. She spent time every night working on her sword, perfecting and honing it. It was not so much that she was a perfectionist, although she was; it was having something legitimate to keep her occupied in a world where she suddenly had no purpose. Sitting and staring at the flames, she pondered what her next steps should be.

She was free, wasn't she? Was she still technically married to Hrafn?

The ache seized her heart again, and she rubbed her chest. The pain was getting worse each day, and she had her answer. She didn't understand how she was bound to her agreement not to run from him when he had violated his half of the agreement by finding a loophole and not releasing her as he had agreed. Tears of anger gathered on her lashes, but she didn't let them fall.

So what were her options? Run until the pain became bad enough to take her? Or return to him with her tail between her legs and be his slave? She thought of her father, a proud strong man; he had raised her to be a fierce and independent woman. She would not dishonor him by allowing herself to be owned any longer. She would choose death on her own over slavery.

The door to the cottage opened behind her, and Bjørn rushed inside.

"Olwen, there is an emissary on the way... he wants a parley."

"An emissary?" Olwen stood from her seat. "Who would want to talk with me?"

"My men say his name is Jeger; he's the Advisor to the Prince. If you'll meet with him, I can have a horse and guide ready to take you to a neutral place. I told them not to bring him here; this place must remain a secret. I'd advise against this, Olwen. I can get you to a meeting, but I can't sacrifice my men to protect you if he attacks."

Attacks? Olwen considered his words. She couldn't imagine Jeger attacking her. Even when he was furious at finding her married to his consort, he had not lashed out at her physically, focusing instead on sulking at Hrafn. He had even championed her when Hrafn was being an ass. Still, what did he want to discuss with her now? Was he just coming to talk her back into going back to Hrafn? He needn't have bothered coming if that was his motivation. She would not go back willingly.

Bjørn stood waiting for her decision. She chewed her bottom lip as she considered. She knew it was a bad idea, but she desperately wanted to see Jeger again. Even if he was furious with her, she wanted the chance to say goodbye to him. Taking a deep breath to steel herself, she closed her eyes and nodded to Bjørn. By the time she opened them, he had left to make arrangements. She was going to see Jeger.

Two days dragged painfully slowly, figuratively and literally. With nothing to do, Olwen was losing her mind in the tiny cabin. It hadn't helped that her pain level was growing as well, making it hard for her to breathe or move. She had spent most of the two days bundled in front of the fire, rubbing at the phantom pain in her chest. Tears threatened to fall at any given moment, but she proudly held them back, refusing to be weak in front of strangers. She could fall apart once she was on her own.

The front door opened, and sunlight spilled into the room, blinding her momentarily.

"It's time."

She nodded at the dark silhouette in the light and slowly climbed to her feet. She was sure that she just looked tired to anyone who saw her, but her truth was much worse. She was close to agony. Wrapping her cloak around her and pulling the hood high, she stepped out into the cold air to join her guide. Their breaths puffed in translucent white clouds, as did the horses, as they moved to mount. She looked back at the cottage with one last moment of indecision before her horse started following her guide, taking her decision with it.

They rode for several hours in silence. She was grateful that the guide wasn't trying to make conversation or get to know her, as her mind was full with all of the emotions and thoughts that she tried to untangle before she had to see Jeger. She was secretly overjoyed to get to see him, and her heart raced with anticipation. At the same time, she was terrified of his judgment. She considered him a friend. She would consider him more, but she wasn't sure that was what he really wanted. She had been forced upon him and his relationship, and yet he had been kind to her. She had truly wished that there was some outcome available to her that did not involve hurting him, but she could see none that didn't involve her sacrificing herself.

The guide surprised her when he brought the horses to a stop suddenly in a small clearing. Olwen looked around but couldn't see anyone else; there were only trees as far as the eye could see. Even through the pain in her chest, she reached to put a hand on the pommel of her sword, just in case.

The guide dismounted and turned to her expectantly.

"From here, I will transport you to the meeting place. Your other party should already be there waiting for you."

Olwen stared at him in confusion. "Transport?"

"Yes, I am a transporter. I can teleport people and things over great distances. We are called for neutral meetings; as both parties will be far from home with no way to track the other, it keeps things civil. Transporters agree that if one party should become aggressive toward the other, they will not transport the aggressor back. It's a failsafe."

Olwen shook her head at her own naivete. Perhaps Hrafn was right, and she was not prepared to live her life on her own without someone looking out for her. There was still so much of the world she did not know... not that she would ever admit that to him.

She slid out of her saddle and walked to the guide, who held his hand out for hers. As soon as she placed her hand in his, her world surged around her. It was as if she was being churned inside out, with everything warping and morphing around her. It wasn't painful, but it was very unsettling, and when they finally regained solid footing, she felt nauseous.

Before she could comment, she was swept into a strong embrace and picked up off the ground. Jeger's musky, woodsy scent filled her nose, and she threw her arms around his neck and cried, despite promising herself that she wouldn't. She wasn't sure how long they stood there like that, but she didn't want the moment to end. She felt like she was home when he held her.

Finally, he gently put her back on her feet, and she straightened. She looked up at him and gasped when she saw the dark circles under his bloodshot eyes. He looked like he had aged in only one week. She knew she looked no better, but it killed her to see him like this.

He ran his palm along her cheek gently, and then moved his fingertips to tangle in her hair.

"You are safe, Ollie?" he asked.

"I am," she answered quietly. "I am so happy to see you, Jeger."

"And I, you. I have a lot to say and not a lot of time, so I'll try to be concise." He stopped and sighed deeply before looking into her eyes again. "Ollie, I am so sorry. Please know that I tried—"

"I know, Jeg. I heard you two talking that morning." She lowered her eyes with her confession.

"Then you know I wanted him to release you. Konungr be damned."

"I do, Jeg. But he wasn't going to. I would still be his property if I hadn't run. You see now why I can't go back."

"Have you been suffering?" He pulled her face back up so he could search her eyes, but he didn't need to. Reflexively, her hand rubbed at her sternum.

"Jeg, I'd rather die than go back and be humiliated as his servant and plaything."

"What if there was another option?"

"Jeg, I don't see—"

"What if there was? Hear me out, Ollie," Jeger kneeled on one knee before her so that she looked slightly down at him rather than him towering over her. "Ollie, Hrafn will release you so that you won't suffer any longer. He would also offer you the position of the royal swordmaker; this would guarantee you customers, as well as grant you the protection of the crown. You could live independently if you wanted to."

Tears streaked down Olwen's face as the hurt she felt seized her heart as hard as the magic of the bargain.

"Jeger, I don't trust him to do that. What if I return, and he refuses again? Then I am trapped once more. I have no power in this negotiation other than distance."

"But distance will kill you both. Ollie, I can't lose you both. He has promised to be kinder to you."

"I don't trust him, Jeger. I don't see a way this will work."

Jeger's eyes creased with pain, and he closed them for a moment as if willing himself to hold back the flood of emotion that threatened to take him. Suddenly his eyes flashed open, a look of realization on his face.

"Marry me." It came out more of a command than a question.

"What?" she asked incredulously, "Jeger, I can't just–"

"Marry me. I mean it. Ollie, become my wife. I will protect you, and I will be your champion. If you want to leave and live independently once this is all settled, then I agree to let you go in advance with no terms or limitations at any time. But I love you, Ollie, and I would be a good husband, even if it was only temporarily while we separate you and Hrafn. This can work. I can keep you safe and make sure that your best interests are protected."

"But you already have a consort, and technically I already have a husband." Olwen bruised her lower lip between her teeth.

"And in this country, members of the royal court may have as many of either as they wish. Lord knows the Konungr doesn't even know how many consorts and wives he currently has."

Olwen wrinkled her nose in distaste. "Jeg, I only ever wanted to have one husband. I don't need a collection. And I certainly do not want to be one of many."

"No, Ollie, it wouldn't be like that. For now, it would be just the three of us, just like it was... until we can abolish your marriage to Hrafn. Then you can decide if you want to be married to me or if you'd rather be unmarried altogether. I will support your decision either way. I can promise you I would not introduce anyone else into our relationship. I would like to say the same for Hrafn, but he has surprised me over these last several months."

Jeger's eyes fell as he considered what he was saying, and Olwen's heart broke for him again. It was hard enough for him to accept her into their relationship, with no say on the subject. What would he do if Hrafn did it again? Or more than once? Would it be the final blow that destroyed their relationship? The thought of Jeger being alone and heartbroken was more than she could bear.

"Jeg, there is so much here that I would never have considered before, but I am learning that I am not the same woman who was married to Henrick in Espar. I had never taken a lover; never mind bedded two at a time. I had never lived in a palace, even one which resembles a dungeon. I had never lived among royalty, and I don't really miss that at all." She paused with a sigh.

"I had never married for love, nor had anyone I cared for enough to marry. I need to know if you have feelings for me before I can give you an answer because I tried to have a marriage with Hrafn based on the terms of a bargain and not a love match, and it did not work out well for me. So I need to know, Jeger, do you have feelings for me, or is this proposal another bargain to suit the situation?"

Olwen kept her eyes on her feet as she spoke, her cheeks flaming. Tears threatened to spill again, and she couldn't meet his eye. If he told her this was a means to an end, she would probably still have to take it; the terms of the existing bargain were going to kill her and Hrafn if she didn't. But she hoped from the depth of her heart that this was not a business transaction for him and that his proposal had come from a place of tenderness for her. She knew it was foolish and idealistic, but she had witnessed the unfettered joy her mother and father had shared in their love, and she wanted that too. It may not be a marriage, and it may not be with Jeger, but she would have it one day.

Jeger's fingers gently cupped her chin and brought her face to his until her forehead rested on his. She closed her eyes and could feel his breath on her lips.

"Ollie, don't you know? Hrafn was the singular beat of my heart for as long as I can recall. He is my other half, and I lived to be his, owned completely by him... until the day you came into our lives. I love you to depths I have never known existed. There is nothing I wouldn't do to ensure your safety, regardless of whether you could ever return my affections.

"At first, I was jealous. You were handed a marriage to him after I had fought, sworn, and killed for it. I was never angry with you; I was angry at him for simply tossing aside that which I had coveted for so long. I had begged him to marry, begged him to acknowledge our relationship. He had refused me, only to hand it to a stranger.

"But I saw, through you, all of the things I had sacrificed, as I saw him overlook all of the wonders that you are. Yes, your swords are amazing, but if you never made another one, I wouldn't miss them. Your heart is kind and strong. You do not seek power over others; instead, you just seek a small place to call your own. Even in your leather trousers and tunic with your hair disheveled, you are more beautiful than a ballroom full of princesses.

"My heart was jaded, and you have shattered it completely. You are genuine and vulnerable in a way I have not seen since I was a child. You have entrusted me with your heart and your body. Throughout all of this, you have asked me for nothing other than friendship. And although I was the consort to your husband, you accepted me into your heart and life immediately, and that does not happen in my world.

"And then you accepted me into your wedded bed..." Here Jeger stopped for a moment as if contemplating. "Ollie... I know you and he do not have a vowed marriage, but you did not have to allow me access to you, and..." Again, he stopped as if he was struggling to say the right thing. "I had always been more partial to men than women. I could fuck either, but given my choice, I would always choose a man. And I still love Hrafn, but Ollie, you are so jævlig divine that I cannot stop thinking about you. You are my consort's wife, but I long to see your body, to feel you against me, to call you my own. I long to wring every last bit of pleasure out of you that exists. I would give anything to have that right.

"And it's not just your sex. I love the way your eyes wrinkle in the morning when you wake. I love the way your smile is higher on the right than on the left. I love the way you feel when your head is resting on my chest. I love the sound of your laughter. Ollie, we have hardly had a chance to know each other, and always around our relationships with Hrafn, but I want that with you. I want you to look at me the way you look at him for safety. I want to be the one who offers you untold pleasures simply because you deserve them. I understand if you do not have these feelings for me, but even if it is only temporary, I would like to be the man you call husband."

"Yes."

"Yes?"

"Yes... I will marry you."

Jeger pulled her down to him and devoured her mouth in a searing kiss, pouring all of his emotion into her. Olwen let the tears flow freely now. It was as if the cork on her emotions had become unstoppered, and everything that she had felt over the last month drained out of her through her eyes. When they finally had to break apart to breathe, Jeger wiped the tears from her cheeks with the pads of his thumbs.

"It's going to be alright, Ollie. I have a plan."

14

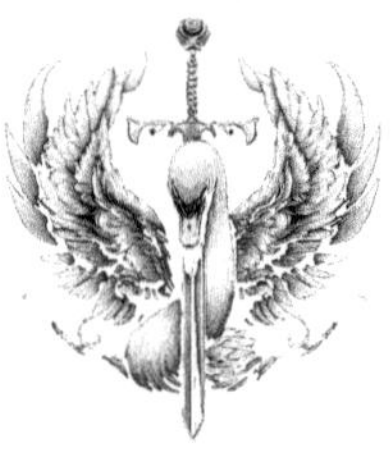

Hrafn

Hrafn knew the moment Olwen was back in camp. The last three hours had been unbearable, and he had been waiting for unconsciousness to take him. Even as he lay on his sleeping mat with a fevered sweat and crippling pain, as soon as she was in his proximity, the symptoms started changing. He couldn't explain how, but he *felt* her, and somehow it was better. He blew out a breath of gratitude. Only moments later, the flap to his inner bedroom was pushed aside as Jeger entered, carrying a very pale Olwen.

Hrafn stared at her as if he was seeing her for the first time. Her normally golden hair was limp and lifeless, and there were dark circles under her eyes. It looked like she had lost weight as well; her cheeks were sunken. Any anger he had felt for her was gone as he took her in. His heart beat faster and felt full, and he had the overwhelming and unexplainable urge to claim her as his own. For the first time in his life, he found himself at a loss for words, suddenly incapable of stringing together a sentence. He simply lay in his feverish haze and stared at her.

Jeger stood Olwen on shaky legs. She leaned awkwardly on Jeger, but she couldn't miss Hrafn's condition. His eyes and cheeks were hollowed, and a thin sheen of sweat made his skin shine with wetness. She looked like her first instinct was to run to him and help him, but she held herself back, as if she didn't know what was appropriate or how he would react. She also wasn't in great shape herself.

"Alright, here is what I am proposing," Jeger said, meeting both Olwen and Hrafn's eyes, "You both need to be close to recover from the effects of the bargain, so I am calling a temporary truce between you. I expect you both to be kind to each other for my sake, if for no other reason. Neither of you is in any shape to argue with me. I will have food brought in, and then we are all going to bed... to sleep." He looked at each of them in turn. When they both nodded, he stepped out of the room to collect food for them.

Olwen stared at the flap Jeger had just walked through, suddenly unsure what to do with herself. She was awkwardly self-conscious and twisted her fingers together.

"Come, Wife, why don't you get undressed and join me? You will be more comfortable here than standing. I promise I will behave."

Olwen spun at Hrafn's words and nearly fell over with a wave of dizziness. His words were laced with humor, but his tone had been more tender than she could remember him ever using with her. He folded down a corner of the blanket as if demonstrating his sincerity.

Olwen began undressing. She turned away from Hrafn as she peeled her trousers off and was considering whether to remove her tunic when Jeger returned with a tray of fruits, cheeses, bread, and meats for them. Putting the tray down, he walked to Olwen and kissed her tenderly before gently ushering her to the sleeping mat. Once she was seated, he reached down to pull her tunic off of her. As soon as the fabric cleared her body, she pulled the blanket up over her chest, her cheeks pink. She was suddenly very modest as if she was starting all over with these two men. She settled back and noticed that Hrafn was studying her curiously. She looked away again as her cheeks darkened.

"You both need to eat" Jeger placed the tray down on the sleeping mat between them, indicating it was not a request.

Hrafen reached out and picked up a strawberry, and before Olwen could pick up her hand, Hrafn was lifting the berry to her lips. She flinched for a moment, not expecting it. His expression wasn't playful or mocking; there was only raw honesty. He wanted to feed her. He held the berry up to her lips, his eyes beseeching her to take it as if it was a peace offering that his soul needed to make. Slowly she opened her lips and took the berry into her mouth. Glancing at Jeger, she noticed a subtle smile on his face.

She took a crust of bread and matched it with a wedge of cheese and reciprocated for Hrafn to return the gesture. They spent the rest of the meal feeding each other, and Jeger, in silence and peace. As they ate, Hrafn became aware that his pain had vanished somewhere over the course of their meal. His first instinct was to think of a sarcastic remark about how the pain disappeared once he attended to Olwen, but he found himself enjoying feeding her too much to allow himself to dwell on that emotion. Already her color was returning, and her eyes had regained some of their brightness. He remembered that Jeger had carried her into the room and wondered if she had been injured or in pain herself as he had been when she arrived.

Before he could ask, Jeger got up and undressed. Hrafn stopped to watch him, and it didn't escape his attention that Olwen did as well. He watched her from the corner of his eye as she gently worried her lower lip between her teeth as Jeger took off his breeches and then strolled back to the sleeping mat in the nude. Even through the blanket, Hrafn could tell that Olwen's nipples were pebbled, and her pupils were dilated wide; she was aroused.

And why wouldn't she be? Jeger was a stunning man and an amazing lover. He was a mass of hard muscle, and he was blessed with an impressive cock. Despite his strength and size, however, he was an attentive and tender lover. He could love you gently, drawing out your release for hours with whispered touches, or he could rut you hard and fast, driving you into the mattress like a feral beast. A man's sexual education begins early in the courts, and there wasn't much Jeger had not seen or done. He was the only man who had ever been able to get, and keep, Hrafn's attention.

Jeger climbed into bed between Hrafn and Olwen, pulling their heads onto his chest as he sighed. Hrafn knew Ollie was aroused, which only made him aroused. Ollie had her eyes closed and was doing her best to just fall asleep, but Hrafn couldn't let it go. If she was aroused, she deserved release.

Lifting his head, Hrafn pulled Jeger's mouth down to his so that he could kiss him deeply. Jeger tried to pull away at first, but Hrafn was insistent. Simultaneously, Hrafn reached over Jeger's body to pick up Olwen's hand off of his chest and bring it down to Jeger's cock. Her hand froze beneath his, and Hrafn gently pushed it down onto Jeger's cock once more. It jumped under her fingers in response, and Jeger moaned quietly into Hrafn's mouth.

Needing no further encouragement, Olwen wrapped her hand around Jeger and began to stroke him to hardness. His moans were steady now as his hand reached around her body to gently massage her breast and nipples while she saw to him. Hrafn continued to kiss Jeger deeply and then moved down to kiss his jawline, his throat, his upper chest, and finally, his nipples. He toyed with Jeger's nipples as he watched Ollie stroking his now fully erect cock. His own cock was stiff just seeing it.

Without saying a word, Ollie pushed herself up and moved down the mat until she was laying between Jeger's legs. Jeger spread his thighs wider to give her access, his head falling back as he felt her hot breath against the soft flesh of his cock. Hrafn couldn't contain his dirty dialog.

"That's it, my sweet Swan. Take his cock all the way down. Suck him dry, Ollie. That's it. Take him all into your throat. Such a good girl. Make him come down that lovely throat of yours, Ollie. Make him shoot his seed deep inside you."

Ollie worked Jeger's cock in her mouth and throat, groaning around him. She could feel it flexing in her mouth, swelling. Her hands massaged his balls as she hollowed her cheeks to provide suction, working him the way he had shown her, bringing him pleasure the way he liked it best.

Jeger was moaning, trying to be quiet but losing that battle. Her lips on his cock was just too much. He pulled Hrafn up and indicated what he wanted. Ollie watched in fascination as Hrafn mounted Jeger's face, his knees on either side. Jeger took his cock into his mouth and sucked him down as he groaned. Ollie could see Jeger's fingers digging into Hrafn's ass cheeks as he pulled his hips down to his mouth.

Looking up and seeing Hrafn's pleasure was all Jeger needed. His body began to tense, his muscles coiling as his climax began to build. His breathing was ragged, and his groans pained. His hips bucked up to meet Ollie's mouth, and one hand snaked down to secure her head over his cock as he fucked into her mouth. His other hand held Hrafn's ass, pulling it into his own mouth as he groaned and sucked him deep. His muscles began to twitch just before his back arched, and he groaned low and long. He pulled Ollie over his cock in a death grip as it spasmed in her mouth, spilling down her throat. After his back hit the sleeping mat, he fucked his hips up, pushing his cock into her a few more times until he had fully released in her. Ollie allowed him his release and then sucked and licked him clean while he turned his attention to Hrafn.

Hrafn dropped his weight onto his straightened arms and then began to fuck Jeger's face with force. Jeger grabbed his hips, pulling him in deeper as Hrafn grunted and pumped. Ollie laved Jeger's cock in her mouth as she watched Hrafn fucking Jeger's mouth with intensity. It was violent, brutal, and primally erotic. She could see Hrafn's back starting to tighten. His cock was swollen large, and his balls were starting to constrict; she knew he was going to explode any second.

Reaching into their night bag beside the sleeping mat, she pulled out the small bottle of oil they kept handy. She poured it down the divide of his ass, and he moaned loudly, turning his head to her in surprise. His pupils were wide and dark, and his expression was full of hunger and need. She stopped.

"Do it, my Swan... Take my ass." His voice was breathy and ragged. Beneath him, Jeger moaned, which caused Hrafn to suck in a breath with a hiss. "Do it!" He urged, pumping his cock into Jeger's mouth frantically.

Olwen spread the oil over her fingers and placed one at the surface of his puckered hole. She had seen them do this, but she had never done it herself. Hrafn pushed his ass back against her finger on his upswings. Gently, Olwen pushed the finger in. Hrafn's response was immediate. His breathing was erratic, and he had all he could do not to groan or scream his pleasure loudly.

"MORE!" he hissed.

Olwen pushed her entire finger into him and worked him the way she had seen the men work each other. She was fascinated with the feeling of his rings of muscles as they tightened around her digit with his excitement. Experimentally, she pushed another finger in with her first, and Hrafn nearly fell over onto Jeger. When she knew Hrafn was on the very edge of climax, she pushed a third finger into him and felt his body shudder around her fingers as he shattered into his release.

There was nothing subtle or quiet about it; Hrafn roared as his body locked up with spasms. He lodged his cock deep in Jeger's throat as he threw his head back in ecstasy. For an endless moment, his body was taut in release, pumping his seed into Jeger. Olwen worked his ass, loving the feeling of him squeezing her fingers hard. Finally, Hrafn did collapse and had to roll to the side to avoid crushing Jeger.

Hrafn was panting and gasping for air, his body still shivering with the shockwaves of his bliss.

"Hva faen," Hrafn finally growled between huffs, his voice low and guttural. "My cock has never felt that good."

"I'll second that," Jeger said, his voice also low and gravely.

Olwen beamed a happy smile. She loved to see these two men sated. She got up and washed her hands before coming back to sit with them.

"You're next," Hrafn said. Olwen looked up to see him looking right at her with that predatory look in his eyes.

"Oh. I–"

"On your back," Jeger ordered.

"Now," Hrafn finished when she didn't move.

"You don't have to–"

"You can either lie back, or we can take you sitting. It's your choice, my Swan, but I will have your juices running down my face before I let you go to sleep. You will come for me, maybe more than once." Hrafn was suddenly serious.

Jeger rolled onto his back and pulled her back against his chest so she was laid out over him. He leaned down and kissed her passionately, massaging her breasts and tweaking her nipples between his thumb and fingers. She moaned into his mouth and arched just as she felt Hrafn settling between her thighs. He picked her legs up and threw them over his shoulders unceremoniously.

She let out a low moan into Jeger's waiting mouth as Hrafn dove his tongue into her folds. Jeger's hands worked her upper body, teasing and plucking at her breasts, sucking on her throat, and pulling her head back by the hair while Hrafn worked her pussy like a man with a mission. His tongue darted inside her, working her walls, and then came to rest on her sensitive clit. She bucked her hips up, but he placed one hand over her hips to hold her in place while he worked her clit with his tongue.

Jeger had to move back to kissing her to muffle the screams of pleasure that rose from her throat while Hrafn laved her clit with his tongue. He pushed a finger inside of her slowly, and she arched against him again. She struggled against the hand that held her down as she wanted to fuck her hips against his finger. He added a second finger, feeling her walls stretch to accommodate him. She groaned with pleasure. Hrafn could feel her muscles starting to tighten, her climax imminent. He made a noise to get Jeger's attention, sending him direction.

Jeger's hand moved to her throat and clamped down firmly. He wasn't cutting off her air; he was dominating her. Hrafn's hand tightened around her hips, holding her in place. With her body immobilized, Hrafn picked up the pace of his hand as it fucked deep inside her. He cocked his fingers, finding that spot within her that made her lose all control. Instantly she was writhing, screaming her pleasure, but the men held her fast as they delivered her into her climax. Hrafn felt her core ripple around his fingers as her back tightened, trying to arch. She was like a spring winding tighter, tighter, tighter... until finally, a keening wail left her as her body convulsed uncontrollably under Hrafn's mouth. Her fluids coated his hands and face and ran down her thighs and ass, leaving them both glossy.

Hrafn lapped at her folds, licking her clean and sending her into aftershocks until she finally had to push his face away from her over-sensitive clit. She gulped for air.

"That's one orgasm, my Swan. I believe I want another," Jeger said suggestively.

"No more," she whimpered, "I'm too sensitive."

"We're not letting you sleep yet, so what do you want?" Jeger asked with a smirk. "Lady's choice."

Olwen pulled herself up to sitting. Her hair was wild, and her eyes were wide. Her legs were wet with her arousal. Hrafn was instantly hard again, Olwen noticed.

"I want to suck Hrafn's cock this time," she said. Without waiting, she reached out and took him into her hand, stroking him from base to tip. His body shuddered with delight.

He rolled onto his back, offering up his cock for whatever she wanted. He propped himself up with his elbows behind him so that he could watch her suck his cock into her mouth. She had the most erotic little mouth he had ever seen, and seeing those sweet pink lips spread around his width just made him want to blow all the harder. Her little pink tongue ran the length of him and swirled around the head, making him groan.

His jaw dropped, and his heart missed a beat when he watched her reach between her own legs, gather up some of her moisture, and coat his cock in it before stroking him again. She was going to be the jævlig death of him.

And then she was on him; her mouth took him deep, sucking and stroking. He groaned as he fisted her hair in his hands experimentally. He had seen Jeger do this with her, and she seemed to like it. Indeed, she picked up her pace, sucking him deep and making him hiss. Her ass was in the air as she launched her mouth over his cock greedily.

But it was when he saw Jeger move to kneel behind her that he very nearly lost it. Just the sight of his gorgeous consort, with his cock hard and ready in hand, notched at Olwen's wet mound, brought him to climax. As he shouted his release, Jeger gently pushed into Olwen's warm pussy. She groaned around a mouth full of Hrafn's cock, his seed now spurting down her throat as she gurgled and groaned. She spread her legs wider, and Jeger pushed in even further. Hrafn could do nothing but watch, transfixed, holding her head on his cock while Jeger took Ollie from behind.

His large cock disappeared into her, only to reappear and then slam back into her with a wet smack. Each thrust of his hips sent her onto Hrafn's cock with a groan. Soon Jeger built up a rhythm, and while Hrafn was not as hard as he was, Ollie's hot groaning mouth slamming down onto him still felt amazing.

Both men were groaning and sharing every dirty thought that occurred to them as if the sensations were so overwhelming that they had to vocalize.

"Faen!... Your mouth!... My Swan!"

"So tight... on my cock!... FAEN!... Come on my cock!"

Olwen just groaned and mewled like a beast, her mouth too full to say much.

For just a moment, Hrafn and Jeger made eye contact; it was clear that both of them were absolutely aroused watching the other get their pleasure with Ollie. There was a tenderness and hunger born of years between them.

Jeger's eyes seemed to settle on Ollie's head as it bobbed on Hrafn's cock, and his own cock swelled, causing her to cry out in pleasure again. Both men reacted as Ollie's body grew tight, her back arching, her cries rising in pitch; the vision had a stranglehold on both of their cocks. And just like that, she was soaring over the edge, wailing and bucking, sucking and clawing in the throws of climax.

Jeger released a choked noise as his own orgasm overtook him, and he drove his cock deep into Olwen. Her walls convulsed around him as she screamed her pleasure, muffled around Hrafn's cock. He continued to pound into her, emptying himself completely, before falling over her body limp with exhaustion.

The three of them lay in a panting pile of sweaty limbs, sated and tired.

"Faen, we have missed you, Ollie," Jeger said tenderly, pulling her by the arm so he could kiss her.

"We have," Hrafn agreed, surprising both Ollie and Jeger. "I didn't realize that we weren't complete without you." Hrafn then pulled Ollie's limp body over so that he could kiss her as well. In the end, they wound up piled together, with Ollie in the middle and one man on each side snuggled up to her. Without a word, they all fell blissfully into sleep.

Olwen

When Olwen woke, she was alone on the sleeping mat, and she could hear Hrafn and Jeger already starting their day in the next compartment of the tent. She washed quickly, frowning as she remembered she would need to bind her chest and resume her impersonation of a male. Her clothing was all where she had left it, so she dressed and made her way to the next room to eat with the men.

When she pushed the flap aside and entered the room, both men stopped talking and stood to face her. She immediately stopped moving, frozen, wondering what was happening. They had never behaved so oddly before when she entered a room. Instantly a feeling of dread pooled in her stomach.

Jeger's face lit up, his smile easy and warm.

"You're up. Why don't we take our meal together in the other room so we remain undisturbed?" He held his hand up to indicate the room which was designated as his sleeping room, although he slept every night in Hrafn's bed. They often used it as a meal room or sitting room. He seemed perfectly content to have her with them.

"Not that there is much likelihood of it, as I made sure that when I returned last night, all of the guards were sent to the other side of the encampment; we are pretty isolated here at the moment to ensure our privacy." Jeger crossed the room to place a tender kiss on her forehead.

Ollie's eyes shifted to Hrafn to find him watching her with a mild look of awe on his face. She wasn't sure what to make of him or his behavior. She had expected him to shout at her; she had expected a fight when she returned. Was he just being nice because Jeger had insisted upon it? He couldn't have simply forgiven her; could he have? Was he going to explode with rage as soon as Jeger wasn't present to temper him? Pulling her eyes back to Jeger, she nodded and turned into the makeshift room.

Breakfast was awkward, and Olwen was beginning to think that she might have made a mistake in returning; truthfully, she didn't have much of a choice. She could stand on her stubbornness and say she would die independent, but she really did not have a death wish. She was also completely taken aback by Jeger's admission of love and his proposal. Still, sitting at the table felt bizarre as Jeger was completely smitten with her, and Hrafn seemed to be in a daze, watching and evaluating her as if she was some strange creature. It made her uncomfortable. She almost preferred it when he was snappish and rude. She wanted to get up and excuse herself to work on swords, but she didn't get the chance.

In the next chamber, the guard called in seeking the prince. Jeger immediately left the room to find out what was going on, leaving Olwen and Hrafn staring after him. It was only a short moment before Jeger was back to retrieve Hrafn, raising his hand in warning for Olwen to stay put and out of sight. Her sense of dread returned two-fold.

Olwen stood and positioned herself closer to the flap door of the room, but the men in the other chamber spoke too quietly for her to make out the conversation. She paced a few steps, then back, before there was silence in the next room again, and the flap pushed inward to reveal Jeger and Hrafn returning. Both of their eyes shifted restlessly with concern, and Jeger fidgeted with his hands as if he didn't know what to do with them.

"We have been ordered back to the palace, as we have been 'unsuccessful' in defending our borders against invasion," Hrafn said quietly, his haunted eyes not meeting Olwen's.

"What does this mean, that we have been 'unsuccessful?'" Olwen hissed. "There IS no invasion to defend against. It is the raving of a madman."

"Lower your voice!" Hrafn whispered with a hiss, but there was no anger in it. It was fear speaking.

Jeger stepped between Olwen and Hrafn, pulling them both to his body. He looked down at Olwen when she looked up with pleading eyes, wanting to understand.

"It means that the Konungr wants to punish Hrafn and needed justification."

"Lower your voice!" Hrafn hissed again, this time with heat. "Talk like this is treasonous and will get us all killed."

"Hraf, I think we are already on that pathway."

When Hrafn looked up, his eyes were wide, but his jaw was clenched tight.

"NO," Olwen whispered, her hand flying to her mouth involuntarily as she gasped. "He wouldn't... Jeger, would he?"

When Jeger looked away without answering, Olwen knew. Her heart stalled in her chest, and she suddenly couldn't take a breath.

Hrafn turned suddenly and began pacing. "I will return, alone. Jeger, you take Olwen and go. Take her away from the court and hide somewhere safe until we know it is safe for you to return."

"I won't," Jeger said flatly, his nostrils flaring with indignation.

Hrafn turned to him, his eyes narrowed. "Don't be selfish, Jeger. Think of Olwen. She does not deserve to be delivered into the hands of the Konungr. Take her and protect her. I will send word once I have discovered what it is the Konungr wants of me."

"Olwen can speak for her jævlig self!" she spit. "I am not leaving you again, Hrafn. What if he imprisons you? My distance will kill you sooner than he would. I am not running like a coward, *Husband*. Whatever fate you face, we face together."

"Ollie, see reason–"

"No, Hraf, she's right. We do this together, or not at all." Jeger pulled them in tight, holding them close. "We are a family, and we fight and die a family."

Hrafn looked absolutely green as he glanced back and forth between Olwen and Jeger. His misery was etched in his face, and Olwen knew that he was expecting the worst. She clenched her own jaw, all of the rage of her unfulfilled life surging through her. She had only just found happiness, and she wasn't about to give it up so easily, not even to a king. She didn't know how, but she was going to put a stop to this fear. She was going to take control of her own life and happiness, and she was taking Hrafn and Jeger with her.

15

Hrafn

The journey back to the palace seemed far too short, but there was no way that Hrafn could delay them any longer than he had. He had made his way back slowly, stopping often and taking any excuse proffered to wait before resuming; in the end, however, he and his men found themselves back at the outer gate of the palace, with the Konungr's guard there to 'greet' them.

Hrafn knew that to the observer, the entire exchange would look civil, possibly even boring. He wondered if Olwen realized the intense amount of drama playing out around her in the guards' casual gazes and indifferent appearances. She was clever; he was sure she understood what was really happening.

The Konungr's guards were not simply there to 'greet' them but to make them aware that they were under observation; essentially, they were under an unspoken order of arrest by order of the high king. They would be allowed the privilege of walking into the castle under their own power, bringing their own items with them. To the observer, it would seem that nothing was amiss. They would all return to their quarters to await their summons to the Royal Receiving Room to debrief His Royal Majesty the Almighty Konungr.

Their quarters would have extra guards posted, for their safety, of course. None of them would be allowed to leave the building in case the Konungr should find himself ready for them, obviously. And they might do well to have someone sample their food before they ate, lest enemies of the Konungr managed to seed the wrong meal with poison, as had, unfortunately, been known to have happened in the past with other heirs to the throne.

Hrafn bit his tongue as the Captain of the Guard ordered him and his men to their quarters until they were summoned. Even though the guard should be taking orders, not giving them, Hrafn knew that whatever actions he took in response would all be used as evidence against him for a paranoid and megalomaniacal king. He would do well not to give him any ammunition.

Hrafn had arranged for Jeger to continue to act as the personal guard to their swordsmith. He quickly retrieved General Lenz, and the three men and Ollie made their way up to Hrafn's quarters. Since General Lenz had been persuaded to assist with the parley between Jeger and Olwen, Hrafn was making use of his situation. Lenz was in a better position to be able to report what the Konungr was intending and what he was doing.

Once they were all inside Hrafn's sitting room, Jeger slammed the door in the guards' faces and threw the bolt.

"I fail to understand what I am doing here," Lenz said without emotion.

"You are smarter than that, Old Man," Hrafn said as he made his way to the bottle of spirits over the mantle and began to pour glasses. "You know as well as I that the Konungr is going to dispose of you now that you have failed to play his loyal lap dog."

"We don't know that—"

"I'd say we do. He would have killed your only son to motivate you to his way of thinking. With no leverage left to him, he will not have a way to save face in light of your refusal to spy for him. If anyone was to find out that you did not willingly act against me on his behalf... He cannot afford for that truth to live." Hrafn delivered his words dispassionately as if he was discussing the weather.

Olwen and Jeger each took a glass from Hrafn and stood quietly. Hrafn offered a glass to Lenz, who accepted it with a slight tremor in his hand.

"How is it you think I can assist you?" Lenz asked curiously, sipping his drink with an air of nonchalance. Only the slight trembling of his fingers gave him away. He was very nervous and for good reason.

"The enemy of my enemy is my friend, General. I have no ill will toward you. I did not order you or your son executed for playing your roles. I am willing to pardon you both if you will swear your allegiance to me and help me in my quest to become the next Konungr."

Hrafn drank from his glass, never taking his eyes off Lenz, who hesitated and then drank. When he spoke, his words were barely a whisper.

"Forgive me, Sire, but I would not want to be mistaken for someone agreeing to commit treason."

"Nor should you," Hrafn quickly agreed, "When your allegiance is to the rightful Konungr. Are you vowed to the current king?"

Lenz blew out a deep breath. "No. My father was vowed to him, as were all of his peers. Of course, none of them lived very long. We were born into service of the Konungr; it was expected. He never saw the need to have us vow our fealty."

"So if you were vowed to another, you would be within your rights to remain loyal to that king?"

"Yes, but that would not stop the current Konungr from ordering my head removed from my body, Sire." Lenz's face flushed red as his anger rose. "I have no wish to die this day."

"Not this day, hmm?" Hrafn paused and sipped his drink again. "How about tomorrow, then? How about next week? How about your wife instead, or your son if he can find him?"

"Are you threatening me, Sire? The Konungr already holds those threats against me; I hardly see how allying with you is to my advantage."

"You miss my point entirely, Lenz. You will not stand with me if it means dying today, yet the Konungr can call your life forfeit at any moment: tomorrow, in two days, next week. Not just you; he can call anyone you hold dear as collateral to keep you cowed. I never took you for a coward nor a fool. We are all pawns in the hands of a madman as long as we are divided. You stand a much better chance of living to see your grandchildren grow up if you are my ally than if you stand with the current Konungr. You know I would make a better king."

"I agree, you would. But how would you deal with the fact that there is already a man sitting on that throne? I doubt very much he will voluntarily abdicate for you. You would not be able to best him in battle; no one can. That is why we have endured him as long as we have, Sire. It has not been loyalty; it has been self-preservation."

"Let me worry about the 'how,' Lenz. I need to know I have your support on this. You can rally the other generals under you; they will listen to you. If you get me the generals, I will find a way to claim the throne."

Lenz threw his head back and swallowed the last of his drink in one gulp. "That is a large ambition, and you are not the first to have had it, Sire."

Hrafn blew out a breath, suddenly looking weary. "Lenz, I am the longest-standing heir. I have seen many fall before me, and I have learned. I will not act impulsively. I will take my time; you know how I work. Let me get through this situation and see what the Konungr demands of me now; once this is over, we will meet and discuss terms again. I will need your answer at that time."

"Are you so sure you will live to discuss it again? The Konungr has a lengthy record of filicide."

"If I do not survive this, then there would be no need for us to meet, regardless. Again, let me worry about that."

Hrafn and Lenz stood with their eyes locked appraisingly. Finally, Lenz sighed loudly and nodded his head. Placing his glass on a nearby table, he made his way to the door, removed the bar, and let himself out. Jeger quickly replaced the bolt over the door once it had closed.

"You don't really believe he will do it this time, do you?" Jeger asked when he finally turned to face Hravn. The color had drained from his face, and his eyes were wide and sad, with a smattering of fear in their depths.

Hrafn blew out a breath and ran his hand down his face. "I don't know, Jeg. Sooner or later, my luck will run out. If not now, perhaps next week... perhaps next year. The Konungr is unpredictable on the best of days."

"What did he mean when he said no one can best the king in battle?" Olwen asked quietly, drawing the attention of both men. "Is he so fierce?"

"Ferocity is not the issue, my Swan," Hrafn said as he approached her. Stopping beside her, he took her hand in his tenderly. "The man is powerful, yes, but he is also unscrupulous. He fights without honor and changes the rules to suit himself. If you are stronger than he, he insists on magic only. If your magic is stronger, then it is weapons. And if he ever feels he has a disadvantage, he feels no shame in calling in reinforcements to ensure he is victorious."

"And no one puts a stop to this?" Olwen asked with outrage.

"No one dares to contradict him or stand against him, lest they become his next opponent."

"But all they would have to do is work together, refuse to bend to him, and they could best him."

Jeger took her other hand in one of his. "True, but he still has many under oath to him, and they are obligated to throw themselves in front of danger before he can be harmed. It would take a lot of men, and a lot of magic, to get through all of his vowed vassals and then his loyal vassals, and even then, how would they decide who would be the next king? No one in court trusts anyone else to work with them to rid themselves of the Konungr, never mind competing with them for the throne. The current Konungr has only to continue feeding them dissent to maintain his rule. So long as they hate each other as much as they hate him, no one will rise up."

The space around them grew quiet.

Olwen

Olwen looked between the two men helplessly, but they both seemed to be lost in their thoughts. Fatigue and sadness were evident in the heaviness of their eyes. Hrafn always seemed this distracted and broody when he knew he would see the Konungr, and now she had a better understanding of why.

How had he survived so long under a king, his own *father*, who was so willing to end his life? How had he endured knowing that he was expendable, that there was no love for him? She couldn't imagine.

"We must plan," Hrafn said quietly.

Olwen met his eyes and then followed as he walked into his bedroom, with Jeger right behind. Once safely in the bedroom, they all sat together on the bed, huddled for comfort.

"In the event that anything... unexpected... happens to me," Hrafn looked up at Jeger, "I expect you to evacuate Olwen from here. He will hunt you both down if you are connected to me in any way. Take her to your cousin Dúfa in Fimbulvetr and seek asylum."

"Hrafn..." Jeger couldn't finish his thought. Olwen could see his heart breaking in front of her eyes.

"I know, Jeg. But we have to be smart. If I am gone, then what is the point in making the two of you targets? You must keep her safe. Promise me?"

Hrafn held Jeger's pained eyes until Jeger nodded. Hrafn put his hand into a pouch at his waist and pulled out a small amulet. He held it up to the light for Jeger to see.

"I need you to spend a few moments orienting this. It will take you to your destination if you have already told it where you wish to go. Have it ready so that you can move in a moment's time."

Jeger took the tiny stone totem and held it in his hand without comment. Olwen could see the wetness gathering on his lashes, but he did his best to focus. She and Hrafn watched as Jeger closed his eyes, focusing all of his attention on the tiny bit of stone in his hand. When his hand glowed with a light thrumming, he opened his eyes.

"You need only hold it and say 'Take me.' The stone will transport you, and anyone touching you, to your destination."

Jeger nodded his understanding again.

"You mustn't come down to the reception hall. Keep Olwen safe up here."

"Hraf, no! You need me! My magic–"

"–Is exactly why you cannot be there. You need to keep Olwen safe."

Olwen looked between them as they stared intently at each other. She had never asked what Jeger's magic was, nor Hrafn's, for that matter. It had never occurred to her that they had magic. It should have; she had magic. She would ask them later.

The mood in the room was somber, bordering on despairing. The three clung to each other, not needing to speak. After an endless amount of time seemed to have passed, Hrafn suddenly spoke quietly.

"I am in need of bathing. Would you join me, Olwen? Jeger, you as well, of course..." He looked hopefully between Jeger and Olwen.

Olwen tried not to let her shock show. He had never openly invited her to join them before. In the past, she had joined them if she was already there with him alone, or Jeger and she had been playing when he joined. It was normally Jeger who facilitated her time with Hrafn. It felt very special that he was asking her.

Silently the three made their way into the washroom, and Hrafn loosed the water into the waterfalls. They undressed, heaping their clothing carelessly, and made their way into the spray of the water. Olwen tipped her head back, letting the water slide over her head and body, relaxing her tight muscles.

"Hraf, what if–"

Jeger never got to finish.

"Don't. Just don't, Jeg." Hrafns mouth was on Jeger's, his lips desperate and insistent. His hands clutched at Jeger's shoulders, massaging his thick muscles as if to hold him in place so that he could never leave.

Olwen closed her eyes, tipping her head back again to give them some privacy.

She gasped, nearly swallowing a mouthful of water, when a warm mouth enveloped her nipple. Then another mouth was on her other nipple. She sputtered the water out of her airway, even as groans worked themselves out of her chest. There were four hands traveling over her body with urgency, parting the flow of the water, massaging and groping her soft skin and tight muscles.

Fingers tightened in her hair, and her mouth was pulled forward to meet Hrafn's.

"I'm sorry for everything I have put you through, Ollie. I want you to know that. I know I was selfish in my dealings with you, and I want to make things right. I free you of your bargain with me and of our marriage. I relinquish my deal with Henrick, so you are no longer my wife by bargain. You are free to live your life as you wish to live it. I have only one small request."

She felt the crackle of energy on her skin. He brought his lips crashing down to hers, his tongue pushing its way into her mouth even as she opened for him. His grip on her tightened, and his free hand cupped the side of her face before slowly sliding down to her narrow graceful neck. His hand rested there, firmly in place.

"I have released you, Ollie, but that does not mean that I can live without you. You have become as much a part of my heart and my life as Jeger has. I cannot bear to lose you. Please... will you stay here with me, with us? You can still be the swordsmith; we will help you with that. Just... please... stay."

His mouth resumed working hers, not allowing her to answer, only to utter deep animalistic groans. And then her pussy lit up with sensation, and she moaned loudly into his mouth, her eyes opening wide, then clamping shut.

When Olwen's groans pitched up and became louder, Hrafn opened his eyes to see Jeger kneeling on the ground between them, his head lodged between her thighs, feasting on her. One arm was slung around her hips to hold her while his other hand plunged into her pussy as his tongue worshiped her clit.

Hrafn moaned loudly, his cock fully erect and ready at the sight. He tightened his hold on her neck and in her hair, pulling her head back and running his mouth along her jaw and neckline as he controlled her. She writhed and moaned under his hands at Jeger's attentions, her body red with the blood rushing to the surface.

Hrafn knew his dirty talk affected her. "Oh, how I love to watch you take your pleasure, my little Swan," he cooed in her ear. "Does Jeger bring your beautiful little pussy as much pleasure as he does to my cock with his talented mouth? I know he loves to eat you, my Swan. He loves to taste your juices on his tongue and feel you squeeze his fingers deep inside."

Olwen heaved another low groan, her body starting to tremble under Jeger's artful mouth. "Please," she begged before groaning again.

"Make her come, Jeg. Make her explode on your tongue. My Swan, you are so beautiful when you are falling apart on our mouths or our cocks. I want to fuck you tonight so hard that you forget any thoughts of ever leaving us, that you wish only to remain our bed partner for the rest of your life, spending your days and nights with your legs spread and in endless orgasms on our tongues and cocks. We will bathe you in our seed, and still, you will beg for more."

Olwen arched her back as much as her body could within the holds the men had on her. Every muscle strained with stiffness as she screamed her release, and then her body shuddered, convulsing with her orgasm. Jeger groaned as he lapped at her pussy, trying to catch every last bit of her sweetness, his fingers still pumping into her, pushing her through another orgasm as it rose.

"That's it, my Swan, come for us. Let Jeger taste your sweet nectar. Let him fill all of your needs." Hrafn placed gentle kisses along her neck, absently massaging her breast, his hands no longer holding her in place, now comforting her instead.

When she had felt the last of the aftershocks, Olwen let the men lather her and clean her gently. When they pulled her carefully out of the water, she followed them. She stood quietly as they both dried her with soft cloths with reverence. She had never experienced feeling so loved in all of her life.

The men's eyes were sincere as they dried her, massaging and pressing tender kisses into her skin as they went. They looked at her longingly as if she was a treasure. There was not a part of her body that had not been adored by one or both of them. She was afraid to say anything for fear that it would break the spell.

Jeger lifted her with an arm under her knees and behind her back and carried her back into the bedroom, where he deposited her onto the mattress with care. He climbed down beside her, cupping her face, before his mouth moved to take hers in a tender kiss. Their tongues danced sensually while his hands resumed roaming her form, teasing her into arousal again.

Hrafn took her other side, his hands working her body as well. Olwen could feel their hardness pressing into her sides. They were both aroused and ready. She plucked up her courage and, pulling her mouth away from Jeger's, she spoke to Hrafn.

"Did you mean it, Hraf? Will you fuck me so hard that I forget that I ever wanted to leave?" She meant to sound coy, but she was too breathless to really pull it off.

Hrafn moaned loudly, his cock stabbing into her side, before he answered. "Ollie, I will fuck you so hard and so long that you forget your own name."

Ollie made a face as if she was considering. "And Jeger, what will you be doing while he is fucking me into forgetting myself?"

"I will be doing anything you ask of me, Ollie. I would take that fuckable mouth of yours with my cock, if it helped you to forget faster."

Her nipples immediately pebbled at the thought.

"Interesting; I had thought perhaps you would suggest fucking my ass, as we haven't done that yet." She returned his kiss and felt both men's cocks lunging at the mention of her ass.

Between panted breaths, Jeger addressed her, "Ollie, that takes some working up to, but if it piques your interest, I can guarantee that I will make sure that happens. I would love to feel my cock in your tight little ass."

A thrill ran through Olwen. She had lived a life without love, where sex was just something you endured for your husband. And now she had not one, but two sexy men worshiping her body and bringing her endless pleasure. She was a very lucky woman, and she knew it.

"Come, *Wife*, prepare yourself to be fucked senseless," Jeger whispered, then laughed as he pulled Olwen up so that he could lay on his back before her. She climbed down his body until she was nestled between his thighs. She placed a hot but tender kiss on the head of his cock, and it twitched with delight.

Behind her, Hrafn pulled her hips up until she was on her knees, her ass and pussy on display before him.

"My beautiful Swan, I could lose myself in servicing your lovely pussy. Look how pink and swollen it is, like a beautiful flower. It weeps honey just for me, and I would gladly be there to catch each and every drop on my tongue and to milk more from your depths.

"But to feel you convulse around my cock, like a tightly gloved fist around my hardness, that makes me lose all sense. That drives me to rut you like a wild beast. I want to bring you such pleasure that you break apart and shatter until you are not even aware of yourself anymore, only the bliss that is my cock inside of you. I want you a mindless writhing creature beneath me, driven only by your need, screaming and wailing like an animal in heat. I will not stop until I have that."

She could feel the throbbing ache between her legs at his words. She was impatient for him to begin.

"Take his cock, my Swan. Take his cock and make him scream your name so that I can drive your body into oblivion."

Olwen gladly dropped her mouth over Jeger's waiting cock, taking him deep and making him cry out. His hands were wrapped in her hair instantly, and his grip was firm as he pulled her over his cock the way he liked it. She had asked him to do this with her, and it drove her wild to feel him stiffen, swelling in her mouth even more. He spit out a string of obscenities, even as he thrust up into her open mouth, his hands guiding her throat over him deeper. She just moaned around him, her own need growing.

She felt Hrafn's cock as it pressed against her slick opening. She moaned more loudly, trying to press her ass back against him, needing to feel him filling her. Jeger always sank into her hard with one swift thrust, but Hrafn was working his way in slowly, pulling back out, and working in a little further. It was driving her crazy with need. She wanted to feel him slamming into her, deep inside. Instead, he teased with a gentle in and out, the friction lighting up the sides of her canal.

Jeger kept a steady pace, pulling her down onto his cock as he groaned and thrusted, and soon even Hrafn bottomed out inside of her, his balls hitting her thighs as he groaned in delight. She delighted in the feel of him as he spread her wide to accommodate him.

"Are you ready, my Swan? Because I am going to fuck you mercilessly."

She pulled her mouth off of Jeger's cock and turned to look at him over her shoulder. "Fuck me already, Hraf. Give me your cock." There was heat in her words.

Jeger snatched her hair and pulled her back onto himself, cursing her for neglecting his cock, but only in a teasing tone. He was soon groaning and thrusting up into her, calling her name, losing himself in the sensations she was giving him.

And then Hrafn unloaded. Bringing one knee up beside her hips, he impaled his cock into her like a piston, hard and fast, leaning over her just slightly so that he drove his cock down and into her, pushing her over Jeger's cock more deeply. Instantly she was screaming and wailing at the sensation. His cock hit the spot inside of her that unleashed the most amazing feelings, and she was at a complete loss. She was helpless to do anything but take it, the feeling overwhelming her. She screamed and moaned, but her mouth was full of Jeger's cock, and he only shouted and groaned at the feeling of it.

She was paralyzed with bliss, positioned between the two men pumping into her from the front and from behind. She locked her shoulders and knees and just held on for dear life as the thrusting continued, both men grunting, groaning, and roaring while they fucked her like wild animals. She had never been so excited in all of her life.

She felt the climax starting to build. Every muscle in her body was responding to some primal call, every bit of her stiffening in preparation as if she was going to explode. The coiling began in her core, hot, wet, and tight. It grew tighter, tighter... the feelings were just too good. Soon she lost all sense of self; she was no longer Olwen. She was just the sensation pulsating out of her pussy and rocketing through her whole body.

With each breath, she let out a long keening wail, each one a little higher than the last. Hrafn continued to pummel her from behind, fucking into her hard and deep, his own groans growing louder in concert with hers.

"Come for me,... my Swan... that's it!... Come... Come on my cock... come NOW!"

Olwen let out a piercing scream as every muscle in her body locked up. Jeger clamped her head down onto his cock as he screamed her name with his own release, shooting deep into her throat. Hrafn continued to pump her pussy hard from behind, her wetness sliding down her thighs through her convulsions as the shockwaves tore through her. Her vision went black, and all she was aware of was the thrumming of the cock pounding into her, driving her further. Finally, Hrafn launched himself into her hard, grabbing her hips in a bruising grip as he roared his release over her, his cock spasming deep inside of her as he spilled his seed into her. He held her in a death grip, sealing his cock deep inside her, before he continued to pump into her again, drawing out the last of his essence and his orgasm into the warmth of her body.

The three of them collapsed into a pile of sweaty bodies heaving for breath, Olwen still convulsing with aftershocks. After a few minutes of catching their breaths, Olwen turned to look at Hrafn.

"I still know my name. You're not done yet."

This elicited a groan and a broad smile from Hrafn and Jeger.

16

Hrafn

Hrafn groaned as his sensitive cock brushed against the sheet. He hissed between his teeth as he jerked his hips to stop the pain. They had fucked far too much the night before. A knocking at the outer door caught his attention.

He quickly pulled himself out of the tangle of limbs that were his lover's and headed for his chamber doors. Behind him, he could hear Jeger waking slowly. He grabbed some clothing and made his way through the sitting room; wrapping a dressing gown around himself, he opened the outer door, but only a crack.

"WHAT?" he demanded. He noticed too late it was the Konungr's messenger. "When does he want me?" he added belatedly.

The messenger stiffened, his nose wrinkling like a rodent. "His Majesty, the Konungr, requests your presence following his lunch this afternoon." He spoke into the air as if making a proclamation, never meeting Hrafn's eyes.

"And when the faen will *that* be?" Hrafn growled.

The messenger finally turned bored eyes on Hrafn and then shrank back at the vicious glare he received. "I imagine when His Majesty has finished eating," he offered, suddenly meek.

Hrafn did not give the man the opportunity to say more, shutting the door with a thud in the small man's face. He rushed back into the bedroom to find Jeger already up and preparing to wash and Olwen stretching like a cat. He must have had a stricken look on his face because both of them ceased movement at his mere presence.

"He's called for you?" Jeger stood like a statue. His eyes were resolute, but one could sense his fear.

"This afternoon. We need to have a strategy in place. I suspect he simply wants to humiliate me, as he usually does. However, knowing that he placed Lenz's son in our ranks, I cannot discount that he will take things to extremes."

Hrafn made his way into the washroom, and once the water was flowing, the other two followed. They bathed, dressed, and ate in relative silence, each lost in their own thoughts and worries. At last, Hrafn addressed them both.

"I will go down alone." He held his palm up to stop Jeger, who opened his mouth, from objecting. "I will go down alone so that you and Olwen are protected. Jeg, if you are there, he can call you out too. He can use you both against me. Please don't do that to me. I would throw myself on a blade before I would allow him to hurt either of you. I will be lost even before I have begun."

Jeger looked haunted, like an animal that was being backed into a corner. They all knew he didn't want to remain in the rooms. Hrafn had to hope that he would honor this request, for all of their sakes.

He turned his eyes to Olwen. "Ollie, you are free to live your life as you wish. When I return from my appointment, I would very much like for the three of us to sit down again and discuss your wishes for the future. I won't lie; I very much want you to remain with us, Jeger and me. I meant it when I said that you have become a part of my heart. I won't ask you for an answer now, but I would like the opportunity to present my case before you."

Hrafn noticed that moisture collected on her lashes, and she spared a brief glance at Jeger, who nodded with a tender smile before picking up her hand and kissing the back of it. Hrafn's heart was full to overflowing. He had never wanted a wife, but now he knew he would never be happy without Olwen in his life. And he had never anticipated that Jeger would befriend her so deeply. After his initial bout of jealousy, he accepted Olwen into their relationship and had even pushed Hrafn to accept her further than he was willing at first. He could never have foreseen that, even with knowing Jeger all of those years.

He looked between the both of them, and he was filled with so much caring that it almost made him want to weep. The seed of a thought niggled in the back of his mind, desperate to grow and take bloom. He had asked Jeger to marry him; maybe when this nonsense with the Konungr was over, he would marry both of them. In his mind's eye, he could see the country coming together to celebrate his marriage to Jeger and Olwen. His heart swelled at the thought...

... and then crashed into a fiery wreck. The Konungr would never allow his happiness. He would have to marry them in hiding, as he had made Jeger his consort, to prevent them from being used against him. Anger and despair threatened to climb up his throat, clawing for release. He choked back the emotion that wanted so badly to make itself heard: it would make no difference how he felt about any of it.

Unless they left.

He looked up to see Olwen and Jeger staring at him with concern. He had been so lost in his own reverie that he had completely forgotten they were there. He tried to smile so that they wouldn't worry, but it didn't work if their expressions were any indication of what they were thinking. In the end, he sighed deeply.

He would have to consider making a plan to take them both and leave the country. It might be the only way they were allowed to be together and to be happy. But would he be happy leaving his people in the hands of a madman? Did he have a choice if it meant Olwen and Jeger's happiness, potentially their very lives? It was not a decision he was prepared to make at that moment, not when he would be seeing the Konungr soon.

Olwen

Hrafn had only been gone a few minutes, and Olwen and Jeger were already pacing and sweating with anxiety.

The messenger had been tasked with notifying Hrafn when the King was served his lunch so that Hrafn could be available as soon as the Konungr was ready for him. This gave them the maximum amount of time together before Hrafn had to leave. When the messenger knocked, the three of them looked up as if the knocking had come from a coffin. Hrafn had pulled them both close, kissing them both passionately as if he would never see them again, before fixing his dispassionate facade in place over his features. The court would only ever see this side of him; he would never again give them an ounce of pain for their amusement.

And then he was gone, on his way to meet the king.

Olwen felt as if her heart was being torn out of her body. Not knowing what was going to happen to Hrafn drove her mind to places she should never go. She could imagine this monster of a king ordering any number of tortures, humiliations, or even death for Hrafn, and she saw each potential punishment in full colorful detail in her brain. Her breathing grew more shallow and rapid by the moment.

"You know…"

Olwen spun when she heard Jeger's voice. She noticed he had stopped pacing.

"I promised to keep you safe; I never promised to keep you here. If we were to disguise ourselves and stay to the outer edges of the receiving room, near the servants, we could still see everything without exposing ourselves to danger."

Without waiting, Olwen rushed to her wardrobe and pulled out the men's clothing she had been wearing to disguise herself. Jeger rushed to his wardrobe, pulling off his expensive court clothing and opting for clothing more appropriate to the noble class. Olwen didn't ask him how he had come to have such things. In only a few moments, they were both changed and heading for the door. Olwen was surprised to find no guards at their doors and assumed that once Hrafn was headed to the Konungr, their work was done.

They worked their way down hallways silently. At one point, Jeger took Olwen by the elbow and led her to a doorway; once inside, they made their way down a staircase and through a long corridor.

"These are the servant's passages. Hrafn and I use them all the time to move about the palace without being noticed."

Olwen only nodded as they both rushed down the corridors. She was glad that Jeger knew where he was going because the endless twists and turns had her lost in moments. She would never be able to find her way back without him. Finally, he slowed their pace. She could hear noise and conversation ahead.

When they emerged from the corridor, Olwen found them near the kitchens, based on the noises and the smells. Jeger confirmed with a passing servant that the Konungr had just finished eating and was heading to his receiving room. Olwen felt Jeger place his hand on her lower back and then pull it away quickly. It might seem odd for him to escort a young man down the hall so intimately. He led her to another series of doors, and then they both walked into a room full of people. They had found the reception room.

A string quartet played quietly in a corner while the Konungr arranged himself on his throne, several servants around him fetching whatever he needed to be comfortable. Olwen couldn't see him over the crowd, but she knew he must be there by the way people fawned. It was a richly appointed room with marble floors and walls so that every noise echoed, making it overloud. There were velvet drapes hung on either side of towering windows that ran along the long high walls. The room easily could have been three stories high, with an arched ceiling high above, far above the candles so that light seemed to dissipate into the darkness.

She and Jeger stood among the upper-working-class and nobles on the outskirts of the room as if they were pressed to the walls to make room for the elite in the center. The bulk of the crowd consisted of nobles and upper-class patrons of the Konungr. They were decked in high fashion with silks and brocades, rings on their fingers, and gold chains around their necks; some even wore tiaras. Olwen had to wonder why they were dressed in such finery for a normal afternoon reception... or perhaps they always overdressed? She looked down at her trousers and suddenly felt as if she was an intruder.

As the people talked in hushed tones among themselves, Olwen couldn't help but remember Jeger's conversation from the night before.

"Jeger," she whispered, pulling him down so she could speak into his ear, "What is your magic? And what is Hrafn's?"

Jeger turned his head so he could speak into her ear and avoid being overheard, "Hrafn can shapeshift into a raven, but his true magic is in somniancy, the magic of dreams and sleep."

Olwen thought back to her first meeting with Hrafn; it now seemed a lifetime ago. He had somehow rendered her unconscious; now she understood how. "And your magic?" she asked quietly.

Jeger hesitated before he responded, "We do not discuss my magic; I am under oath not to reveal it to anyone. Only Hrafn knows what it is, as he was there when it... presented itself." She didn't have time to consider it further before a large gong was sounded, and the noise in the room vanished like a whiff of smoke.

Someone Olwen couldn't see announced the Konungr's itinerary for the court, and there was a small noise of softly spoken approval from the courtiers. Right on cue, Prince Hrafn was announced, and the doors opened with a boom. A collective gasp was heard as one set of footsteps marched across the marble floor toward the throne.

Jeger kept Olwen near the door at the wall in case they needed to make a hasty exit. It was a good strategy, to Olwen's mind, but she wished she could get just one glimpse of Hrafn. She recognized his voice the moment he spoke.

"You have summoned me, Konungr?"

There was none of the acid or heat he had used earlier when talking of the king; his voice was tamed and respectful.

"Hrafn, indeed I have. I have been advised that you have not performed your latest duty as I have requested. Tell me that is not so."

"I am afraid it is true, Your Highness." Olwen could hear the tension in his voice.

"Why, Hrafn? Why have you disobeyed a direct order? It has not been in your nature to displease me in the past."

"Your Highness, I searched the borders myself. We looked high and low, even in the areas which would be to no advantage for an enemy force to enter our lands. I found no evidence whatsoever that anyone has trespassed onto our lands, and I do not know who has been advising you otherwise. I could find no sign at all. I cannot fight a force that does not exist, Your Highness."

The collective gasp was louder, with whispered talk murmured through the crowd.

"Are you suggesting that my advisors are lying to me, Hrafn?"

The king's tone was mocking, and Olwen's blood turned to ice. She looked at Jeger to see him equally unsettled beside her, a thin sheen of sweat building on his brow. His jaw was clenched tight, making the tendons in his neck stand out.

"I am not suggesting anything, Your Majesty, except that there are no enemy forces on our Northeast Border. I have seen it myself."

"I see," the king said in a low voice, drawing it out. "So it is your opinion that we are not under attack at all, that we should do nothing, as there is no threat."

To Olwen's ear, he sounded condescending, as if he was baiting Hrafn. She couldn't understand why he would, though. What could he possibly gain? If there was no enemy at the border, he should be glad of it. Unless...

"Doing nothing is never an option, Majesty. I am merely pointing out that there are no enemy forces lying in wait, requiring a military response at this time. Vigilance will keep it that way." Hrafn spoke slowly and clearly, and Olwen could tell he was choosing his wording carefully. It was a tricky verbal sparring dance that he was engaging with the king, and one wrong word could be his last.

"Well, I am so relieved to hear that you believe we should remain vigilant," the Konungr announced as if it was some punchline, immediately bringing sniggers and laughter from his sea of sycophants. "Especially as you, yourself, have seen no sign of the enemy at our borders."

The laughter and guffaws continued with no comment from Hrafn. Olwen cast a confused eye at Jeger, only to find him red in the face with anger. His body was tense beside her; his hands clutched into fists at his side. When Hrafn remained silent, the Konungr spoke again, and the room went silent with seeming delight at hearing what he would say next.

"I find it convenient that you have found no evidence of enemy incursion. You have said this yourself. And yet I know it to be a fact that we have enemy forces on our borders at this very moment, waiting to catch us unaware. I must surmise from this that you are working in collusion with our enemies, Hrafn. How else would you explain reporting to me so falsely?"

"I have never worked against you, Majesty. I have always been your loyal servant. If others report contrary to mine, then THEY are the traitors, not me. I cannot say it any more clearly."

"So you say, and yet you leave us vulnerable to attack. Did you think you could lead me to believe that we are safe, that I would simply lower my defenses at your word alone? No matter. I now have the swordsmith I need to carry us to victory; I no longer need you.

"Hrafn, I sentence you to death for treason against the crown, to be carried out on the morrow at dawn. Say your farewells tonight, for it shall be your last."

He delivered the sentence as if he was bored, and the reaction of the crowd was sudden and loud. There were gasps, whispers, and shouts for and against... mostly for. Olwen couldn't hear herself over the noise.

"Then you leave me no choice: I challenge you for the right to the throne." Hrafn's voice rang over the din, and there was another loud gasp bordering on a scream.

Hrafn

Faen i helvete! Hrafn knew that his calm facade was slipping, but there was no way he was going to his death calmly and meekly. He might not be able to defeat the Konungr, but he would die with honor trying.

The Konungr smirked as if he was overjoyed to hear that Hrafn wanted to fight him for the throne; perhaps he was. Perhaps this would give him the spectacle he wanted to feed the minds of his followers. A fight would both entertain them and squash any other thoughts of rebellion with his death, while simultaneously ensuring his place as the alpha warrior in the court.

"So you admit that you do wish to usurp MY throne?" the king asked loudly.

"I wish nothing of the sort, *Majesty*, but I also do not wish to die for a falsehood; nor do I wish to enlist our people into a war that does not exist."

"Enough talk!"

Hrafn was relieved to see that at least the king, too, was losing his mask of indifference, his true anger bleeding into his remarks. The Konungr stood and stepped to the edge of the dais before pulling out his sword.

"Let us argue with our steel."

Hrafn pulled his own sword, angry with himself that he had chosen a more decorative one than he would normally use for battle. The king took a few lunging steps down and swung the first blow. Hrafn blocked it easily and swung around for a return, only to be met by the king's sword again. He knew the Konungr was a master fighter, but he was as well, and he had been training and working the fields for years while the king sat on his cushy throne. Already the king's breathing became heavier.

The crowd cleared away, giving them a wide berth, as they swung and advanced on each other. Both managed to get small shots, but neither could seem to inflict much damage; the only saving hope was that the king seemed to be losing steam more quickly than Hrafn. Their martial dance continued in circles around the room, sweeping people out of their path until Hrafn successfully parried an attack, only to have one of the king's guards on the outskirts sweep his sword out of his hand. He suddenly found himself without a weapon.

The king smiled triumphantly, lowering his sword slightly, undoubtedly readying himself to launch into his victory speech. Before he could say a word, Olwen's voice was shouting Hrafn's name. He turned his head slightly to see her pushing her way through the last of the crowd and throwing her sword to him. He reached for it, and just as his hand tightened on the hilt, the Konungr realized what was happening and made his move. The king's strike struck Hrafn's upper arm, slicing him and starting a fresh flow of blood down his sleeve.

Hrafn wheeled on the king with Olwen's sword. He could feel the power emanating from it, and it gave him renewed hope. The guard behind him tried to interfere again, and Hrafn ran him through as he made his way after the Konungr, who was actively retreating. Although the room was full of people, the only sound was the heavy breaths of the two fighters, the groans and grunts as they swung their swords, and the clashing of steel on steel.

Hrafn pressed his advantage, pushing the king further and further back. The Konungr no longer looked confident; in fact, he looked very unsure of himself. His breathing was labored, and sweat ran in fat beads down his face. As Hrafn worked him back toward a corner, where there would be no escape, the Konungr finally saw that he was outmatched. Not one to lose gracefully, he immediately searched the crowds around his strikes until he made eyes with several of his men. He only nodded at them as he continued swinging furiously. It was enough.

Soon several men were moving out of the crowd and taking a defensive posture around the Konungr, who had the audacity to smile. There were five men against Hrafn, and Hrafn was already beginning to fatigue. He held his sword aloft, not willing to concede.

The first of the guards was easily dispatched as they ran in to attack Hrafn. Four to go. The next two fought Hrafn in tandem while the last remained to guard the Konungr. Hrafn sustained more superficial wounds, but ultimately wounded one so that he could not stand and fight and killed the second.

Two left, including the king.

The last guard moved forward, trying his hardest to appear determined, while nothing but fear lit his eyes. Hrafn recognized him as one of the guards he had worked with in previous years, one who was a good and devoted warrior. In a moment of mercy, he swung and cast a sleeping spell to make it appear as if he had struck the man down. As the guard's body hit the floor, he faced the Konungr again.

"Do you concede?" Hrafn called, his breath ragged from effort.

"Oh no, Hrafn, I have only just begun," the Konungr answered. He laughed out loud, and then he began to shift.

Olwen

A shriek lit the room as it devolved into chaos. People began screaming and scrambling for the exits, pushing and pressing those ahead of them in a terror. Hrafn looked from the corner of his eye, and he could see Olwen and Jeger still there behind him. He wanted to turn and scream at them for not following his order and for placing themselves in harm's way, but he knew he would never have time.

In front of him, the Konungr's joints and bones snapped and popped as his body reformed under his skin, jutting and rolling. The skin itself shifted and formed into a shield of scales, clothing tore and fell away, and the large grey dragon slowly took shape. He wasn't as big as a true dragon, but he was several times larger than a man and much, much heavier. The dragon flicked its tail and huffed what sounded like a laugh while small plumes of smoke rose from its nostrils. It took one menacing step toward Hrafn, and the remaining guards in the room all pushed back away from him.

The dragon inhaled deeply and then shot a stream of fire at Hrafn, which Hrafn managed to avoid by ducking and rolling away. The dragon recoiled to do it again, and Hrafn realized his mistake; he had rolled himself into a corner, and there was no way to avoid the next blast. As the dragon shot the next volley at him, Jeger suddenly jumped in front of him, taking the brunt of the attack so that Hrafn could jump to the side and escape again. Jeger screamed with pain, and the air was filled with the smell of burning flesh and hair while Olwen screamed from where she stood.

Hrafn had barely a moment to get his footing before he was launching himself away again, this time with less precision and preparation. His leg was caught by the blast, causing him to cry out as he landed.

Olwen looked on helplessly. Both of these men were going to die unless she could do something. Her mind raced as she searched the room for some way to take the advantage. She wondered if she could simply tear the floor underneath them, but that would probably injure Hrafn as well. If she could get close enough, she could stab the king...

Did she need to be closer?

She had sung metal to her before, had it flow over short distances: from the pile to the bench. Another blast sent Hrafn scrambling, this time crashing into a chair and overturning a table. She didn't have time to wonder.

Olwen opened her mouth and trusted that the magic knew what to do. She saw what she wanted, and her song came out like a cross between the wail of the banshee and a scream of terror. It was loud and imbued with so much power that the walls and floor trembled. The noise caused the remaining people in the room to cover their ears as it invaded their minds. Hrafn looked up to see all of the swords, spears, and ornaments behind the dragon around the room begin to shimmer and melt into a gelatinous form. The dragon seemed annoyed but, seeing nothing else happening, moved on him again with a large smile. He was unaware of the metal in motion.

The guards all dropped wherever they still held of their weapons, most of the metal floating like streams with the spring runoff, forming large puddles of metal in the air behind the dragon. Then the metal began to reform. Olwen continued to scream, the sound issuing from her chest like cannon fire. Long darts of metal took shape with wicked sharp points, like a dozen large needles in the air.

The dragon took another menacing step toward Hrafn and opened its maw to finish the battle. Olwen let out one last blast of sound. As the dragon inhaled, a dozen shafts of sharpened metal flew through the air like missiles and launched themselves into the dragon. They were so sharp that even the scaly hide was no protection, and the dragon stopped mid-breath to look down in stunned stupidity as the stakes made their way through his back and out his belly. It made a horrific roaring and burbling noise in its throat as it flailed and then fell to the floor, dead, its blood puddling beneath it on the marble.

Olwen rushed to where Jeger had fallen, dropping beside him and weeping. Hrafn picked himself up and limped over to them. Jeger was still alive, but his burns were severe, and he was suffering.

"Clear the room!" Hrafn shouted, looking at the remaining soldiers. They wasted no time in running to the doors and out. Soon it was only the three of them.

Olwen sobbed uncontrollably as she tried to comfort Jeger.

"Do not cry, Wife," Jeger held her hand tightly, his breathing shallow and sharp. "All is well. It will be alright, Ollie." Olwen just cried harder, unable to say anything.

"*Wife?*" Hrafn's voice sounded behind her. "You called her that last night too. What is the meaning of this?" Although he was exhausted, he sounded very angry.

Olwen tried to speak, but couldn't, so Jeger sputtered, "We... married. Both... married her." He dropped his head back, the effort of holding it up too much.

"So this whole time I have been concerned with her welfare, with making sure you protected her, you have been *married* to her? You went behind my back and married? Without telling me? Tell me, Jeg, were you hoping I died today so that you could take her away and live in peace without me? Is that what you wanted all along? ...To finally have your marriage.

"I feel such a fool! Here I was thinking I loved you both, that I would marry you both, and the whole time you have already been married. You have been enjoying each other while I bore the burden of the Konungr's demands. Should I just go now and leave you two to your life together?"

"It is not like that, Hrafn!" Olwen finally managed to get out. "He married me as a part of a bargain to get me to come back to you, so you would not suffer from the bargain."

"Oh, so it was HIM you came back for. You only fucked me because I happened to be in the room, is that it? This is the greatest betrayal I have ever faced, and I have lived with the Konungr. I do not know that I can ever forgive either of you. I am finished."

With that, he picked up his sword, even while Olwen argued. She screamed as he raised it, and Jeger raised a hand as if to defend himself. The sword came down swiftly and so hard that it went through Jeger's chest and into the marble below. Olwen's hysterical screams continued as she scrambled to pull the sword out of Jeger. Blood pooled in his mouth and then ran down his cheek as his life left his body.

"GUARDS!"

Olwen turned to see the guards cautiously returning to the room at Hrafn's command.

"Traitorous *Wife*, I–"

"YOU listen to ME!" Olwen shouted, her voice on the verge of hysteria, "Don't you DARE blame me for the situation you find yourself in, Hrafn. You took a woman as a WIFE through the collateral of a bargain. You have been unfaithful to your consort for your entire life. You meant to cheat me out of our bargain when the terms no longer suited you rather than simply discussing it with me.

Your entire life, you have had other people's lives to play with like a game, and I am DONE being your pawn. I would not have returned to a life of slavery under your rule except that Jeger was kind and sweet, and he ASKED me to. He offered to marry me so that I would have proof of his sincerity in caring for my well-being. Yes, I married him, and I love him. I would have remained married to him.

"I had considered staying married to you as well after I returned and after you had changed so much, mostly at Jeger's prompting. At least, I had thought you had changed. I had thought perhaps you had found your heart. But I see now I was wrong. That you could kill your own love just to deprive me...

"Tell me this, Hrafn, did it never occur to you to wish us happiness? Or was it only and always all about you?"

Hrafn glared at her, unable to answer, though whether it was due to shame or fury, she could not tell.

"Take her." Hrafn motioned to the guards, and they started moving toward her.

"Yes, take me," Olwen said sadly as she held the amulet in her hand for Hrafn to see, her sword in her other.

"No!–" His outraged expression and shocked voice faded as Olwen felt herself churned inside out, the density of reality molding into her and around her, spitting her out in a courtyard. Her legs gave out, and she fell to the flagstone, a sob bursting from her chest. Safely away in Fimbulvetr, she allowed herself to crumple and mourn the death of her lover and her love.

The story will continue in Kingdom of Swan and Sword.

17

About the Author

Fay Smith has had a passion for writing and communication for as long as she can remember. In college she majored in English, before switching gears to learn foreign languages and work as a linguist. As an army brat she traveled the world and saw many different customs and people, giving her mind a fertile growing space for the worlds she would write about in the future. She lives in New England with her husband, three dogs, and one cat.

18

Also by this Author

Blue in Boston, the Color of Love Series, Book 1
Spicy Contemporary Romance
Amazon: https://www.amazon.com/dp/B0BNGKXGNS

The seductive first tale in the Color of Love series of dark and spicy adult romance novels!

Jenna had faced darkness, so she liked living life on her terms. Meeting an entitled rich lawyer was never a part of her plan; especially when proves he can take what she was dishing out.

Max is a self-described workaholic. As a partner at his law firm, he doesn't have time for relationships or drama; if he needs company, he hires it, like any other service. So why does the sharp-tongued, blue-haired woman who put him in his place haunt his dreams? Maybe it's her passion and sass, or maybe it's that her desires rivaled his own?

When their strengths suddenly became weaknesses, is there hope for someone who is broken to find love?

Red in Richmond, the Color of Love Series, Book 2

Spicy Contemporary Romance
Amazon: https://www.amazon.com/dp/B0BWSNPSR7

The scorching second tale in the Color of Love series of dark and spicy adult romance novels!

Nat was doing her best to just survive and stay under the radar, so pursuing the hottie she saw at the gym was a big no-no. To make matters worse, he's a fed! She knows it can't end well if he discovers who she really is, and what she's done.

Baxter was sent to Richmond to follow a lead on the mob family he investigates for the FBI, but he never expected to meet a seductive redhead whose passion runs hot, and whose secrets run deep. He knows nothing good can come out of pursuing her, but he just can't stop himself.

When the truth about her past is brought to light, and the dust clears, will there be anything left for them together?

Amber in Atlanta, the Color of Love Series, Book 3
Spicy Contemporary Romance
To Be Released, Summer of 2023

The blistering third tale in the Color of Love series of dark and spicy adult romance novels!

Amber had made a mess of her life. At eighteen she was sick and tired of being everyone's second choice or backup plan. She had thought she could just run from her life and her problems as a teenager, and start over, but life has a way of bringing our lessons back around until we learn them.

Victor had just had a bomb dropped on his world: his first real love had told him she had not only left him when they were kids, but she had also taken the baby he never knew about. A chance reconnection brought them together briefly for a friend's wedding; neither was prepared for all of the lies from their past to surface and drag them back under.

They say there is a fine line between love and hate, and Victor and Amber can't help but crush that line as their passions flare.

Is it desire, revenge, lust, hatred, or love? They have to figure it out before it consumes them completely.

Heavenly Scent

Fantasy Romance, low spice

Amazon: https://www.amazon.com/dp/B0BX1D5TCX

When one small-town girl turns out to be a mixed-blood hot commodity for an evil kingdom of Fae; it will take her long-absent Fae Father, and unknown Angel grandfather, as well as her sexy Fae warrior, to secure her freedom. Her life changes in an instant, as she fights to avoid a life of slavery. Is she strong enough to survive one crashing blow after the next? And if she can make it to freedom, can she resist the growing passion which threatens to devour her heart?